THE PARIS MAID

BOOKS BY ELLA CAREY

STANDALONES

Beyond the Horizon

Secret Shores

The Things We Don't Say

SECRETS OF PARIS

Paris Time Capsule

The House by the Lake

From a Paris Balcony

DAUGHTERS OF NEW YORK

A New York Secret

The Lost Girl of Berlin

The Girl from Paris

The Lost Sister of Fifth Avenue

THE PARIS MAID

ELLA CAREY

New York Boston

This book is a work of historical fiction. In order to give a sense of the times, some names of real people or places have been included in the book. However, the events depicted in this book are imaginary, and the names of nonhistorical persons or events are the product of the author's imagination or are used fictitiously. Any resemblance of such nonhistorical persons or events to actual ones is purely coincidental.

Cover Design by Shreya Gupta
Cover Photos: Woman © Richard Jenkins; Hotel by Eye Ubiquitous/Alamy Stock Photo; Planes by Shutterstock

Grand Central Publishing
Hachette Book Group
1290 Avenue of the Americas, New York, NY 10104
grandcentralpublishing.com
@grandcentralpub

Originally published in 2023 by Bookouture, an imprint of Storyfire Ltd., Carmelite House, 50 Victoria Embankment, London EC4Y0DZ

First Grand Central Publishing Edition: October 2024

Grand Central Publishing is a division of Hachette Book Group, Inc. The Grand Central Publishing name and logo is a registered trademark of Hachette Book Group, Inc.

Library of Congress Control Number: 2024938244

ISBNs: 978-1-5387-6850-1 (Trade paperback)

Printed in the United States of America

LSC-C

Printing 1, 2024

To all my readers, with my love and thanks.
I appreciate each and every one of you very much.

PROLOGUE

PARIS, SUMMER 1944

Louise

The townsfolk's scornful taunts rip through the air in the grand old square: "Femme tondue! Femme tondue!" Shaven woman. Woman of shame. I bow my head and stare at the rain-soaked cobblestones, tears blurring my vision beneath the small wooden stool where they have forced me to sit.

My head jerks with every slice of my tormentor's razor as it grazes my scalp, and I wince as the sharp tip comes too close and threatens to cut the thin skin on my head. My fair hair falls to the ground like feathers from a plucked bird, hovering in the air before coming to a gentle rest. The sight of my blond tendrils lying helplessly on the ground lodges deep in my soul, and I remind myself that I am simply one person in the grotesque circus that is captivating the towns of France.

It is not the Nazis who are shaving my head. No. Paris has been liberated and I am debased by France's own jeering countrymen. I am surrounded by the newly free citizens of France.

When it is done, and my head is shorn, my self-appointed barber stands back and admires his work. Slowly, I lift my head and meet his glare. He folds his arms like the satisfied town butcher, and the crowd roars to life.

I feel overwhelmed, hunted. The faces around me mist and blur and the noise swells to a crescendo.

A pair of rough hands yanks me up and drags me along the street. The crowd parts and I am pushed onto the back of a truck and dumped unceremoniously on a hard wooden bench.

I am staring at two other miserable young women, also bald, who are seated opposite me. One has tearstained cheeks, but their faces are expressionless.

A drum beats steadily in the distance as if it is an omen. A man hurls himself onto the truck and rips off my white blouse, holding it like a trophy. He throws my top and it flies into the crowds as if it is a billowing sheet, and a young man picks it up, waving the fine cotton garment above his head before bringing it down in front of his face and inhaling it as a connoisseur would sniff a vintage wine.

I wince and shudder as yet another pair of rough hands daubs me with sticky black tar. Black streaks mark my cheeks, and a red swastika is painted on my forehead and my arm. I am branded, just like the victims the Nazis sent away to the camps.

I am shaking uncontrollably by the time a team of men on the ground sweep our fallen hair into a pile. I shudder at the smell of burning hair when they strike a match and stand around the pyre, gloating until our lost tendrils transform into exquisite purple and orange flames.

I turn my eyes away, but the acrid smell of something that is never supposed to burn hurts my nose and settles in the back of my throat.

The truck rumbles to life. It is as if we are adulterous women accused of witchcraft from a time we thought had passed.

The French people who have been humiliated by the Nazis' occupation of their country stand by and watch, their expressions hungry, as if doing to us what they could not do to the Nazi occupiers. Like air-raid sirens gone wrong, their catcalls sweep through the still afternoon air.

I cower in my seat.

These people have been oppressed and abused by a terrifying occupying regime, so now they have turned full circle and stolen their own women's dignity, humanity, and truth.

Slowly, I lift my head to meet the beaten-down gaze of my fellow accused. Our jaded eyes flicker against each other's. There is little hope. But as the truck begins to move through the square, and I sit here, stripped of everything, I realize there is one truth they cannot take away from me. There is one secret no one will ever know.

CHAPTER ONE

LONDON, PRESENT DAY

Nicole

My phone pings in the queue at the supermarket. I forage about in my handbag. There is a message from my aunt Mariah and an image lights up the screen. And the message: *Place Vendôme, Paris, 1944. Found this during my research into the family history. Astounded, obviously. But it explains everything.* A young woman stares out at me from the photograph. Her head is shaved, and even though the image of her is in black and white, I can tell the blood has drained from her lips. A Nazi swastika is branded on her forehead. My heart contracts as I peer at the photo until I realize that her features are more familiar and dearer to me than anyone else's.

"No," I murmur out loud.

Trolleys clatter, registers beep, and supermarket attendants wave people into the checkout zone.

I stand still as a telegraph pole.

Granny Louise.

The girl in the photograph is my beloved grandmother.

I try to remember what she told me.

Granny only had a few faded photographs from after the war when she married my grandfather, standing on the front steps of a church, Granny smiling and smiling with her blond hair waved and pinned back from her face. She wore a white, drop-waist dress that trailed to the ground. There was a large satin bow on one hip and she held a bunch of bright white lilies so big they were almost falling out of her hands. I remember photos of her honeymoon in Cornwall, that deep-red lipstick they all favored back then, only visible in the black-and-white photographs as a deep stain. Then there were pictures taken by the sea when the bracing wind was blowing her hair, her Marilyn Monroe smile giving away nothing except joy.

People are staring at me, and I must move. I inch toward a cash register and scan my purchases, reach for my credit card, pay the grocery bill, and, somehow, walk out the sliding glass doors. A stiff breeze blows bits of rubbish around the supermarket parking lot. I unload my groceries, sliding my large brown paper bags into the back of the Land Rover. It's a sensible car, the one we bought when we found out I was expecting a baby.

My hand floats to the tiny bump beneath my dress and I climb into the car, slide into the seat, fasten my seat belt, and swallow down the panic that writhes inside me like a basket of cut snakes.

Rain begins to patter on the windshield. The memories come thick and fast. Granny reading to me until I fell asleep, sitting on the edge of the bed she kept for me in her spare room with her legs crossed at the ankles, her faded hair still waved like it used to be in the 1940s, and her blue eyes crinkled in concentration. We went through all the fairy tales, the 1930s adventure stories when children used to disappear into the countryside, munching on apples and chocolate and messing about on boats until sundown. Granny tucking me into bed until I was safe as a caterpillar in a cocoon. Granny's breakfasts of toast and marmalade and the best hot chocolate in the world.

I force myself out of my reverie and back to the harsh reality of Aunt Mariah's message.

As I drive home, the rain thickens and starts to fall in unusual patterns, blowing this way and that, and the houses in my street merge into a shimmering mirage. Everything takes on a glassy tone.

I turn into the driveway of our small, semidetached house in Abbey Wood with its yellow climbing roses cascading all over the façade, and I sit for one moment. Granny's house in Sussex was covered with climbing roses, her garden was filled with herbs and vegetables and cottage plants, and when I first laid eyes on this semidetached house, it was the roses that drew me in.

I pick up my phone and start typing a reply. *Mariah, there must be a mistake. Granny would never have been complicit...as a...*I cannot even bring myself to write the words. And then I do. *Nazi collaborator.*

Three dots appear on my screen. A few seconds later, nothing. I undo my seat belt and frown. I know too well how women who had allegedly collaborated with the Nazis during the Second World War were paraded around France on the back of trucks after the Allied liberation of the cities and towns. They were spat on, ostracized, and thrown into prison and tried.

The front door opens. Yellow, watery light streams out onto the veranda, followed by my husband, Andrew. He puts up a huge black umbrella, and soon we are lugging the groceries out of the car.

As I walk through the rain, tears start to fall down my cheeks. I plonk my shopping bags down on the wooden floor just inside the front door.

"Darling?" Andrew's brow wrinkles, and he searches my face, his brown eyes serious and his red hair sticking up in tufts, the way it always does when he has been out in the wind. I love his unmanageable hair. "It's the anniversary. It would get to anyone, sweetheart."

I shake my head. Mariah has sent her message three days before the anniversary, the first anniversary of my mother's death. The timing is clear. I lean into Andrew's hug, resting my face against his shoulder, my forehead pressed against the softness of his gray woolen sweater, the old one he favors when he is teaching applied science to his younger students at the local comprehensive school, because sometimes they make a bit of a mess. "It's not just that," I say. Reluctantly, I pull my head away from his shoulder and show him the picture on my phone.

"What is this?" he whispers. His head flicks up and his eyes lock with mine. "How on earth did your aunt Mariah get hold of this? I don't understand."

"I have no idea."

"You haven't heard anything from Mariah recently? Other than this?" He holds the phone out in front of him.

"No. Nothing since..." The funeral. Mum's funeral. Neither Mariah nor my cousins came. There was an excuse about not being able to get away from Paris, where Mariah moved not long after Granny's death ten years ago. And flowers. Exquisite flowers from one of the best florists in London. Flowers that were far grander than the ones that trailed around Granny's garden.

"She looks exactly like you." He tucks a stray strand of my own blond hair behind my ear, and runs his hand down my wet cheek, wiping away my tears with his thumb.

I pause and brace myself. I had noticed that the picture of Granny in Paris looked very similar to me, but I almost had to swallow the thought down. It was too much to bear.

"Well," I say, gathering myself and trying to muster some of Granny's pluck, "something smells wonderful in the kitchen." Homey scents fill the house. Roast lamb, rosemary, new potatoes. I pick the shopping bags up off the floor.

Andrew scratches his head. "I'm sorry. I'm dumbfounded. Why would Mariah send such a thing?"

The woman who did not come to her mother's funeral, to Granny's funeral, when the church in the village was full to bursting at the seams. Mum and I had to sit alone in the front pew. I'll never forget the heartbroken expression on Mum's face. The woman who made us sell Granny's house, because Mariah wanted to put her half of the profits toward an apartment in Paris.

I pull Andrew into another hug in the kitchen. I love him and his uncomplicated, happy family. I love the home that we have built together.

"I know," I say. "It's all so sad."

Andrew pulls the deliciously crisp roast leg of lamb from the oven, along with the potatoes, carrots, and steamed fresh green baby beans. He sets two plates out for us, and there is a small white jug filled with his homemade mint sauce, using herbs from the pots on our kitchen window.

"This is gorgeous," I say, meaning it. How Granny Louise would have loved him, had she had the chance to meet him.

Once we have finished, and we have cleared up companionably, I take Andrew's hand. "Come with me," I whisper.

I lead him down the hallway to the bookshelf that stands near the front door. My eyes go straight to the book I am seeking. I know where every book is placed, because I arrange them just like Granny did, in alphabetical order. She liked to do things that way. I do too. I reach for the copy of *Grimm's Fairy Tales* and solemnly open it up to the title page. There is an inscription that I found when I was cleaning out my mum's house after she died. Neither Mum nor Granny ever mentioned it, and now it's too late to ask.

Inside the cover of the book in faded sepia ink are written

the words I pushed aside, as I was too consumed with grief to pay real attention to them:

To my darling Louise, the Ritz Hotel, Paris, 1944

A frown line appears between his eyes.

The book is clutched tightly to my chest. I do know that Mariah's latest project is ancestry. Several years after Granny's death, but before Mum became ill, Mariah went to a major fashion magazine that used to feature her daughter, my cousin Pandora, on the cover when she was modeling in her twenties. Aunt Mariah told them of her research into her late husband Ed's family. The magazine published a two-page spread, complete with photographs about how Pandora's mother had discovered that the famous fashion model's grandmother on her father's side of the family had been captured by the Nazis in Poland. The article had gone on to describe how the eldest daughters in many Polish families were sent to work in forced-labor concentration camps. And there was a photograph of Pandora's paternal grandmother, all white-blond tousled hair, like Pandora's.

I hold the copy of *Grimm's Fairy Tales* close to me as if I am clutching Granny herself. "I'm worried that Mariah will take the image of Granny and go to the press," I say. I shake my head.

"You knew your granny. That's all that matters. Ignore it." Andrew gently wipes a stray tear from my cheek with his thumb.

I shake my head. "I can't. The image itself is enough to haunt me, but the implications behind it are already preying on my mind. I can't believe that my grandmother was a traitor."

Andrew rubs a hand across his beard. "But I don't think there's anything that can be done."

I shake my head. "There is something I can do. I can get on a train, go to Paris, and prove that Granny never collaborated."

"Darling—"

"You are right that I knew her. And that's enough. But if I must prove it, then that's what I'll do." My hand moves protectively to my stomach. Proving that Granny was no Nazi is not only about the past, but also about the future. I want my baby to know the truth about the woman I loved more than anyone in the world.

CHAPTER TWO

PARIS, SUMMER 1944

Louise

The leather banquettes in the bar of the Ritz Hotel are empty. Paris's spies and her double-crossers, the glamorous secret-keepers who rub shoulders in the oak-paneled room and plan their murderous crimes, are all tucked away for the night. But the smell of expensive whiskey and brandy lingers in the air, and Frank Meier's bar is polished to a gleam. His bottles of liquor, spirits, and fine wines glimmer in the half-light.

I try to look nonchalant as I walk through the empty, hushed place toward his closed office door. I knock several times in a quick rhythmic pattern, following the code that Frank changes every week.

Frank opens the door, the fine lines around his eyes easing into the smile of a man who could be sitting in a deck chair staring out at a blue sea, but the heavy bags beneath them reveal the weariness that envelops us all. His hair is neatly combed to one side as if he has just stepped out to begin a shift, but I know he has been up all night.

Frank leans forward, kisses me on the cheek in traditional Parisian style, and ushers me into the office.

Claude Auzello, our hotel manager, nods at me from an armchair in the corner.

We are about to get down to business when the door swings open and Blanche Auzello is standing there. Claude's wife makes no attempt to lower her voice. And yet, rumor has it, Blanche is far more than just Claude's wife. I have heard whispers of bravery that goes well beyond her role here in the Ritz Hotel.

"Popsy? Are you going to come to bed for ten minutes before you must get up and do it all again?" Blanche flicks her long dark hair and turns her mesmerizing face toward Claude. Her accent is American, and everyone knows her story. She grew up in New York and was an actress before she married the manager of the Ritz Hotel. It is said that she hid her Jewish identity to make herself safe. Apparently, Blanche invented a completely different childhood for herself than that which she really had. Blanche's brown eyes flash. "I *miss* you, Popsy," she says to Claude and pouts like a schoolgirl.

Frank looks down at the floor, and I try not to giggle.

"Of course, my darling," Claude replies. He is, famously, never ruffled, and he doesn't seem the least bit worried about this. "You will excuse me." He attempts a formal bow to the rest of us and leaves the room.

I can't help my smile. Everyone knows that Claude is called Popsy by his wife because his eyes pop every time he looks at her.

After they leave, Frank does a wonderful fluttery imitation of Blanche. It's well meant and we need laughter at the moment. But then he turns serious. "I have a new list for you this morning. The delivery truck was early today."

Frank pulls out a sheet of paper and hands it to me.

On it are rows and rows of numbers. My heart starts racing.

Fancy dresses might be anathema to me, but when it comes to numbers, I just look at them once and I know every single one by heart.

Frank first heard of my strange talent when the other maids were gossiping in the hotel staffroom about how I could remember exactly who was in every room of the hotel, that I could recall who came to stay months ago, and even who visited them on which day. I'd even been able to recall guests' identity card details if I'd had a little look while I was cleaning their rooms.

Frank viewed this with fascination. He got me to remember strings of numbers and names of hotel guests overnight (all Nazis), and then when I recalled them all perfectly the following day, he asked me to start working with him, and with Claude, who oversees the underground operations in the hotel.

Jean-Paul, our head chef, organizes four sets of what appear to be mysterious codes to arrive with his deliveries, and his waiters report Nazi conversations to Frank from the hotel restaurants. The Nazis who stay here are both overconfident and indiscreet. I don't know whether they think we are fools, or beneath their notice, or both.

I run my fingers down the rows of numbers. My hand, with its spattering of freckles, is quick. My brain fires up, and I feel truly alive for the first time today.

"Hans Jürgen Soehring." I stop about one third of the way down the page and begin pointing out specific rows of numerals, instantly remembering the corresponding Nazi names. "Colonel Hans Speidel. Hans Günther von Dincklage. Carl-Heinrich von Stülpnagel, Reichsmarschall Hermann Göring."

Frank transcribes the numbers onto another piece of paper, which will be sent on to the Allies in neutral territory, without saying a word. Even though Frank has never told me what we are doing explicitly, I am certain that we are sending coded messages about which Nazis are staying in the hotel and when.

Sometimes, I must translate vegetables from French into German. Lists of vegetables. I find it hilarious as they're all codes. Göring is a potato. Often, I am asked to provide more detailed information, given my knack for languages. I speak French, English, and German fluently.

I told Frank the other day that I am better at numbers and letters and remembering things than I am at life. Frank told me this was life; I love him for that.

I was always going to try to go to university. The plan was that I would move to Paris and work as a maid while studying. I wasn't sure what subject yet, so I had hoped to enroll in a course in liberal arts. But then the war came. Four years later, the university part of my plan has grown old.

"Josée de Chambrun had a private lunch in the suite of Carl-Heinrich von Stülpnagel yesterday," I say. "I knocked on the door, and because there was no response, I went in to clean. Von Stülpnagel looked furious. I heard nothing of their conversation because they turned silent the minute I walked in the door." I had been trying to tuck my unruly blond hair into my maid's cap because it had escaped. My face had reddened at the sight of them.

A shadow passes across Frank's face.

"They dined on steak tartare, salade Niçoise, quiche, and crepes," I add. Not sure if this is helpful, but I always like to give a bit of extra detail, and I think Frank appreciates that.

Josée de Chambrun is the aristocratic daughter of the Vichy French government's high official, Pierre Laval, and Carl-Heinrich von Stülpnagel is the German military governor of occupied France. I don't see it as unusual that the two would be lunching together, given the Vichy government's loyalty to Germany and to Hitler's rule. But Frank is frowning over his numbers.

I move over to the window that in the daytime looks out over

Rue Cambon. The blackout curtains are thick and ruthless. Not a flicker of light is allowed inside the hotel. We are protecting ourselves from the Allies' bombing raids. They are targeting the bridges and the military bases in northern France in preparation for what we are told will be a mass invasion to liberate the country from the occupying Germans.

I'm not sure what I'm going to do at the end of the war. What keeps me awake at night is the fear of losing the little Résistance family I've found in here: Frank; Claude; the head chef, Jean-Paul; and the ever-elusive, fabulous Blanche, who hovers around and above us like a dream.

Frank rubs his fingers over his chin. "I've been thinking..." He swallows and appears to be choosing his words. "The Allied attacks. Saint-Germain-en-Laye. Have you heard anything from your mother?"

Pain slices through my insides, as if someone has taken a sword and slashed a diagonal cross through me, and I think back to when I spoke about my mother to Frank a few months ago.

It was late, or early, whichever way you want to view it, and we had been working together. I had reported to Frank about Coco Chanel and her Nazi lover, Hans von Dincklage, and a conversation I had overheard between them about a trip to Spain.

Afterward, Frank and I began talking about family. I told Frank the heartbreaking truth about my father, how he had walked out and left when I was twelve years old.

I almost told Frank another awkward secret that I carry about my father and that I have not shared with anyone else. But it did not seem safe to do so and instead I told Frank how my mother, my practical, darling mother, began taking in customers after my father left and selling beautiful dresses that she sewed from the pretty fabrics she had always admired. I told him how she used to covet lovely soft and silky materials when I was young. After we went to church on a Sunday, she would stop outside the draper's shop, her eyes drinking in the florals, the spots, the pretty striped silks. Her face would become dreamy on the way home. Then, she would cook a beautiful Sunday luncheon for my father and me, but her expression would still hold that faraway look, and I was certain that she was dreaming of making something magical out of those fabrics in the window of the draper's shop.

So, when my father left, my mother put her head down and began to sew. Maman and I had to move from our little farm in Normandy as we could not afford to keep it, and my father had driven it into the ground anyway, so my mother chose Saint-Germain-en-Laye. And soon, the customers came, and kept coming, and my mother went from being a married woman to the owner of a small business. It suited her.

My relationship with her was never overly affectionate or demonstrative, but we understood each other. She was always there for me, and I for her. Maman approved of my dream to go to university and she was behind me wholeheartedly when I moved to Paris to work as a maid to support myself. The closest we came to outright declarations of love was once when she put a note under my bedroom door and told me she was proud of me when I did well in my final year at school and had earned a place at the Sorbonne. That was 1939.

I keep the note in my bedside table, even today.

I have written to my mother every single week since I started working at the Ritz. And yet, she never replies. At first, I thought it was just one of her odd quirks. I imagined her asking me why we would bother writing to each other when there is nothing of any interest to say.

I didn't worry about it for the first few months, because my mother doesn't grieve or yearn for the past. But now the silence from her is like a mountain ravine that gets wider every day and I have no idea what is going on.

• • •

Frank folds up his papers. He looks at his watch. "I must go and hand these codes on...Louise, keep writing to her. I shall try to get in touch with my contacts in the area to find out whether she is safe."

I nod.

Frank holds the door open for me. I slip back out through the empty, silent bar and through the swinging double doors to the staff area of the hotel. I can navigate my way around the back corridors like a mouse. I know every nook and cranny, and it is in the shadows that I feel truly safe.

I am adjusting my maid's apron before breakfast, just two hours later, when there is a soft tap on my bedroom door. I freeze. Billie Holiday's "I'll Be Seeing You" swells through the room and I wait. I love a bit of Billie Holiday before breakfast. In fact, I think everyone should try it. It does one no end of good.

Perhaps I imagined the sound. But there it is again. Distinct. Three knocks, followed by a pause, before another four taps.

I stay still. We maids have been trained never to answer to anyone except our supervisor, Juliette. If the inhabitants of the hotel are not Nazis, then they are underground. If they are not underground, then they are collaborators. Only a fool would answer their bedroom door in the Ritz.

In normal circumstances, one would assume that no guest would have any interest in knocking on the door of a mere maid. In normal circumstances, no guest would be able to make their way into the staff quarters of a magnificent hotel. But these are no ordinary circumstances, and the Ritz is not just any magnificent hotel. The Swiss-owned hotel is officially neutral, but the reality is that everyone is tied to one side or the other, sometimes both.

I hear Juliette's voice through the door, and I'm relieved. I move over to my wireless and turn my music off. The silence washes over the room like a coat of white paint. I straighten my black maid's uniform, check that my apron is pristine and sitting perfectly straight, and ensure that my thick blond hair is not exploding out of my cap. Even knowing it's Juliette, goose bumps rise like tiny mountains on my forearms and a strange pattern plays in my stomach.

"Louise?" Juliette calls through the door, more purposefully this time.

I reach for the tarnished handle and lower my gaze as the door opens, silently as silk.

"I never thought of you as someone who would listen to jazz, Louise. I request that you be a little more discreet with your wireless. There are rules."

Yes, rules set by the Nazis as to what we will not listen to. The Yankee Doodle station is strictly forbidden, and jazz is degenerate. If she'd come a few minutes earlier, she would have caught me enjoying a cigarette, leaning out the window of my attic room, looking down at the people on the Rue Cambon. Already, the air is hot and sultry, and my room is stifling.

I raise my head and look up at the implacable gaze of my superior. Her lips widen in a determined smile, and her eyes crinkle with a sense of something I cannot fathom. I would say that she looks excited, like a cat that has caught a mouse.

Juliette folds her hands with their red-painted nails in front of the pale blue two-piece suit she is wearing and steps aside.

A young woman stands behind Juliette. Her long blond hair clasped at the nape of her neck, the blue eyes that sparkle in a way I have not seen in four years among French people, and the healthy pink sheen on her cheeks all tell me one thing.

Nazi.

I fold my arms. What horror is this?

"So. I would like to introduce you to Sasha Hoffman," Juliette says, and the girl and I stare at each other.

I narrow my eyes, but she, audaciously, smiles.

"From now on, you will be sharing your room with Fraulein Hoffman, Louise. Please make her feel welcome."

My hands ball into two tight fists at my sides. I need another cigarette. The second single bed in my room has been empty since I moved here. I am singular, and I like my own space. It means I can sneak out at five o'clock in the morning to meet with Frank and Jean-Claude. I cannot share my room.

"This is impossible."

Juliette flushes at my gumption, but I have long given up pleasing others. I used to try, so very hard. I tried at school, and at home, when my father was living with us, and yet it made no difference. He still left. These days, I do not begin to bother.

"Do call me Sasha," the girl says.

I send her a withering look. We are all aware of the Nazis' tricks to make us think we can trust them. Tricks to lead us down the dark labyrinth of deception to Germany to meet our deaths.

The German girl's blue eyes light up, and she smiles. It is captivating. She has two rows of pearly white teeth, small teeth, and there is a spattering of freckles across the bridge of her nose and on the tops of her cheeks. I think how hard I used to work to remove my freckles with lemon juice.

"This will not work." I keep my voice firm.

"The orders are from above." Juliette sends me a little nod. Her dark hair is pulled up into a French roll, and she clasps the string of large imitation pearls around her neck. She has been influenced by Chanel and her love of costume jewelry. Does she know what Chanel is doing in this very hotel?

My stomach drops, and there is something eating away my insides. Am I being watched? Most likely. This means that not only I, but Frank and Claude, and Blanche and Jean-Paul, are also at risk. I cannot have that. I cannot lose these people. They are all I have.

"Sasha joins us as the assistant to Carl-Heinrich von Stülpnagel," Juliette adds. "The military governor of occupied France."

"You don't need to spell it out." I send Juliette one of my cultivated stares, but I fold my arms around my waist as if I am hugging myself.

Juliette ignores my rude reply. "I shall leave you to get to know each other. Once Sasha has settled in, please show her down to breakfast." Juliette issues orders as if she is talking about cleaning the Imperial Suite.

She turns on her heel and disappears.

Only the sound of her footsteps breaks the eerie silence in the empty corridor. Everyone else is down at breakfast. I like to go down last, eat efficiently and quickly, and not linger. I hate the other maids' chatter about the large families they have left behind. I don't wish to get involved because I can't cope with their conversation. My life is made of silences, and no one is going to understand that.

Time is moving strangely, and the German girl is already in my room. She places her smart brown leather suitcase with its brass ornamentation on the spare bed and opens it with one crisp click.

I curl my lip at the expensive-looking suitcase, this representation of ostentation that the Nazis have thrown in the face of the Parisians these last four years. Outside this hotel, the true citizens of this city have been left to starve in their freezing homes.

The Nazis have treated Paris as their personal playground. Trainloads full of German officers have arrived daily on the direct route from Berlin to entertain themselves in the most beautiful city in the world. It only took them a few days to commandeer Paris's most famous hotel.

Sasha sits down on the bed next to her smart suitcase, crosses her legs, opens her handbag, and pulls out a cigarette. She lights it and regards me through the smoky haze, then she closes her eyes a moment and tips her head back.

I let out a wry laugh.

"Something amusing?" She is speaking French.

I will never give away that I understand German.

"No." I am firm.

She opens and narrows her extraordinary blue eyes. They are two sapphires shimmering in the smoke.

I hold my ground.

"I love Billie Holiday," she says. "In case you're wondering."

I turn on my heels and move toward the door. "I am not wondering."

But as my shoes snap along the bare wooden floorboards of the women's staff corridor, one thing becomes starkly clear. I will never, ever be able to relax now, not when I eat, sleep, or clean the rooms of the top-ranking Nazis, and especially not when I slip downstairs to Frank's bar. I have a sinking thought. Perhaps I should stop working with him. I cannot give Sasha any reason to become suspicious or to investigate when our lives are at stake.

But even as I walk along the corridor and Sasha's footsteps click along behind me, I realize that Blanche Auzello would not be intimidated. I remember the flash and the confidence in her eyes, the way she ensnared us all in that room and had us twirled around her fingers like jeweled rings. I have heard tales of Blanche dressing as a German nurse and accompanying a badly wounded British air force gunner across Paris to help him to a barge on the Seine. No, cowardice and fear will not end this occupation, and we in the Ritz have a role to play just like everyone else. It's just that the Nazis are in our building. Even in our bedrooms, it seems.

We come to the set of white-painted double doors that leads to the kitchens, the hotbed of underground resistance, and I pause, my hands resting lightly on the two handles of these closed doors. I'm about to bring in a viper.

But I hesitate only for a moment, and then I push the doors open wide, and lead Sasha into the staff dining room, where everyone is sitting sipping coffee and eating freshly baked white bread with preserves, in a way that the hungry Parisians outside this gilded, guilty cage cannot even begin to contemplate. And it is as if I am walking on thrilling air, while my stomach has turned to a block of determined, steely ice.

At the long table in the staff dining room, Frank is chatting with Claude.

I slip into a vacant chair, deliberately choosing a place with a maid and a bellhop sitting on either side of me, so there is no room for Sasha to sit nearby.

I pour myself a cup of coffee. Frank is looking down the table at me.

I raise my cup and send Frank a little nod.

His eyes avert to Sasha, who has seated herself right opposite me so that she can see every move I make. His face whitens slightly.

But I don't quake. Fear has left me.

CHAPTER THREE

STANSTED AIR FORCE BASE, UNITED KINGDOM, SUMMER 1944

Kit

Kit placed his razor down on the basin below the long mirror in the latrines. Next to him, his younger brother, Charlie, wiped a hand towel across his own neatly shaven face. Kit gazed at their reflections. He and Charlie could be twins, with their dark blond hair cut short in the military way. Their green eyes were almost identical, but Charlie had dimples in his cheeks and Kit was beginning to get fine lines fanning out around his eyes.

The light in the bathroom was garish, but outside, dawn was yet to break over the air force base. Kit stretched his arms high over his head and yawned. He had not expected to be woken up at four o'clock in the morning to be sent out on a mission over France. Two other pilots had fallen ill, and Kit had grimaced when he had found out that his younger brother would be flying with him today.

He rested a hand on Charlie's shoulder. "I'll be taking extra care today," Kit said. "The Jerries are moving all their guns to the north coast of France."

"I thought most of their weapons were concentrated north

of Paris?" Charlie asked. He tapped his razor against the side of the basin and splashed water over his face just as Kit had taught him to do all those years ago.

Kit felt an ache at the way Charlie had followed him into the military. He knew Charlie would much prefer to be back working in the bookshop in Bloomsbury where he had been so at home while studying English literature at university until Pearl Harbor was bombed. Kit, as the son of expatriate Americans in London, had spent the early years of the war in London driving ambulances, carrying stretchers, rescuing people from bombed-out buildings, and helping the Red Cross, but when the United States had been drawn into the conflict, Kit had flown back home to California and chosen the most dangerous mission there was. Training to be a bomber pilot. He'd been devastated when Charlie had insisted on coming, too, out of loyalty to him.

"The country's transportation hubs merge to the north of Paris," Kit said. "We will be targeting the capital's outskirts today, I suspect. Time to go face the inevitable plate of Spam and eggs."

Charlie straightened up. "I'm bright-eyed and bushy-tailed," he said.

Kit threw an arm around his brother's shoulder as they walked out into the rising dawn toward the mess.

Once they were sitting at one of the long tables that stretched along the room, Kit stared at his own plate of Spam and eggs, while next to him Charlie chatted with one of the gunners and ate heartily. It was rewarding to see Charlie's confidence having picked up so much since they'd joined the military, but it was Kit who received the anxious letters from their mother about looking after themselves. She had sailed back home to her family in the United States for safety before the war broke out, but

Kit knew that his mother worried day and night about them both because, should their airplane go down, she could lose both of her sons at once.

But it wasn't as if their mother was not used to having family in the military. Their father, Anthony, had enjoyed a successful career in the navy and had been highly decorated in the Great War. He was working now in a highly skilled role in London in the War Office as an expatriate American.

Not only did Kit want to take care of his younger brother, he didn't want to let his father down, and that meant he had to come home safely with both Charlie and a distinguished military career under his belt. He and Charlie had undertaken several missions during their time in the air force, but things were escalating in France, and Kit couldn't help feeling especially nervous today.

In the locker room, Kit put on his bib over the light green trousers and shirt he wore, pulled on his leather jacket, threw his escape kit over his shoulder, and placed his dog tags around his neck. With Charlie close behind him, Kit checked in his wallet at the counter for safekeeping and went to the briefing room.

He sat down next to Charlie at one of the double desks among the rows of men who were going out on today's mission. The major traced a red line over the big operations map from the coast of France to Paris. Kit had been right: They were aiming to blow up a bridge on the northern outskirts of Paris near Saint-Germain-en-Laye.

Nerves flickered through his system. There was no way of knowing how many guns would be aimed directly at their aircraft from Paris as they flew over the coast, and they may be getting fired at from new areas today as well.

He focused on the major, but he was more aware than ever

of Charlie's presence next to him. Every time they went up together was a deeper reminder of how young Charlie seemed for his years.

The major looked at them and folded his arms. "Escape from Paris is impossible now. The Germans are determinedly, deliberately picking up fallen Allied airmen from the streets, so avoid Paris at all costs if you land in trouble. What the Nazis want is to make the air force stop raiding their munition depots and their bases. But we will not be intimidated. We will continue to send you up."

Kit caught Charlie's eye and read the question there. *How were they supposed to bail out if they were hit and not land in the city below?*

He sent Charlie a far more confident smile than he felt.

Out on the tarmac, the flight crew were subdued. Kit checked out a parachute, put on his flight helmet, and jogged over to one of the trucks with his brother. The six B-26 aircraft sat waiting for them. The mile-long runway that the plane needed to take off stretched out like a pathway.

Kit set his mouth into a firm line. He'd lain awake and dreamed of becoming a fighter pilot after Pearl Harbor was hit.

Nowhere in his dreams had his kid brother been right next to him.

CHAPTER FOUR

PARIS, SUMMER 1944

Louise

"What do you have planned for today?" Sasha asks.

I turn around to look at the German girl, but she stands perfectly still in front of her bed, the expression on her face opaque.

"I am cleaning." I roll my eyes. As if she had to ask.

"Perfect. I shall come with you."

I grit my teeth. "And what of Colonel von Stülpnagel?" I ask her. "Are you not needed in his employ? Why would a Nazi secretary want to clean rooms?"

"I have various duties," she replies. "Just because I'm in the employ of the military governor of France, that doesn't mean I don't enjoy certain things—cleaning. Billie Holiday."

I turn and march out of the room.

Once we have collected the trolleys and have checked in with Juliette, we make our way down Temptation Corridor, the passageway that connects the Rue Cambon side of the Ritz to the other half of the hotel that backs up against it on Place Vendôme.

The usual curl of apprehension I feel as we approach the side of the hotel where the high-ranking Nazis live is tripled with von Stülpnagel's accomplice trotting alongside me as if we are taking a walk in the park.

Four years of German occupation have not dulled the sense of menace that lurks in this part of the grand hotel. Once, this side of the Ritz was a palace; now, it hosts some of the most sinister murderers in the world.

Our trolleys are filled with lemon-scented cleaning products, feather dusters, and immaculate brooms that are fit only for the grandest hotel in Paris. They glide as quietly along the floors as a pair of Reichsmarschall Göring's soft-soled slippers. From the Imperial Suite in the Ritz, he's pillaged art, run the Nazi war machine, and tried to avoid the temper of Adolf Hitler, who blames him for the Nazis' weakened position in the war.

I force myself to focus on the sound of our muted footsteps on the rich carpet of the passageway, but the hush that has enveloped the German side of the hotel since talk intensified of imminent Allied landings in France is eerie and strange.

I distract myself from the rattle of the trolleys and the sound of Sasha's footsteps by averting my eyes toward the gorgeous array of luxurious items set up in glass cabinets that line the corridor. This corridor is not called Temptation Corridor for nothing. But the sight of jeweled slippers, fur coats, antique jewelry, and perfumes on display only serves to remind me that the Nazis stole, and now flaunt, France's greatest luxuries.

We bring our trolleys to a stop outside the closed doors of the magnificent Imperial Suite. I close my eyes as I always do when I am standing here and say a little prayer in the hope that Herr Göring will not be in residence today. All the staff know how he lounges in there, outlandishly dressed in silk kimonos, addled by his addiction to morphine, and dousing himself in exotic perfumes made by the nearby house of Guerlain, while eating excessively. Meanwhile, outside the protective walls of this building, Paris is almost descending into civil war. At night, I curl up in a ball in my bed, knowing that local gangsters are directing day-to-day operations of terror for the French police, who are at war with the swelling numbers of Resistance. Us.

Sasha and I wait a few seconds after I knock until there is no answer from inside Göring's suite. I sigh with relief when the eerie silence hanging over this half of the hotel is not broken by one of his staccato shouts. We swing open the wide doors to the exquisite suite.

The sight of the bedroom that replicates Marie Antoinette's boudoir in the Palace of Versailles never fails to enchant me, even after four years, even after cleaning it nearly every morning under the exact same routine.

My shoes sink into the supple Aubusson carpets, and it is all I can do not to sag into one of the gilt and silken Louis XV chairs. Like a footman in a choreographed ballet, I come to a stop at the end of the bed that is crowned with eggshell-blue silk draperies with an oil painting set into their folds. The room is filled with the scent of the pale roses that sit in a crystal bowl on a small inlaid antique table, and I stand face-to-face with my and Sasha's reflections in the pair of white-framed mirrors that are set into the wardrobe on the white-paneled walls. Here is a fairy-tale world complete with a resident ogre.

"First, we must change the sheets on the bed."

Sasha opens her mouth as if to say something, but I send her a firm look in return.

I am certain that Sasha is hoping to find out which side I am on.

She will never know.

She bites her lip a moment and then seems to think better of making conversation, and we remove Herr Göring's bedding from the luxurious mattress. I show her how to turn and rotate it to ensure even dips. I have been schooled to do this regularly;

otherwise, the mattresses will sink in the places where the guests sleep.

I move past the pile of sheets that I have scattered on the floor and throw open a window to further air the vast bed, stopping for a moment to gaze out at the timeless serenity of Paris's wealthiest square, the Place Vendôme.

Sasha tidies a lavish gown trimmed in ermine that Göring has left on a chair, placing it in one of the mirrored closets among his sumptuous collection of stolen emerald brooches, jeweled sandals, and diamond earrings that he leaves lying about.

As well as conversing freely in the brasseries, the Nazis leave papers lying around in their rooms. Usually, I pick the papers up and scan the contents, which I relay back to Frank, but I will not risk that today. If our Nazi occupiers try to throw their weight around and hold haughty, imperative discussions among themselves when I arrive to clean, I listen to them and report every word. Power is their purpose, but too much power can come back to bite.

I watch Sasha. She picks up the crystal bowl on Göring's bedside table filled with tablets of morphine, alongside another bowl that contains a mélange of black pearls, opals, garnets, and rubies.

I keep moving—I have to keep moving—and we shake out the sateen cotton sheet, tuck it and the cashmere blanket in neatly, and carefully lay down the silk bedspread. I hold each pillow over my forearm, to check they do not flop down on both sides. Satisfied that none of them need replacing, I arrange them beautifully on the bed.

"Did you grow up in one of the big German cities, or in a little town?" I ask.

"I grew up in Heidelberg."

My hand stills at the mention of Heidelberg.

"You were at the university?" I ask. I keep my voice as casual as possible.

"I was studying psychology."

"You have progressed a long way if you are working for von Stülpnagel," I say. "You must be revered in the ranks."

Sasha raises a brow. Again, she does not react.

I move to the bathroom and start on the porcelain basin, wiping away traces of Göring's makeup that are scattered and spattered on the marble surrounds. Perhaps, as he was orchestrating the Blitz over London from this very suite, Göring wanted to pretend he was some seventeenth-century pompadour.

"You take pride in your work." Sasha surveys the room. "Tell me, do you have ambitions beyond all this?"

"I have no ambition," I lie.

Once I am finished, and the bathroom is sparkling and perfect, I turn on my heels, place both of my hands on my trolley, and, even though my breathing is shaky, I hold my head high and walk out of the bathroom.

"I have another question," Sasha says once we are in the glorious salon.

I pause as I take a polishing cloth out. If this is a game of cat and mouse, she is playing by the book.

"How did you come to be a maid?" She looks at me quizzically.

"You think I had a choice?" I ask. "You think any of us had a choice?"

Sasha sinks down into one of the deeply cushioned cherry-red silk sofas. This is strictly forbidden, of course, but she throws her head back and looks up at me. "You blame the Germans. But your esteemed Vichy government has hardly demonstrated loyalty to the citizens of France."

I glance around the Imperial Suite. Everything is perfection. I gather my trolley and start rolling toward the door, ignoring her. I will not be drawn in, and Sasha has no choice but to follow me.

Out in the corridor, we move back to the Rue Cambon side of the hotel. We come to a stop outside the room of Chanel. Coco Chanel has openly lived here with her German lover, Hans von Dincklage, throughout the war.

"Why don't you clean this room on your own? Please adopt the same methods that we used in Göring's suite." I must distract her with something far more interesting than me, and what could be more interesting than Chanel?

Sasha places her hands on my trolley for one moment, her eyes locking with mine and staying there. But I do not budge, and I do not lower my gaze like a good French person should when in the company of a Nazi.

Finally, Sasha turns and disappears into Chanel's room, and I hold back the bile that sticks in my throat as I move toward the next room on my list.

If I am a target, I will not be shot down without a fight.

CHAPTER FIVE

PARIS, PRESENT DAY

Nicole

The apartment I'm renting in Paris came with a vase of yellow roses and a set of beautiful French windows that open out onto a tiny, perfect balcony. There is a cheerful fire station across the road, complete with two red engines sitting gleaming in the entranceway. Thankfully, I haven't yet seen them dash off anywhere. My favorite part is that I get to enter my apartment through a set of curved wooden doors into a classic Parisian courtyard, flooded with sunlight, and then climb a winding flight of stairs until I come to the third floor. I make my way down the stairs and across the courtyard now.

I still have a little time before my appointment with the archivist at the Ritz, so I wander through the Tuileries Garden, where children are already setting up small boats on the pond.

The Louvre sits like a grand dame overlooking the manicured garden, and like a good Parisian, I stick to the paths. A bank of daffodils turn their faces to the sun, and white, frothy blossoms sprinkle down onto the raked gravel, creating a carpet of petals.

Soon, I am out of the timeless garden and walking up the Rue de Castiglione toward the Place Vendôme. Rubies, emeralds, and diamonds sparkle from the windows of the luxurious jewelers that overlook this most majestic and wealthy part of Paris, and the Ritz Hotel sits imposingly in the heart of the famous square. White canopies curve elegantly over the French doors of the hotel, and serpent-shaped green plants curl up the walls between the windows in planter boxes.

The doorman steps aside to let me enter through the sparkling glass doors into the vast marble lobby with its sweeping staircase that leads up to the beautiful rooms. I smooth my hands over the black linen dress I've chosen to wear. I'm hoping it is classic, like this old hotel, but, right now, I only wish that I had my cousin Pandora's gorgeous height and jaded allure.

A staff member approaches me, dressed in the livery of a bellhop of days gone by. "Bonjour, Mademoiselle," he says.

"Bonjour."

I tell him briefly, in French, that I have an appointment with their archivist, Arielle Blanchet.

"Bien sûr."

The bellhop disappears, and I take the opportunity to gaze around the magnificent space. The grand staircase is exquisite, curving up in perfect proportions and laid with a stunning carpet from the Middle East, and the curling, elaborate, black wrought-iron banister is a work of art.

I busy myself taking in glimpses of the grand salons through the open doors. Through one of these, there are floor-to-ceiling bookshelves lining the walls of the high-ceilinged room and sofas that must be perfect to sink into after a long day exploring Paris. The leather-bound books look so enticing, and I can only imagine Granny Louise loving such a gorgeous space.

A woman comes toward me in a deep green silken shift dress and high heels. She reaches out her hand. "Mademoiselle

Beaumont?" she asks. "My name is Arielle. I am the archivist at the Ritz, and I'm charmed to meet you."

"Enchantée," I murmur.

"Come with me." She swings around, her glossy dark curls bouncing.

Soon, we are sitting at a table in the *grand jardin*. A wide strip of deep green lawn is bordered by box hedges, and a row of trees are covered in blossoms. Tables are set around the circumference of the charming interior square underneath the verandas.

We sit in the sun, and Arielle turns her face up to the sky in appreciation. "The weather is wonderful," she says.

"Much warmer than in London. Thank you for meeting with me, Madame—"

"Arielle. Please. I am an employee, not a guest."

Our eyes meet, and something anchors itself between us.

My shoulders drop. It is difficult not to be intimidated by such opulent surroundings. My aunt Mariah and my cousin Pandora would be far more at home here than Granny...

"I was intrigued by the email about your grandmother." Arielle leans forward in her seat. "You have reason to believe she was in the hotel in the summer of 1944? It was an extremely volatile time in Paris, and in the Ritz. Why do you think she was here then?"

I reach into my handbag and pull out the copy of *Grimm's Fairy Tales*. Silently, I open the cover and turn to the title page, and the inscription and message written all those years ago: *To my darling Louise, the Ritz Hotel, Paris, 1944*. I pass the book across to Arielle.

She opens it and checks the publishing date. "This is an early edition and valuable." She frowns at the sepia handwriting inside the front cover. "The dedication certainly looks genuine," she says. "So, yes, it looks like whoever wrote this could have been here in 1944."

Coffee arrives. I bite back my questions.

It is espresso, and the waiter chats with Arielle. I take a sip for fortification.

"Your grandmother was French?" she asks after he leaves.

"I don't know. She never mentioned being French...or anything else. The past was something she never discussed. She never talked about the war. It sounds awful now, but I never asked."

Arielle looks away across the square. "No, that is understandable. There is so much silence among that generation about the war. There are many French families who do not know how their ancestors survived the Nazis' brutal occupation of Paris."

"I lost my mother a year ago," I manage. "So now I can't ask her or my grandmother." I can just talk about it now, without tears rolling down my cheeks.

Arielle shakes her head. "I am sorry."

I place my empty coffee cup down in the tiny saucer. The photograph that Mariah sent me gave me nightmares for a week. But I know I must deal with it. If I don't show it to Arielle, she won't be able to help me.

My fingers are steady as I scroll through my photos, and my hand does not shake as I show her the image of my grandmother, a swastika branded across her forehead.

Arielle glances at the phone. She gasps. "Mon Dieu," she murmurs. "Where did this come from?" She winces and brings her hand up to cover her mouth.

I know it is distressing. "The photograph came from my aunt. The relationship she had with my grandmother was troubled. But I adored her, and I'm struggling to believe this could possibly be my grandmother, you see. And yet, the photo bears such a striking likeness."

Arielle still stares at the phone. "Extraordinary," she murmurs.

I watch her. She has turned quite pale.

"Is everything all right?"

She frowns and looks up from the phone, cupping her coffee cup in her hands. Finally, she shakes her head. "Please, would you send me this image by email?"

"Of course," I say.

She nods. Clears her throat. "Let us focus on the book. *Grimm's Fairy Tales*. The book is printed in English, but the stories in it obviously originated in Germany. If it was a gift, it would be a strange one from an Allied beau. It was not uncommon for French women to have affairs with Nazis."

I stiffen, and my throat sticks. "I knew my grandmother," I manage to say, my voice tight. "I could never believe such a thing of her."

"I know this is hard to comprehend, but, Nicole, the fact is, it might have been a gift from her lover," Arielle offers gently.

"I cannot accept that. I knew her." But then...Those times when Granny's eyes held a faraway expression. The fact that she never wanted to leave England. Never had any desire to travel, was happy to spend her days at home in the small village where she knew everyone and they knew her. And loved her. She was a master of diversion if anyone asked her where she grew up. But that does not mean anything sinister. "I..." But I'm stuck. I simply have no words. No proof. I clear my throat.

"The way these women were humiliated after the war was thorough." Arielle gazes out at the lawn.

A beautifully dressed family are shown to a table nearby, and the children pull out coloring books. I watch for a moment while the little girl chooses a selection of pencils and turns the pages of her book, her face full of concentration.

"I understand about the women who were accused of Nazi collaboration," I say. "I teach history."

But Arielle seems to be miles away.

"I need to find the truth, because this is a part of family

history that could haunt future generations." *Could haunt my child.*

"She might not have been in love," Arielle says, but she still seems absent. "Women lived in the hotel and slept with Nazis, because, in return, they were able to send extra ration cards and food to their families, who were starving."

I shake my head.

"Other women were terrified, particularly those who were alone and who had lost their careers because of the Nazi occupation. They saw living in the Ritz and sleeping with Nazis as a means of survival. As a means of getting by."

Granny loved life so much. She always saw the good in things, people, situations. And she was protective of herself and those she loved. But even so...

Arielle continues, her voice soft, understanding. "Women had to do desperate things to survive. And they were often the only ones left at home while their husbands, sons, and uncles were away at war."

I bite my lip in order not to cut her off. This is like a runaway train, a story I can't contain. It's moving in a direction I cannot cope with, and I have no means of stopping it now.

"Their homes were freezing, and coal was severely restricted, so people were dying of malnutrition and cold. Added to that, they were living in terror that if they put one toe wrong, they would be deported to Germany to the labor camps, as they called concentration camps back then."

I know all of this, but I search frantically for a way out of this hole into which I feel I'm being buried, a parallel narrative running through my head. The woman I knew showing immense bravery and courage in times that were impossible...

"I do understand, thank you. Would you look through the archival records for me and see if there was a Louise Bassett staying in one of the hotel rooms?"

Arielle folds her hands on the table. I start when I see how the archivist's hands shake. What is wrong with her? Is she the nervous type?

"I am not sure that anything adds up here apart from what I have just told you." She frowns and pushes back her chair. "Please."

I stand up, too, only to stumble on the edge of the table and put my hand out to stop myself from falling.

Arielle catches me. She grasps my hand and my eyes meet hers. We stare at each other for a few seconds, and it is as if neither of us wants to look away.

"This is more important to me than I can say," I murmur. "If you could search the records of the guests during the occupation, I would be grateful."

Arielle lets go of my hand. The moment of honesty when we were looking at each other is over. She pats her hand down her dress as if she is dusting herself off and nods formally. "I shall see what can be done, but I cannot promise anything." Arielle indicates that we should go back out to the lobby. The meeting is over.

"Thank you," I say.

She nods at me, but her expression is still troubled, and the thought that my grandmother collaborated with the Nazis makes me feel vulnerable, as if all my foundations are made of sand.

CHAPTER SIX

PARIS, SUMMER 1944

Louise

I decide to push my worries about Sasha aside as I enter the rooms where the famous French actress Arletty has passed the war. I find her sitting at her dressing table in an oyster-colored silk bathrobe, a gift, I imagine, and I know who from.

Arletty turns to me, arching her fine eyebrows. Deep shadows bloom beneath her beautiful, deep-set eyes. Her long hair is styled in soft waves. "Louise," she breathes. "Thank goodness you are here. I have a terrible dilemma, and I have no idea what to do." She reaches for a silver cigarette case, a slow and languid movement with her soft, perfectly manicured hands, and flicks the case open with a dramatic gesture. She lights her cigarette and waves it in my direction as if she is raising a glass.

I wonder, *Is she acting all the time?*

I fold my own dry, cracked hands, fingers reddened from too much contact with water, nails peeling, and palms roughened, in front of my plain black dress.

Arletty stands up and moves to the window, where she is

perfectly framed by the pretty silk floral curtains, smoke curling artistically from the latest of her endless Gauloises.

Legend has it that Arletty was born into a humble working-class family, and after her father's death, she left home and pursued a modeling career. She moved from modeling to acting, working in music halls and then plays and cabarets. For ten years, she worked hard as a stage performer before debuting in the cinema houses as Blanche in *A Streetcar Named Desire*.

Arletty reinvented herself after her father died by being visible; I have done the opposite, shrinking into the background. Who could be more invisible than a maid?

I pause at the fine antique table opposite the film star's canopied silken bed. It is a bed of gold where a once golden film star sleeps. I've always preferred the smaller rooms here on the Rue Cambon side of the hotel, for the obvious reason that the guests tend to be French, but also because if I ever was able to afford to stay here, I'd much prefer to curl up in one of these cozier rooms rather than rattling about in one of the grander Place Vendôme suites. When the Nazis took over the hotel, they commandeered all the magnificent suites, sending all the French guests scuttling away to the smaller rooms.

"Louise?"

"Madame." My heart starts to dance in anticipation of what she is going to confide. As much as I detest what she is doing now, I love it when she tells me stories about her past, such as when she starred opposite Michel Simon in *Hôtel du Nord*, working under the direction of Marcel Carné. Of course, I must pass everything that Arletty tells me on to Frank, but that is in her best interests as well.

"I have a delicate matter. It is my..."

"Liaison?" The word slips from my tongue before I can pull it back in again.

Her eyes narrow. "You are full of euphemisms."

She strides across the room and checks that the door is fully closed.

"Hans has started to urge me to leave Paris. He says it is not going to be safe for me to remain."

"Has he?" I keep my expression neutral.

Hans Jürgen Soehring, the handsome German Luftwaffe officer who had started studying law in Grenoble before being recruited by the Nazis, is Arletty's wartime German lover. He came to Paris as one of Göring's trusted men. Arletty's horizontal collaboration with Herr Soehring and her visits to the Parisian theater and the opera with him have earned her the hatred of the Resistance and the condemnation of Parisians. While they starve, their previously adored French film star has passed the war in comfort in this hotel, often seen out with her German lover. But, despite all of this, I know she trusts me. This is the trouble with working here. It's harder to hate people you get to know.

She has told me, and I have told Frank, how Soehring introduced her to German books over cozy evenings here in the Ritz and how their romance blossomed over long lunches nearby in the Café Voisin.

In the face of hostile Parisian criticism, Arletty insists she is nothing more than a Gauloise, a fan of the cigarettes, and that is that. This is her way of shrugging off her collaboration, as one might shrug off cigarette ash with the flick of a hand.

"My friends are warning me that I must make a choice," she murmurs. "A terrible choice between the man I love and my country. They say I must choose between Hans and Paris when the war is over." She looks at me in anguish. "How am I supposed to choose between my two great loves?"

"If any of us come out of this war with just one of our great loves, we will be grateful. You could look at it as a privilege to be able to make a choice, madame." I take my typical honest approach with her, because while Arletty is privileged, and a collaborator, she also has the ability to relate to me as a working maid. This is one of the reasons that my feelings about her are complicated. She does not treat me with complete disdain.

Arletty moves around the apartment, wringing her hands and frowning. But then, she turns to me. "If I were to go to Germany, Louise, I would have to take a little piece of Paris with me."

A little piece of Paris? Have not the Nazis already looted half the countryside? I am sure that if she goes to Germany, she will be surrounded by French treasures.

"Perhaps were you to go there, you would consider bringing a large piece of Paris back?"

My sarcasm seems to go over her head. "Were I to accompany Hans to Germany, I would like you to come with me."

A breeze stirs the curtains with their pretty sprigs and roses, and I close my eyes. For one moment, I allow myself to remember the holidays we took in the countries of Europe before my father started drinking. Countryside with rivers that threaded like ribbons through valleys all covered in deep green trees, sun sparkling on fat grapes in vineyards. Picnics with my parents, my young mother with her long blond hair flowing down her back, in her blue-and-white-striped cotton dress, and my father, handsome and wearing a white shirt undone at the collar. Walks with just the three of us along quiet country roads while they swung my arms between them, lifting me so high above the ground that I thought I could fly.

I still dream of traveling again one day. But Germany is not on my list.

Arletty is puffing on her Gauloise with no pretense of elegance now. When I look at her, I see the strain of small lines around her big, intense eyes and around the contours of her generous lips.

"I could bear to leave Paris, if you came with me," she whispers.

"Madame." It is all I can say at this turn of events. I am shocked.

"I fell in love with Hans," she continues. "What could I do about the fact he is a German?" She shakes her head. "It is impossible to obliterate such feelings, even in the face of war. Especially when we are all in danger," she murmurs, looking down at the floor. "Love is all we have left."

And right then, the wail of air-raid sirens blooms across the Paris skies.

"Come, we must go down to the basement." I grab her hand, glad of the opportunity to release myself from this awkward and uncomfortable conversation. The sound of the sirens is terrifying, but it has saved me from having to respond.

Outside in the corridor, Sasha runs out of Chanel's room and Arletty falls into line with Coco Chanel. Madame Chanel is immaculate in a cream linen suit, and she sniffs audibly at the sight of the former film star trailing along in her bathrobe.

Sasha has been tasked with the job of carrying Chanel's gas mask on a satin pillow. Despite the fact that she is German and my enemy, I stifle a laugh as she holds the famous fashion designer's items out like a dead animal.

"The targets are far away from Place Vendôme, out by the railway yards in the towns north of Paris, it seems," Sasha says as if to calm me down.

I reach out and grasp the wooden paneling in the hallway. Not again. It has been a year since I last tried to go to visit Maman at the little apartment where we lived in Saint-Germain-en-Laye. The first few times that I went, the apartment was empty. Or she was not opening her front door. It has been two years since I last heard from her, or saw her. I have no idea what is going on.

The air-raid sirens wail. Arletty rushes ahead.

We are swept along, guests and staff alike, because even at the Ritz, an air raid is an event. I catch a glimpse of Arletty slipping down the gracious staircase, her silk bathrobe billowing behind her, while Chanel glides, her bejeweled hand sliding down the banister. Neither of them seems interested in looking to see where their German lovers are.

Love—is it love, or a matter of convenience?

Sasha walks close beside me down to the basement, and I sense her gaze flickering toward me again and again, as the sounds of airplanes and gunfire intensify.

"Chanel says that the deaths from the air raids in Paris this summer will rival those in the Blitz in London," an elderly doorman tells one of the middle-aged waiters.

At the bottom of the narrow servants' staircase, we wait while the hotel guests and management file into the basement. Frank holds the door open. He sees me with Sasha, and his expression does not change.

There is a crash, and someone inside the basement squeals.

But I know they will all be comfortable in here. This is an air-raid shelter worthy of the Ritz, equipped with fur rugs and Hermès sleeping bags.

"Louise?" Arletty calls to me. "I am cold. Help me work this *vêtement* out." She is holding up a silk sleeping bag.

I walk over to her, help her to unbutton it, and she climbs in, gathering it around her like a protective cocoon. Chanel has taken herself off to a private corner, and there is chatting and murmuring among the guests as I sit down next to Arletty.

Sasha settles herself down on my other side. I cup my hands over my mouth and blow into them. I want Sasha to go away, but pictures of my mother, our little home, her dressmaker's model, haunt me, along with the sound of sirens, the distant rattle of anti-aircraft guns, and the keening call of Allied aircraft. I do not have the energy or the capacity to dismiss Sasha.

Arletty turns to me from where she sits on my other side, her eyes wide in the semidarkness. "I could never leave my beloved Paris without taking a part of her with me, someone who will look after me in the way I am accustomed. I am offering you a ticket to safety and security, Louise. When they come, the Allies will not imagine that anyone living among the Nazis in the Ritz has been neutral."

I glance at Sasha, but she is staring intently at Arletty.

"Please, madame," I whisper.

Arletty leans her head back against the wall and closes her eyes.

I press my cold hands into the cellar floor. The sound of distant gunfire rattles Paris. But it is not my safety that I'm worried about, nor Arletty's. As we feel the ground quake above us, I send up urgent prayers that my mother, the little dressmaker, is safe.

CHAPTER SEVEN

SUMMER 1944

Kit

Kit pushed his plane higher and broke above the cloudline. At the sight of the other aircraft merging out of the clouds, Kit rejoined his formation of six planes. Despite the mission they were about to carry out, there was a part of him that enjoyed this freedom and the wonder of flying. In what seemed like no time, the city of Rouen spread out below like a picture-perfect French town. The great cathedral was clearly visible, but as they fast approached the railway yards and bridges north of Paris, the sound of the aircraft engine rumbling was accompanied by the deep beat of shells.

Kit's nerves tingled in his insides as they drew closer and closer to their targets. As ever, the thought that anything could happen to Charlie loomed strong in his mind. Silently, he repeated his instructions to calm himself. *Keep your hands steady and the speed at 195 miles per hour.*

But the barrage of German anti-aircraft gunners and the crack of explosions was almost deafening.

They drew closer to the target, a bridge at Saint-Germain-en-Laye. The aircraft rattled and Kit set his teeth.

He focused on the target, which was just visible among all the smoke from the bombs. He swooped down, and the planes in his formation carried out a deadly acrobatic dance, descending like birds of prey in a perfectly choreographed storm.

But Kit could not hold in his shout of horror when the lead plane in his formation took a hit from an anti-aircraft gunner. The aircraft was headed straight for the ground and smoke billowed from the rear escape hatches. Kit's stomach rolled as out of the corner of his eye he glimpsed the pilot, the co-pilot, and the gunners tumbling through the sky. One by one, their parachutes trailed out, and they sailed down toward the ground.

Kit forced himself to focus on the instrument panel, and his determination to carry out the mission strengthened in spite of the terror he felt that the men would be tumbling straight into the Nazis' hands.

The acrid smell of smoke from the burning plane nearby filled the cockpit, stinging Kit's nostrils and forcing him to choke and cough. His eyes flickered from the airspeed to the altimeter, while sweat dripped from his forehead down his cheeks and he licked at his dry, cracked lips. He glimpsed the parachutes of his crewmates as they disappeared into the smoke and gunshot from the German anti-aircraft men on the ground.

And then he saw it. A perfect view of the still-intact bridge below.

"Retreat!" The instruction came through on the radio.

"Negative. I've got a perfect sighting." Kit ground out the words. There was the bridge. If he was going to lose men, friends he had lived with for the past few years, he was going to make sure the job was done. "I'm taking a diving attack!"

"Negative!"

But Kit knew his own plane's strength. He had not trained

to bail out at the last moment. Gritting his teeth, and gripping the controls until his knuckles turned white, he sent the plane into a steep dive, so they were descending at a near-vertical angle as low as he could fly. Kit kept the target in sight and as soon as the weapons released, he pulled the aircraft up. He'd done it. They'd done it. The weapons plummeted straight toward the bridge, and the massive explosion boomed through the aircraft.

But then, another blast wrenched Kit's hands on the controls. Grayish black smoke filled the cabin. Kit wheeled around for one split second, taking his focus off the instrument panel.

Flames flickered from the side of the plane. Enemy fighters were all around them, and ground fire sent bullets ricocheting through the air. The gunners were shouting. Charlie's voice mingled horribly with the others, and Kit's stomach liquefied while acrid smoke and the smell of cordite burned his lungs. And yet he fought to maintain control.

When he whipped his head around a second time, he saw the men in the rear battling valiantly with fire extinguishers, until the plane lurched again, left, hard.

Kit whipped his pounding, thumping head around, wrenching the corded muscles in his neck, to see a huge hole in the left wing where a shell had pierced it.

They would be going down.

Smoke, noise, and yells seemed to blur together.

Gritting his teeth, he stared hopelessly at the instrument panel, his hands gripping the wheel while his whole body shook and rattled with the engines, and he looked back to see Charlie trying to put out a fire in one of the bombing bays. His loyal gunners were still in the bays, and the engine keened and spluttered, still determined, it seemed, like them, to keep forging on.

But it was hopeless.

The cockpit filled with billowing, stench-filled smoke and there was an earsplitting sound as his window smashed. Kit gasped for air and his head was thrown backward. And then he wrenched his gaze downward to where air gushed up from below. There was a hole in the fuselage near his left foot. The bullets had missed his toes by barely half an inch.

Kit risked turning once again. The fire in the bomb bay was still blazing. They would have to abandon ship.

"Bail out! Bail out!" Kit yelled on the radio. "The fire is too bad in the bomb bay!"

He felt Charlie's hand on his shoulder for one searing second, and then he wondered if he'd imagined it, because everyone disappeared.

"Mayday! Mayday! Mayday!" he yelled into the radio.

Kit peered at the back of the plane, and when he couldn't see anyone left, and the fuselage started cracking and heaving with the awful sounds of a ship that was about to sink, Kit stood up, battled to the side of the plane, leaned down, and jumped.

There was a moment of silence before he pulled the rip cord open, but nothing happened.

He pulled the cord a second time, and then came the shock of the parachute opening, and the silk canopy ballooned into the air. Charlie was nowhere in sight. None of his crew-mates were.

In the smoke, Kit had no way of seeing more than a few inches, and no way of telling whether his crewmates were safe. They were all defenseless now, floating above a sea of Nazis battling to kill them from the ground.

As the plane he'd flown for every single mission since he had arrived in Stansted nose-dived to the ground, and Kit floated down helplessly himself, desperately trying to catch even one glimpse of Charlie, one thing became clear: He had not only let his crew down, but his family, and more than anyone, his brother.

CHAPTER EIGHT

PARIS, PRESENT DAY

Nicole

The woman behind the counter in the town hall shakes her head when I tell her that I don't know where in France my grandmother was born, or whether she was even born in France at all. I have been waiting in a queue for over two hours, and I'm beginning to flag. I would love a cup of tea.

"Our birth, death, and marriage records are stored in the civic offices of each regional department. The different regions of France are all organized into departments, and you would have to go to each individual department around the country and try to find her birth details." She looks at me through her thick glasses. "If you do not know which part of France your grandmother may have been born in, then I think this is going to be a very difficult search. If not impossible."

I nod and close my eyes wearily. I'm over the morning sickness stage of my pregnancy, but fatigue is starting to kick in.

And then I remind myself that I've waited two hours in a long queue. "Would it be possible to search the Parisian records for a Louise Bassett, born October 12, 1922?"

"Of course." The woman indicates the line with a wave of her hand. "This is the general inquiries queue. To make a specific search, please join the queue over there and my colleagues will assist you."

I nod faintly. I'm not up for another queue. And I feel completely deflated.

The woman calls the person who's been waiting behind me, and I make my way back out into the sunny Parisian afternoon.

The sun is glimmering on the river Seine and a barge is chugging past. I linger on Pont Neuf, savoring the fresh air before I go in search of some sustenance.

I turn away from the river and wander down past the little artisan stalls selling black-and-white photographs of Paris. I buy a photo of a curved, elegant lamppost in the rain, with the famous Metro sign behind it.

Near Rue Montorgueil, there is a little café selling the exquisite pastries that Parisians make so beautifully. Soon, I am settled at a round table with a hot chocolate and a macaron.

I reach for my phone, and before I can stop myself, or think, I'm calling my cousin Pandora. She married a Frenchman, which is why Aunt Mariah moved to Paris.

"Pandora?"

I can sense her registering the sound of the voice.

"Nicole. It's Nicole." Your cousin, I don't add. The girl you used to play with when Mum and I used to visit you in London. Until everything went wrong.

We used to spend hours in Kensington Gardens, pretending that I lived in one tree, and Pandora in another. We would go visiting each other like a regular pair of elderly women and pretend we were drinking several cups of tea.

I swear it takes a full five seconds before she speaks.

I bite my lip. "It's been a long time." I laugh nervously.

"Nicole? Where are you? Is everything all right?"

"Yes, of course. Pandora, I'm in Paris."

"You are here? What a surprise!"

I close my eyes. Deep down, despite the differences in my family, I want to reconnect with my cousin. I look down at my swollen belly and smile. *What are you doing to me already, little one?*

I remember wandering around Hamleys toy shop, my hand in Pandora's. Once, we got lost together in the teddy bear section.

"I was wondering...Could we meet?" I'm sure I stop breathing for a moment, but then she rattles off an address in the Marais district and tells me to come over tomorrow at eleven o'clock in the morning.

"Great," I say. My shoulders fall about ten thousand feet, but my heart is racing.

"Au revoir," Pandora almost sings.

I hang up, and the sounds of the café and Paris and waiters laughing come back to life.

You missed out on so much, Pandora, after your mother fell out with Granny. I want you to get to know her memory. I want you to know how wonderful she was.

And right now? I take a small bite of my delicious raspberry macaron. Well, the idea of a cousin who lives in Paris and might be able to navigate her way through the labyrinth of French red tape, while being utterly at home in the Ritz, seems like an opportunity too good to miss.

CHAPTER NINE

PARIS, SUMMER 1944

Louise

We, the hotel staff, have been asked to move away from the guests, and to sit the air raid out on hard benches in the cellar like birds on a perch, with our hands folded on our laps. A group of Nazis arrived late and have been allocated seating, so we staff are not allowed to sit with them. The French and German hotel guests lounge on velvet sofas and gossip their way through the ordeal.

I can only begin to imagine how the sky around Paris pulses violently with orange, yellow, and vermilion, blinding against the summer sun.

Finally, the sirens stop, and the crashes of shellfire turn quiet. After a brief, eerie moment of silence, the all-clear sounds. Light sweeps into the cellar when one of the gloved, uniformed bellhops opens the door.

"Accompany me, Louise." Arletty appears next to me as if by magic, her silk bathrobe wrapped neatly around her slim frame. She startles me out of my reverie. "I am only familiar with the parts of the hotel where one can procure oysters and champagne. Show me how to return to civilization."

Her hands grip mine like a steel-cold vise, and the jewels on her fingers glimmer in the half-light.

I notice Sasha watching me as she helps Coco Chanel to her feet.

I grit my teeth. "I will guide you," I say. My voice is wooden, and I turn my back on Sasha's gaze.

Arletty's hands begin to shake violently. "Hans says these attacks will only get worse," she whispers as I scuttle along next to her while she glides. "He says when the Allies come, they will show no mercy, and neither will our own countrymen."

"I am sure it will not be as bad as you imagine." I lead her through the slow-moving line toward the doorway.

Coco Chanel sails past us, and Sasha carries the designer's gas mask, still on its pillow.

The Nazis whisper and shake their heads about what the Allies are doing to Germany.

"But I do believe that Hans might be wrong," Arletty continues, speaking in whispers. "He underestimates the Americans and the British. They are coming to save us. How could they denigrate a national treasure such as me, or Chanel?"

I choose my words with care. "The French people love you," I lie to Arletty. "You still have many supporters here."

Arletty shudders violently.

Her handsome Luftwaffe general appears as we arrive in the grand foyer. Hans Jürgen Soehring is formal, dark, and handsome. His hair is swept back, and his pressed suit is immaculate and sharp. He takes Arletty's hand and tucks it into the crook of his elbow.

I try to slip away from the man who is working as a member of the Reichskriegsgericht, the court-martial system of the Reich, a tribunal that deals with those who are charged with high treason and aiding the enemy.

"Mademoiselle?" he says. "Thank you for looking after my darling."

I stare at the ground. My stomach curls with distaste.

He chuckles, probably interpreting my reticence as fear, and he turns back to Arletty, leading her back to the confines of her room, where no doubt he will find a way to soothe her.

Revolted, I hurry away. I move out of the grand entrance hall through the door that leads to the Rue Cambon bar. It is already filled with the sounds of German conversation. Glasses clink, and Frank is installed behind the bar, chatting easily with both the German and the French clientele.

He sees me, and I stop in the middle of everyone. I indicate that I need to speak to him, urgently, and he pats an elderly barman on the shoulder, whispers something privately into his ear, and follows me out into his office, closing the door with a gentle click.

"They have sent someone to spy on me," I say. I'm still catching my breath, invigorated from my flight through the hotel.

Frank leans against his desk and waits while I explain.

"The spy is posing as a German maid, and they are making me share my bedroom with her."

Frank's gaze darkens, and he shakes his head. "You will have to stop working for us. It is not worth the risk. Lesser members of the underground have been provided with protection in situations like this." He shakes his head. "No, we must cut you free of any association with us. Don't come down to see us, keep your head down, just do your job, and forget everything that you have learned."

I implore him with my eyes. "Asking me to stop working with you is like asking me to stop breathing. Helping you is the only thing of any worthiness that I have." I mean it.

He walks around the side of the desk and places his hands

on my shoulders, as if he were indeed my father. "Dearest Louise, there is no substitute for your life."

Gently, I remove his hands from my shoulders and stand up to my full height, which is diminutive, I know that, but still. "Blanche would not give up because of this."

"We must prioritize your safety."

"If Blanche can rescue refugees dressed as a nurse, then I can too. Her husband is the hotel's director and she will be under far more scrutiny than me. I say we defy them. I say I do more."

"I'd risk myself, anyone, before I risked you. Your mother—"

I cut that thought off. "Blanche and other women of the Resistance have been finding safe hiding places for those refugees of the Third Reich who are stranded in Paris. Please, Frank, let me do something more than remember codes and fancy numbers. It's defined me for long enough. It's not who I am." I whisper the last words, and I don't know where they've come from. But they came out, and they sound convincing to me. "I want to be more. I want to do more."

Frank's expression is grim.

My voice is barely a whisper. "Don't you see why this has happened? Even the Nazis think I am odd. None of the other maids will share a room with me because I am too strange, too different, with my memory for numbers and the fact that I don't engage with them when they talk about their families or their beaus. This has been going on for years. And now I've ended up having a German secretary in the bed next to mine. Things need to change. *I* need to change. I need to prove to myself, and to everyone, that I'm worth more. That I am as brave as the next Frenchwoman. It is all I am asking, Frank."

Frank looks at me sadly. "I cannot risk it."

I spread my hands out. "I scurry around like an invisible beetle by myself scrubbing hotel rooms. Let me spread my wings."

CHAPTER TEN

PARIS, PRESENT DAY

Nicole

I take my time wandering through the cobbled streets of the Marais district, where I catch glimpses of hidden courtyards and gardens. My guidebook tells me that this district remains untouched by Haussmann's nineteenth-century rebuilding of Paris. There are no grand boulevards or big parks, but the maze-like streets are charming and soon I'm lost in old Paris.

Pandora's apartment is set off one of the secret squares. There is a pair of elaborate wrought-iron gates and I press the intercom to the side. I feel rather intimidated. This was the way I always used to feel when I went to stay with Mariah's family in London. The country girl. Never good enough. I remember how Granny Louise used to laugh this away.

The gate opens automatically. Inside the charming courtyard, there are pots of roses and lavender. I walk up a curving staircase to the left, and there is one of the beautiful Parisian balustrades that could almost be a miniature of that in the Ritz Hotel.

Pandora's front door is wide open on the top floor of the

building, and my cousin is standing ready to greet me, her flashbulb smile all lit up. Her long blond hair is tied up into a messy ponytail, and she is wearing jeans and an oversized pink linen shirt in that effortless way she has. Pandora looks like a model, even with a baby on her hip.

"Nicole." Her greeting seems warm and genuine, and I lean forward to accept her embrace. She holds me close for a few seconds, which is unexpected, and I breathe in the scent of her Chanel No. 5. She kisses me twice in the French style.

"Hi," I say helplessly. "What a beautiful little one." It's easy to cover up my awkwardness by making a fuss over Pandora's gorgeous baby girl, who has huge blue eyes. Already there are traces of the family's blond hair.

"Nicole, meet Mia Louise."

My breath catches hearing the baby's middle name. I feel momentarily resentful but then decide to think the best; maybe Pandora wants to honor our grandmother.

Pandora leads me straight into a magnificent salon with shining parquet flooring. The white-painted walls are lined with black-and-white photographs of Pandora during her modeling days and of her husband, who is a handsome anesthetist, and a few of little Mia Louise.

We walk through to a stunning high-ceilinged dining room with French doors and a small balcony overlooking the pretty street outside. There is a gleaming table that seats a dozen and bowls of yellow roses on the table and the sideboard. I bite my lip and think of the tiny, perfect apartment where I am staying with my own yellow roses. It always seems I'm set to live a miniature version of my cousins' lives.

We come to an enormous kitchen, and there, sitting on one of the stools at the breakfast bar, is my aunt.

"Aunt Mariah," I say. I fumble about for words. "I wasn't expecting you to be here." I feel almost apologetic for my presence. I know I shouldn't, but I can't help it. I am so out of place.

Mariah stands up and comes to take the baby from Pandora. "Yes, I know why you are here. And I thought it was appropriate that I be in the house while you talk to Pandora."

Pandora busies herself in the kitchen. There is a smell of filtered coffee, and she clatters about with plates and cups.

"I'm sure you'd have nothing to say to Pandora that you couldn't say to me," Aunt Mariah adds.

She kisses the baby on the nose, bringing her perfectly coiffed blond head close to Mia's face. The baby gurgles delightedly, and I notice how Mariah's skin is tanned from the sun.

"So, I understand you've been in touch with Arielle, the archivist at the Ritz."

I open my mouth and close it again. I'd forgotten how Aunt Mariah can pull the rug out from under me. But then she's already floored me with her photo of Granny. So why am I surprised she is doing it again now?

"Yes," I say evenly.

Mariah used to get me to help with chores when I went to stay with her. I always ended up carrying her shopping bags when we were out or dashing down to the shops when she had run out of some expensive ingredient. Aunt Mariah always liked to be fashionable and to keep up with whatever trends were of the moment.

I remember Granny Louise once telling me that she found Aunt Mariah exhausting, and I can recall the humorous glint in Granny's eyes. I remember loving the fact that Granny Louise was sharing a secret with me.

"Surely, Nicole, it was hardly a surprise when you first laid eyes on that photograph. My mother was always full of secrets." Aunt Mariah tosses her head as if challenging me to contradict her.

I bite back my smile at the coincidence that I had just been remembering sharing a secret with Granny Louise. "Arielle at the Ritz told me that it was common for French families not to know exactly how their loved ones lived out the war years."

Aunt Mariah sniffs. "Well, we didn't even know that she was in France!"

I sigh. She is right.

Pandora brings over a tray set with coffee and some of the tiny pastries I was admiring yesterday. Pandora and Mariah settle the baby into her high chair and Pandora ushers me to sit down.

As Pandora pours coffee, Mariah busies herself chatting to Mia, tapping her manicured nails on the table. She helps herself to an exquisite little custard tart and places it delicately on her white plate. "My mother, the collaboratrice. The woman who was too cowardly to face up to the German occupation, so instead, she tucked herself up in the Ritz, and made herself comfortable with one of the officers."

I press my lips together. Granny genuinely wanted to reconnect with Mariah before she died. They had not exactly lost touch, because Mariah still rang Granny up every now and then and tried to boss her around, but Granny wanted to rekindle the loving relationship she felt she had lost with her eldest daughter. I remember her showing me photographs of Mariah and my mother when they were girls, and I remember how sad Granny was.

I glance at Pandora, but her expression is neutral.

"Why do you judge her so harshly and rush to assume the photograph means she was guilty?" I ask Mariah.

Mariah sits back in her seat and folds her arms across her chest. I notice that she is wearing a rose gold necklace with a ruby pendant. My mother had one with a sapphire, and now it is at my home. My grandfather gave each of his daughters these necklaces on their twenty-first birthdays. So Mariah does have some family loyalty. How can this woman begin to suggest that her own mother was capable of morally reprehensible acts?

Granny always described Mariah as complex. I'm beginning to wonder whether I will ever be able to unravel the layers she wraps around herself. I'm still not clear as to why she was so angry with her mother.

"I'm coming with you to see Arielle. We both know she is going to produce records that Mother sequestered herself away with a Nazi," Mariah says.

"Arielle has only told me that she will look into the archives to see if she can find any evidence that Granny stayed in the hotel during the war. She warned me..." But even as I speak, doubts crowd my mind.

Arielle was clear that she thought the copy of *Grimm's Fairy Tales* would have been a gift from a German lover.

I press my fingers to my temples. Suddenly I have a sharp headache. I'm taking deep breaths to calm myself, but the torrent of words is battling within me and wants to come out. "I only lost my mother a year ago. Please, would you have respect for our family? Why can't you leave Granny alone?"

Pandora goes to the baby and lifts her out of her high chair, talking in a soft voice, and Mia Louise grins back toothlessly at her mother, gurgling nonsense.

I take a deep breath. "You must stop blaming Granny," I say, my voice dangerously low. There is a rough edge to my tone that I don't like, but I see this happening with some of my teenage students at school, girls who blame their mothers for things that they are not responsible for. "You have a wonderful life, Mariah," I murmur. "Why do you have to pin so much anger on Granny?"

Mariah tosses her head and sniffs. "I'm not going to respond to that. Clearly, things were very different for your mother and you."

"Thank you for the coffee," I say and stand up. "I have somewhere to be," I lie.

"Of course," Pandora says.

I leave my aunt sitting mutinously silent at the table and walk with Pandora to the front door.

"I don't want this for our family," I say.

Pandora has her hand on the door handle. The baby smiles

widely at me and I swipe at tears as I smile back at her. What a mess.

"Goodbye, Nicole," Pandora says. She leans forward again and kisses me on both cheeks in a perfunctory way.

"Au revoir, Pandora," I manage.

I slip back out into the courtyard, and I feel the swish of my baby moving inside my womb. Those little shuffles have come to mean so much to me—to mean everything, actually—in the last weeks. I am five months pregnant, and my aunt was so busy putting her own mother down that she did not even notice I was about to become a mother.

I have no idea how I would cope if my own child were to turn against me, were to blame me, when all I know is that the love I feel for my unborn baby is stronger than anything I have known in my life.

I don't know where this will end. But I do know that my grandmother genuinely loved Mariah and my mother; she loved her family, and I believe there is more to the story than my granny's supposed betrayal. But if I am to discover why things have ended up the way they have for my family, I need to find out where it all began.

CHAPTER ELEVEN

NORTHERN FRANCE, SUMMER 1944

Kit

The sounds of gunfire belted through Kit's ears, and the wail of sirens called like curlews. Overhead, planes swooped and screamed while Kit floated toward the ground. The sound of screaming aircraft softened as he approached a bank of tiled rooftops, and Kit's heart rate slowed a little. What remained of the Eighth Air Force Squadron had turned and flown back to England and the German anti-aircraft stations had stopped sending up heavy flak.

From where he was floating, Kit could see people on the ground starting to emerge from the labyrinth of air-raid shelters beneath the city streets. German trucks loaded with soldiers swerved around a corner and raced toward him. Sweat poured from his forehead in the searing summer afternoon, and Kit pulled on the lines, curling his knees to miss a chimney, only to land facedown on a roof.

He shrugged off the parachute to the accompaniment of German voices shouting orders in the street. The racket of bullets had been replaced by the rattle of orders being barked in a language that sent shock spiraling through Kit's system, because Nazi voices were like a bogey that had scoured his imagination for the last five years. Now, he was about to be thrown into their midst, and he had no defenses except his own wits.

Where Charlie was, he had no idea. With all the smoke, the noise, and the chaos, he'd not been able to see any of his crew floating toward the ground. Kit's breathing was shaky. Where was his brother? Had he made it to the ground? He would give anything right now to see him, to know he had landed. Safely. Right in the middle of Nazi territory where Kit had propelled his little brother because of his own determination to go ahead and bomb the bridge in the face of their formation leader's aircraft having been shot down!

What a stupid decision.

Kit stared down from his perch on the roof. People were returning to the marketplace below him. Elderly men in white aprons pulled cloths from tables. There was no place to hide, no place to run, and nothing for it but to hurl himself down to the street below.

Hastily, Kit pulled off his leather jacket. Next, he removed his overalls, throwing them onto the roof. With barely a glance back, he braced himself, bent his knees, and jumped.

He landed on his side, and his right arm burned with a smarting pain that ran like an electric shock from his shoulder to his fingertips.

Nazi voices were accompanied by the sound of car doors slamming, and the terrifying pounding of jackboots on the cobbled streets. He couldn't stay here for long.

Kit had to remember the advice they'd been given. Blend, blend. He moved toward the marketplace, his eyes raking the tables and the growing lines of Parisians queuing for food.

Pain reared up Kit's arm and burned through his groin where the harness had almost ripped him in two when he landed on the roof. Kit slipped in behind a table next to a man who looked to be in his sixties. The gentleman was pulling a white cloth from his table in front of an old shop that had signs in German written all over it.

He wrenched his gaze toward the circling Nazis. They had fanned out and were systematically scouring the marketplace, barking orders at the stallholders, who quietly carried on.

Kit felt the long hard gaze of the market trader's eyes boring into him. Slowly, he turned his head to acknowledge the man, but as he did so, his eyes closed for one brief second and he prayed that the Frenchman would take pity on him. There was no doubt it was obvious who he was, and he could feel the wet warmth of his own blood dripping from a telltale cut on his cheek.

Kit measured his own safety against the measure of his neighbor's gaze and slumped with relief when the man reached underneath the table and, wordlessly, held up a white apron for Kit to put on.

"Merci," Kit murmured, thanking goodness for his schoolboy French, and sent up a prayer of silent thanks for the man standing next to him who had probably saved his life.

The RAF instructor had advised them to pick up a bucket and pretend to be a plumber, or to grab a paint can and start slathering white paint on a wall. Well, here he was, a market stallholder. At least he had followed some of the advice he had been given, even if it was too late.

Kit stared at the meager pickings in front of him, a few wizened turnips, a handful of potatoes, a bowl of misshaped peas. Just this morning, he had sat in front of a plate of eggs and fried Spam back at Stansted.

Gaunt, impossibly thin women patiently queued to try to feed their families out of the hopeless supplies on the table.

And when an elderly woman dressed in a pale blue summer dress that looked like something Kit's mother would have worn in the 1920s, threadbare at the seams and hanging off her shoulders, asked for one potato and produced her ration book, Kit's heart contracted at the way she looked down at the ground in shame.

Nazis beat their way around the market, their uniforms pristine and their well-fed bodies brimming with health and a vitality that no French person in sight could begin to emulate.

Not wanting to draw attention to himself, yet having no idea what to do, Kit turned to the man next to him.

But then in one swift movement the woman reached out and pressed her hand onto his arm.

"Serve the customer," the man said.

Sweat beaded on Kit's forehead and for a moment he swayed violently. He felt a bolt of panic about Charlie. He shouldn't be standing here, serving customers, when his little brother was somewhere, defenseless. Or, Charlie could be dead.

Kit's throat seized up and he couldn't speak when he tried. He handed the woman a potato and stamped the ration book.

The man next to him reached into his pocket and pulled out a packet of cigarettes, offering one to Kit.

He accepted, leaning forward and cupping his hand over the end of the cigarette while the stallholder struck a match.

Out of the corner of his eye, he watched while the Nazis stopped people and insisted on inspecting their identity cards, the infamous *Kennkarten* that citizens of the Third Reich had to carry. If they failed to produce them, they were hustled away to some dank, dark prison, where they were interrogated using the famous Nazi methods that had terrified thousands into confessing to crimes they'd never committed.

The reality of the French people continuing to try to carry out the most rudimentary of tasks, selling simple food to their countrymen, seemed achingly moving while terror hung down over them like an eagle, talons stretched, about to pounce.

A few moments later, one of the Nazis shouted, held up his

hand, and gave that dreaded, arm-straight-out salute that Kit had heard about but had never witnessed until this day: *Heil Hitler!* And the searching Nazis moved to attention and disappeared.

Kit swung around, dry-retching into the spare baskets that sat along the ground behind the stall. He straightened up, forcing himself to swallow the bile that wanted to course from his throat, trying to tame the nausea that threatened to sink him down to the ground like a deflated balloon. He had to find Charlie. He had to find his crew.

He wrenched his gaze back to the stallholder, and in the split second when there were no Nazis in sight, he pulled the man into a hug, holding his bony frame and closing his eyes.

"You go now," the man said, in halting English, but English that Kit was more than grateful for. "They will be searching for the crew from your downed aircraft until they find every single one of you and," he said in a lower voice, "they will not question you first."

"Yes. We were warned. I can't thank you enough. Honestly."

The man nodded.

Kit walked as normally as he could, given the burning pain in his groin and arm, out of the market, and into the suburb that had just witnessed the terror of his contingent lighting up the sky overhead with orange flames. Had the bombs they'd hurled from their airplanes met targets that were innocent? What of children who had been sitting in class, or walking home from school for lunch at the wrong time, when the air raid had begun?

Kit tore these thoughts from his embattled mind. He had carried out missions over Germany. But after bombing civilians who were on the Allied side and already suffering more than enough, guilt bit and gnawed at him. Seeing starving customers only served to highlight how war was not discriminatory when it came to victims or perpetrators. Everyone was caught up in this savage game. The innocent side ended up feeling responsible for the devastation affecting people's lives...women with baskets, children going back to school.

Kit strode down the main street, his own boots seeming to clatter alarmingly, while he made every effort to keep his tread soft. Heaven help him if he scared the innocents around here with the sounds that the Nazis made. He ran his hands down his green shirt and trousers—he had to get out of those, must find something more suitable to wear—and when he saw a contingency of Nazis coming up straight toward him from the other end of the street, his eyes darted left and right, this way and that, like a lizard's. Hardly thinking, he turned and opened the door of a café and shuffled inside.

The café was full, and jazz drifted from a wireless. Groups of Nazis sitting in uniform were sipping what was no doubt the unpalatable wartime pretense for coffee, "ersatz" coffee. At some tables, women, smartly dressed, their lips ruby red and their cheeks flushed in a way that no other French person in the vicinity could carry off, sat with the Nazi officers. Kit's stomach churned.

Then Nazi shouts split the buzzing room in two. Kit lurched across the room, grabbing a chair on the way and lining it up underneath a bulb. A pen lay on a nearby table. Kit picked it up, stood on the chair, and began poking the light with the pen with his back to the room.

The Nazis pounded around tables, yelling at people and demanding their papers. Sweat slicked Kit's fingertips as he maneuvered the pen around the perfectly functioning light. Behind him, he could sense, and did not need to see, the feeling of terror that pervaded the room, as Hitler's forces searched for him, Charlie, and the rest of his crew.

Someone turned the music off, and the crowd went quiet.

Voices barked, chairs were thrown back, and at one point

a woman's screams rent the air, filled with the scent of spilled coffee.

But nobody noticed the electrician who was fixing a light.

Kit almost fell off his chair when the Nazis left, and with his legs buckling underneath him, he placed the chair back under the table and set the pen down where he had found it. He lowered his gaze to the floor and wound his way through the tables to the glass door. He was going to have to find a hiding place.

Outside, he leaned against the wall of the café for a moment, gasping in the fresh air. He watched the backs of the Nazis who had raided the café as they disappeared around a corner like a flock of baton-wielding sheep.

Kit moved in the direction of a vacant orchard he'd seen from his parachute, which still lay strewn across the rooftop where he'd landed and was half draped over the chimney of some poor unsuspecting person's house. His heart beat in his chest like a hammer against a snare drum, but he pushed forward and eventually came to a small open space.

Nazi voices barked through the sultry air, and Kit's arm reared up in pain. He scoured the orchard. Gnarled trees, their leaves dripping toward the ground, had been stripped of the plums and apricots that should otherwise have hung like jewels in the glorious French sunshine. They were no good as hiding places; their bare trunks would in no way serve to camouflage him.

Kit spotted a dilapidated shed sitting forlorn and dusty against the back fence and made his way over to it.

There was an old wooden box behind the shed, dusty and with a rusty, unsecured latch. Kit pulled open the lid and climbed inside, grimacing when he reached up to close the lid at the feel of shooting pain up his right arm. He'd somehow lost his emergency kit when he'd parachuted out of the plane, so he had no compass, no bandages, and no salve to treat his wounds. He also had no medication to keep him awake, which he sorely needed now.

Kit sank down into the dark corner of the empty box, not

caring whether flies or lice were sharing his temporary abode. Instead, he tipped his head into his hands and prayed again for Charlie, and the rest of his crew, hating to think that they faced one of three options: evasion, captivity, or death.

Kit eased his wounded arm down onto his knee.

The temperature in the wood box must have burned to over 100 degrees, but the day wore on and Kit hardly knew how high the sun was in the sky. He tried to get comfortable in any way he could, stretching his legs to ease his aching groin and leaning his head back against the sides of the box. The only thing that kept him going through the burning thirst and the heat and the fear was the most enormous sense of thankfulness that he had survived the airplane crash. No broken back, no broken bones, no major head injuries, and he was well hidden here.

It wasn't until dusk fell that he heard voices outside.

Kit braced himself. He sat up enough to ease the rough lid open. Across the back fence of the vacant lot, two German soldiers stood.

Kit dared to lift the lid open a tiny bit more and he tried to listen and understand some of the rudimentary German words that he had learned at school. When he heard the word *Amerikanisch,* he almost fell back into the box. He and Charlie were the only American pilots in the Eighth Royal Air Force Squadron.

Oh, let Charlie be safe, and away from harm. Let him have found someone who would be kind enough to help! His yearning to know that his brother was safe was almost a physical pain.

The two Germans didn't spend long in the orchard. Perhaps like most other workers, no matter what their nationality, these men only wanted to go away to whatever home there was for them right now and have a drink.

When dusk gave way to twilight, Kit eased open the lid once

more. This little pocket of France was pearled with a soft evening glow. Kit closed his eyes, and it was all he could do to wrench his mind away from the shooting pain in his arm and the wretched memory of that last bombing dive that he never should have taken. As he sat there in the heat, his mind started to wander, and he closed his eyes and prayed that he could go back in time and make a different decision.

A decision that would not have left him wondering whether he'd ever see his brother again.

Darkness fell over the wood box, and everything turned strangely still. A hush descended, presumably due to the darned German curfew.

He was going to have to stand up and stretch or his body would almost break in two. Taking in a breath and steeling himself, with his good arm he opened the lid of the wood box wide. He licked his cracked, dry lips and raised his head, a strange sense of nausea and dizziness almost overwhelming him.

And right then, he came face-to-face with someone in the shadows, in the darkness.

"Anglais?"

Kit swallowed, his dry throat scratching. Opposite him there stood a young girl, aged perhaps thirteen.

"Pilot?" she whispered.

"Oui." She was risking her safety, horribly, for him. He knew he had to find the underground, the networks of Resistance that had sprung up all over France. But was it made up of children, risking their lives in ways that the young never should?

The girl indicated a pile of wood next to the box on which there sat a carafe of wine and one of the heaven-sent long French sandwiches that Kit had dreamed of while he'd been encased in the coffin-like confines of the wooden box.

"You eat," the child whispered. "I am back in two hours' time, when the Germans patrolling the buildings in my street have their changeover. And then you move. We move. I help you."

Kit almost slumped with relief. "Thank you," he managed, his voice barely audible. "Thank you."

His young helper nodded, and she turned and fled as silently into the darkness as she had come.

Kit reached like a starving man for the sandwich that looked to be filled with pork and cheese. He took the carafe of wine and eased himself out of sight behind the wooden box, where at least he could stretch his legs and stare at the open sky.

He tipped his head back and let the tears splash down his dirty cheeks and run over the gouge in his face.

He was at the mercy of the kindness of strangers, and it seemed an angel had come in the guise of a little girl.

Kit could tell by the moon that it must be around midnight. A soft sheen of light pooled on the trees in the vacant lot that had become his world and threw strange shapes and shadows all over the ground.

Everything was quiet. And yet the memory of the air raid still rang like a gathering of buzzards in Kit's ears. He had eased himself into a position just outside the wooden box, but he was wedged into a corner against the fence and well hidden, should anyone decide to take a nocturnal ramble here.

Every couple of hours, he had taken the risk of standing up and stretching the muscles in his back and neck that had corded tightly for far more reasons than just the accident of his fall.

Kit stirred to attention at the sound of footsteps. It was the young girl, he knew it; he recognized the pattern of her steps.

She appeared around the corner of the old shed that was in front of the box. Her hair was highlighted in the moonlight, and she looked even younger than she had before.

"Anglais?" She hesitated, and a myriad of expressions crossed her face. "I have a question," she whispered. "I'm sorry. It's something I must ask."

Kit waited.

"I need proof that you are who say you are. You see, Germans are posing as *Americain and Anglais,* to find out things about the underground..." Her voice trailed off and she watched him hesitantly.

In the pearly darkness, Kit thought he detected a faint flash of embarrassment on her cheeks. He pulled for his dog tags that were still resting underneath his shirt. He slipped them over his head and held them out in the palm of his hand for the girl to inspect.

She took a step closer and gingerly reached down and took them, turning them over, almost with wonder, in her small hands. Finally, she lifted her gaze and simply nodded.

Following the line of the fence, she eased her way out of the lot and led Kit up the street, then around the corner, until she stopped and pointed at a house with a flat roof and parapets about halfway up the street. "The German sentries patrol on top of that house," she whispered, turning her serious eyes to lock with his gaze. "They are on a break, and we have precisely seven minutes left to get home."

He stayed quiet, still in awe that young children were the ones aiding the underground.

"When you leave tomorrow," she said, "I will make sure that you go when the sentries stop and change guard."

"Thank you," Kit whispered, and he followed his young companion down the dark street.

Every house, every garden, was silent. He took in his surroundings, checking for places to hide, places to find shelter, places in the street that were farthest away from the Nazis' prying eyes if their time ran out.

The little girl turned into the driveway of a simple suburban house and crossed the lawn. Kit followed her as she slipped around to the back and to an outhouse sitting flush against the back fence. The girl opened the door and let him into a small space. There were garden implements inside and in one corner there was an old table and a dusty chair.

"You can sleep here tonight," the girl said, and as she turned to go back to the door, a woman, perhaps forty years old, appeared. She had a shawl wrapped around her shoulders and her brown hair curled softly against the floral dress she wore. The child's mother. He hated the fact that he was putting these people at risk.

"Anglais," the little girl said, in rushed French. "C'est vrais."

Kit closed his eyes at the verification that was coming out of the mouth of a child.

The woman nodded as she stepped inside the outbuilding. "They are looking for you already." Her eyes darted up and down the length of Kit. "By tomorrow they will have posters set up all around Saint Germain-en-Laye. You cannot trust that people will not turn you in. You must leave in the morning. You can only stay here overnight."

Kit nodded. *How on earth did the Nazis know he was American? Had they captured Charlie and fathomed his accent? Worse, had they tortured him?* Kit's mind reeled with unanswered questions, but then he bent double in pain. His arm burned where he had fallen, and his entire body felt like a plank of wood. His groin ached from his landing on the roof.

"You are injured, and your cheek is cut," the woman murmured. "I shall get you some warm water." Her eyes searched his face, which must be filthy. He knew there was dried blood streaked across his cheek.

"Thank you." They were words he was going to utter repeatedly.

The woman returned a few minutes later with a bowl filled with steaming water and covered with a cloth. Behind her, the little girl carried a tray bearing another carafe of wine and a plate of pork, beans, and potatoes in what smelled like a mouth-watering sauce.

"Are you sure?" he whispered, memories of the people he'd seen out in the markets flooding his mind. "I would hate to deprive you of any food."

The woman looked up at him with a practical expression. "You will need sustenance. Tomorrow is going to be challenging, and you must get as far away from here as possible—and soon. You will try to get to Spain?"

"Yes." They had been advised to travel southwest to Spain if the worst happened. Given he had gone down north of Paris, this would be a journey of some 750 miles.

Kit slipped the cloth from the bowl of steaming water and bathed his face. His arm ached, but his joints were moving and the warm water bathing it was like a balm.

The woman and young girl talked quietly in low voices while Kit ate every mouthful of the delicious meal they had provided for him.

After he was finished, the girl left bearing the empty plate and wine glass, only to return with an odd assortment of clothes.

"This is all we have," the woman said. She looked at him. "These are my best offerings to make you look like a Frenchman. But be warned, you look American."

Kit heaved out a sigh.

The girl handed him a beret in brown wool, and a light coat of pale blue that would cover his khaki-green shirt and trousers. He pulled the beret onto his head and the little girl produced an old, cracked mirror, which she held up for him.

"Parfait," she said, her eyes dancing. "Except you must have the French tilt."

Kit chuckled, leaned forward, and let her adjust his beret.

"You can stay here for one night," the woman told him. "But in the morning the leader of the local underground movement will come to collect you. She will be on a bike, and you will follow her on foot. It will be a long walk."

There was a silence.

"You will only know her as the dressmaker."

CHAPTER TWELVE

PARIS, SUMMER 1944

Louise

I sit with Frank in the small office as the day ends. The Yankee Doodle station plays quiet news of Allied bombing attacks directed at the bridges and Nazi airfields around Paris. We are waiting in silence for the announcement I dread yet desperately yearn to hear. What were the casualties among the French population? How deadly had the Allies' attacks been in this latest raid? And had there been any direct hits on civilian houses? My hands are clasped tight in my lap as I listen.

I picture Maman now with her dressmaker's model sitting in the dim light on the bare floorboards, while she toils at her old sewing machine and loses herself in her pretty creations.

Frank is in the armchair by the blackout curtains in the corner of the office. He is polishing a crystal decanter, which just this evening he'd used for some of the fine wines that he'd served to the discerning German clientele. His neatly parted and combed graying hair frames the weary yet determined expression on his face, and the pouches under his eyes look especially pronounced.

"These should've been the best years of your life," he says. "You should be out dancing, meeting the one."

I hand him my translated messages.

He is quiet a moment, but then he raises his eyes from the codes and searches my face. "Just because your father was not... there for you does not mean that you should give up on love, Louise."

I lift my head and stare at him. But then I lower my gaze and fold my hands neatly in my lap. "It is not for me." I won't risk it. Not ever again. I adored my father. I never want to feel the way I did when he abandoned us and left us with nothing but the clothes on our backs.

Frank reaches out and places his hand atop mine.

Later, much later, I wake and know sleep won't return for me tonight. I will go back down to Frank's office and offer to translate the return codes that will have come in. He has assured me that he's mentioned my name to Blanche Auzello, and he's promised me that she knows I am keen to help her in a more direct manner.

I ease myself out of bed and reach for the pair of soft sandals I left on the threadbare rug between the beds. Sasha's slim form is barely visible.

I know it is just after two o'clock in the morning, even though I cannot read my little wristwatch in the dark. Barely leaving this building for several years and learning to sneak around it has sharpened my senses. I can tell what time it is to the minute, because even with blackout curtains, I can sense the weight of the night. Now, it is the darkest hour, the deadliest time for the deadliest thoughts and deeds.

My feet pad silently on the bare wooden floor and there is an urgency to every movement, to every tread. I reach for the door handle to get out of the bedroom.

There is a shuffle in the opposite bed.

Sasha sits up.

"I am going to the bathroom," I say, the lie coming quick-fire. "Go back to sleep." My fingers grip the door handle.

"Very well," she replies, her voice sleepy.

I sneer at her in the dark, turn the handle, and outside in the corridor I momentarily sink down against the wall.

Gathering myself, I continue downstairs, but my heart pounds. A few minutes later, I am slipping down the famous staircase that is not for the use of the staff. My hands glide down the black-and-gilt-decorated banisters, all aswirl with curlicues, and my feet sink into the rich red carpets that are edged with gold. Dim carriage lights shine my way down this breathtaking *escalier,* and I am reminded of days gone by, of golden carriages and film stars and princesses making entrances into the exquisite foyer of this wonderful hotel. Centuries of history in Paris go far beyond the dark days that the city is seeing now. I live alongside the enemy within these walls, but I remind myself that I am surrounded by hundreds of other members of the Resistance in the city outside.

I make my way to the beam of light that shines under Frank's office door. Of course, I expected him to be awake. He is nocturnal, and I have become the same.

I knock on the door of his office and when I am inside, he pushes a piece of paper across his desk.

"We have a downed Allied pilot who will be arriving in Paris, in a car delivered by the underground drivers from the north."

Anticipation stirs in my stomach. "I want to help."

Frank's weary expression deepens, and he holds my gaze. "Blanche Auzello is going out to meet him. She has agreed that you can accompany her. You will be a mother and daughter and he will be your deaf brother. I *wish* you wouldn't! Please!"

I give him a reassuring smile. "I have to do something more.

It is too safe sitting here in the hotel, when my mother could be..." I gather myself, swallowing hard to drown my fear. What if I never see her again? What if this strange silence between us is all there will ever be? Not only do I want to be as brave as Blanche, I need a distraction from the worry about Maman and the bombing that keeps me awake at night. I have to take this on.

"I want to keep you alive so that you can safely go back to your mother. I feel a responsibility for my staff, and especially for you. You are so young, too young." Frank frowns.

"We are all too young, or too innocent," I murmur. "And the war has made me old enough to do what hundreds of others are doing."

He stares wearily at the floor.

"Come back down this afternoon after your shift," he says. "In the meantime, I shall only hope that you change your mind."

I reach out and press my hand into his arm.

Silently, he hands me some codes to translate, and I settle down to work while he turns away and pours himself a glass of brandy.

Later, once I am back out in the gloom of the bar, feeling strangely relaxed after decoding vegetables into the names of Nazis, my heart lurches.

In the shadows, I catch an unmistakable glimpse of a blond girl disappearing out through the door of the bar into Rue Cambon.

Sasha.

How long do I have until she catches up with me? How long do I have before she discovers my secret? And if she finds out, what will she do?

The following night, I slip back to the maids' section of the hotel after my shift. I have memorized the instructions telling me where to collect the downed Allied pilot. I know the exact route I am to take by heart. Blanche Auzello will be with me, so there is nothing to fear. The pilot is going to remain silent, so he will not give away any traces of an accent. If anyone stops us, we are to tell them that he is deaf.

Once I am back at my bedroom, I open the door and hover in the entrance. Sasha is resting on her bed. Her blue eyes are smudged with tiredness, and she is wearing a dress of pale blue with polka dots, in a style similar to those of the well-dressed German women who are in Paris, and the French women who consort with Nazi officers. I have not seen her since she slipped out of the bar in the early hours of this morning.

I pull the door closed with a soft click. If things are going to be said about her disappearing out into Rue Cambon, and what she might have seen, I do not want them to be overheard by prying ears. I remain standing between the beds, and it is Sasha who invites me to sit down.

One of us has the power to drop the axe, and that is not me.

"You need to be careful," she says simply. She raises her head, and her eyes clash with mine.

I stiffen. A bolt of fear darts through me. But I stand ramrod straight.

She stands up, turns her back to me and removes her dress, puts on her nightdress, and climbs into bed, facing away from me. "Good night, Louise."

I know that I cannot say a word. Anything would indict us. Finally, I slip down onto my single bed as quietly as I can and stare at the confines of the ceiling. I am starting to feel claustrophobic in the place I have come to see as my home.

The sands have shifted. The Ritz that was once safe is no longer safe.

But when I finally fall asleep again, my dreams are haunted by the Paris that I used to know. I dream that my father comes to find me in the hotel. He takes me in his arms and carries me out of here like a little girl. But then the city closes in on us, and all I can see is the river Seine flowing as a pool of red blood. I am rushing toward it with my father, only to stop dead at the sight of the ribbon of scarlet.

I wake, sweating. The air in the room is stifling. It is all I can do to stop myself from running to the window, throwing open the sash, and sticking my head out to take in great lungfuls of air. I turn and face the wall. In the bed next to me, the German girl breathes softly.

Why can she sleep, when I cannot?

Somehow I doze again and I am woken by knocking on my door. The code is Juliette's and she is calling my name. Slivers of white light line the blackout curtains and I leap out of bed, my eyes dashing to Sasha's bed, only to see it made up. She must have moved silently. I am coming to realize that silence can be more intimidating than action. It can be more intimidating than words.

I put on my bathrobe and go to open the locked door, finding myself face-to-face with Juliette waving a newspaper and bursting into the room.

"I shall not comment on the fact that you are late this morning because today is a momentous day." Juliette grasps my hands and holds them. Her lips are pale as if she has been too frantic to be bothered with lipstick. "It has happened, Louise. We are all celebrating down in the staff kitchen."

I stare at her.

"The Allies have landed on the beaches of northern France."

I sit back down hard on the bed, one hand flies to my mouth, and I shake my head. It seems impossible. I can hardly believe it. Surely this is not the beginning of the end of the war? Juliette squeezes my hand, as if to make me believe it.

"So!" I say. I am unable to utter anything else. Anything comprehensible has deserted me and I am only able to sit and stare at the woman standing next to my bed. And yet, there is a great sense of possibility welling inside of me. This is what we have been waiting for. This is what the Allies have promised. Liberation. Life.

As the news sinks in, I beam at Juliette. Oh, how I will look after our pilot. He is a hero. So brave.

"The Allies have dropped numerous parachutists onto the beaches of northern France and have followed this up with multiple landings. It is predicted by the end of the day they will have established a foothold in France!"

I cannot help it. I rush toward her and enfold her in my arms.

Later that morning, I am making Arletty's bed and singing some old French songs. I tremble excitedly at the thought of Blanche and our plan for later today. And I wonder, when the war is over, whether the spirits of all the famous people who have lived in the hotel throughout the war will remain, and whether anyone will spare a thought for the maids and the bellhops, and the bartenders who looked after them all.

The door to Arletty's room bursts open and she flutters in wearing a silk dress. Behind her comes Hans, his handsome brow knitted. He is holding a folded-up newspaper, which he throws on a coffee table before going to the window and staring out at the street below.

"Louise, I am so pleased you are here," Arletty says. She grips my arm, and her eyes mist with tears. "Hans says that the Allies may not make it to Paris for two months."

I look over at Hans's determined profile and I keep my thoughts to myself. *One month, two months? We have survived for years!*

"Hans says that the German ambassador to Paris and his wife are leaving for Germany and that Hans himself will be departing at the end of July."

"I must go and clean the bathroom." I have pushed Arletty's bizarre request that I accompany her to Germany aside, thinking of it as the ridiculous notion it is. "I am afraid I am running out of time this morning as I slept late."

"The point is that we must leave Paris. The orders have come direct from Berlin," Hans says. He strides across the room and picks up his newspaper again. "This is the combined efforts of twelve countries setting out to destroy us. It is perfectly deliberate, calculating, and will set out to annihilate all we have achieved." He shakes his handsome head.

A question forms on my lips, and for a moment I am terrified to ask it, but then, like the sea rushing into a tidepool, I cannot hold it in. "How are the Nazis planning to treat the Parisians in the meantime?"

"Harshly. Naturally," Hans says. His lips curl into a sneer and he does not even look up from his newspaper. "You all need to watch yourselves."

My hands shake as I nod quietly and push my trolley toward the bathroom.

I slip down to Frank's bar after my shift. There are a few quiet tables of Germans clustered about in the bar. Nobody turns to look at me and the door to Frank's office is resolutely closed. Just as I raise my arm to knock, a hand reaches out and clasps mine, pulling me away.

"Come."

A delicious sense of anticipation rushes through me. I know exactly who this is, without even having to turn and face the woman standing behind me.

Blanche Auzello takes my arm and tucks her hand into my

elbow. She walks through the bar with me with her head held high as if we are a pair of fashionable Parisian women, not a mere maid and the wife of the manager of the hotel. Charmingly, and with no hesitation, she greets guests from both the German side and the French side of the hotel.

She whisks me out into one of the grand corridors. I am about to turn one way when she pulls me in the other direction.

"You wouldn't imagine that I could ever live in the German side of the Ritz," she says, tossing her head of lustrous brown hair. She tightens her grip on my arm and we come to a stop outside a suite I have never been inside before. She pulls a key on a white ribbon from underneath her dress. "Now, we shall prepare."

She takes me straight into her rooms and, with a nonchalant wave in the air, she leads me into her dressing room. There are rows of silk and satin dresses, suits with little jackets and pencil-thin skirts, lines of high-heeled pumps and a variety of bathrobes.

"Choose," she says with another wave of her sparkling hand, covered in jewels.

I feel like a fool standing here staring at Blanche's clothes. She is a head taller than I am and her long legs make my short ones look like they belong to a child. If I am planning to be inconspicuous, I may end up looking ridiculous instead.

"If you are going to be my daughter, then I think it would be perfectly permissible for you to have borrowed one of my outfits, to my complete annoyance."

She pats my shoulder as she steers me farther into the dressing room and holds out a fabulous black trouser suit and white silk blouse.

"We could say that you were hoping to be an actress before the war, and that you like to dress up and practice your lines in some hope that, one day, your dreams will be accomplished. I like to go into character as much as possible," she adds with a wink.

"I'm sure that is a great help," I say. I can't take my eyes off the black ensemble. There is a pretend satin rose peeking out from one of the pockets, and I imagine myself with my hair combed to one side and a great deal of kohl on my eyes. What fun. "I love the suit. Are you sure?"

"Delighted. You dress here, and I shall go and get changed in my bedroom. I will see you in ten minutes, and when we go outside into Paris, all you must do is follow me." She disappears with a teal-green silk suit and a hat that looks worthy of the races at Longchamp in the heady days of the Belle Époque.

Ten minutes later, I'm staring at myself in the full-length mirror at the end of the long dressing room. I couldn't feel more conspicuous if I tried, and I'm sure this is not what Frank would advise, not at all. I've had to roll the trousers up so that they sit properly on my shoes.

"Perfect," Blanche says. She struts into the dressing room in a blond wig, with a great deal of deep red lipstick on. She looks completely at home in the green suit and is walking confidently in a pair of matching high heels with a fascinator pinned to her hair. "You see, what this does is create a diversion, Louise. Nobody is going to be interested in the man walking with us. The Nazis will be so fascinated by our outfits that they won't care about anything else. And, you know, you can flirt with them. They are not above a little attention, if you know what I mean."

I nod. I only hope her audacity will work.

"It will be marvelous," Blanche says, as if reading my thoughts.

Next, she unclips her handbag and produces two perfect replicas of the dreaded Nazi *Kennkarten*. She hands me one.

"Here we are. I shall be Madame Rizzolet, you shall be my dearest Claudine, while our pilot, to be known as Henri, is my wayward son. He already has his documentation, so that will be his name for as long as he stays with us. He will keep his

Kennkarten, so if the unthinkable happens and someone discovers he is residing at the Ritz, we shall simply say we had no idea and that he is a guest. You see?"

"Madame Auzello—"

"Blanche, dear. I am allergic to the word 'madame.' I never wanted to get married, you know. The idea of settling down was always impossibly boring to me. But I did so fall in love with Claude..."

"I want to ask whether it might be possible for me to help shelter Henri once he is in residence in the hotel. I'm extremely discreet. Nobody notices me."

"Well, everyone notices me. Opposites. We shall make an excellent team. And I don't see why not. I shall inform Frank."

I grin at her. I feel excited for the first time in months. And I love the way she simply tells people what is going to be done.

"Let's go and get our man, *Henri.*" She tucks her arm into the crook of my elbow again. "Now, we must leave the hotel without being noticed. And we must avoid that dreadful simpering bore, Juliette, at all costs."

I feel like I'm walking high above the clouds as we saunter back out into the glamorous corridor, down the grand staircase like a pair of fashion models, even if I am a tiny one. We glide out through the glass doors while the doorman opens them with a flourish, bows, and takes off his hat. A man I've known for years and it feels exciting to imagine that he doesn't recognize me at all.

Blanche squeezes my arm. Once we are outside in Place Vendôme, she speaks with a lowered voice. "The doormen are all on our side. They will let us in, they won't comment, and all we need to do is make our way to the assigned room with our guest."

We parade down Rue Saint-Honoré, down Rue d'Alger, toward the Tuileries Garden. There is a sense of anticipation and excitement in the streets, even though people don't dare to demonstrate openly, and the shop fronts along Rue Saint-Honoré are still marred by Nazi slogans proclaiming German control. I don't see any of the Resistance who are supposed to be hiding in the windows of buildings, and pointing guns down at the street, according to the Vichy government.

At an elegant café with wicker chairs, Blanche sails toward an elderly waiter, greets him warmly, and settles us down at a table overlooking the gardens across the road.

He murmurs something in her ear, and she leans forward to kiss him on both cheeks. The piece of paper she hands him is tiny and discreet, and he slips it into his pocket with a flick of his fingers and disappears.

Minutes later, he appears again with ersatz coffee and a young gentleman wearing a beret at the oddest angle I have ever seen. He appears to have materialized out of nowhere, and as he reaches up and adjusts the red bandanna around his neck, I swallow down my laugh at the sight of his enormously baggy trousers and oversized white shirt. He looks like an artist from the nineteenth century. But he is undeniably handsome, and it is a little thrilling to see a good-looking young man who is not German for once.

I watch him under my eyelashes. His dark blond hair is cut short, as they do in the military. He is taller than average, his slim body seems to fold into the chair, and his green eyes are fringed with dark lashes. There is a twinkle in them, despite his precarious state. He leans his forearms on the table. His skin has an olive tone.

Blanche kisses him on the cheek. "Henri, dearest! You must be exhausted after your ordeal. We shall not linger here, but we shall enjoy the coffee as it must not go to waste."

She tips back her head and drinks her espresso. I follow suit, and Henri does the same.

I chew on my lip, not sure what to say, slipping back into the mode of the quiet maid, and yet wishing I had an ounce of

Blanche's audacity. Something witty and amusing. But I am tongue-tied and my stomach is in knots.

"Very well, we shall go and get settled. Au revoir," she says after ten minutes. She waves perfectly conspicuously to the waiter, as if she is not hiding herself or trying to be covert in any way.

I glance toward Henri, but his expression as he catches my eye is only one of amusement.

I can't blame him. Why would he take me seriously? Especially as I am dressed in a black suit almost like a man!

We push back our chairs.

"My children. Back together at last." Blanche holds out one arm for each of us, and we walk like a strange little party back to the Ritz Hotel. I can't help feeling that we are taking Henri into the lion's den. I only hope that Blanche and I are enough to protect him.

But my stomach takes a delicious dive at the thought that I will be looking after him, and that he and I will be a team of sorts.

CHAPTER THIRTEEN

Kit

Kit took the last sip of the real coffee that his hosts had made. The young girl had brought it out in a little jar to the outbuilding in the garden where Kit had spent the night rolled up in a blanket on the floor. The child sat in silence while Kit sipped the coffee and ate his breakfast, a good slab of French bread.

When the door opened and the girl's mother entered, Kit stood up. Another middle-aged woman slipped in as well and hastily closed the door behind herself. There was a frown line between her widely set green eyes, and the scattering of freckles across her nose and cheeks gave her the appearance of a girl in her twenties. Her frame was slim and spare like all the French people Kit had encountered since he had landed so conspicuously in France. And yet the dress she wore was made of attractive red and white pinstripes, and fitted her small frame perfectly.

"This is the dressmaker," the girl's mother said. "She is one of our bravest Resistance workers, for whom we only reserve the riskiest of cases. I will not give away any further details about her."

Kit reached out and shook the dressmaker's hand.

She regarded him with her wide eyes and nodded, but did not say a word.

"We cannot impress upon you enough the need for you to protect the dressmaker and her family in the same way that we're protecting you," Kit's host said.

"I understand."

The dressmaker's expression was grave. "Brace yourself," she said. "I only wish that I had better news."

Kit felt his hand turn cold.

"We have intelligence that your air crew have been captured by the Germans."

The ground felt as if it were shifting like sand underneath his feet, and Kit staggered backward. *No. Charlie.* Heaven help them.

"From what I understand, there will be no mercy for them." She lowered her eyes, and her pale eyelashes swept across the light scattering of freckles on her cheeks.

Kit gasped and reached out for the table behind him, ignoring the searing pain that shot through his arm when he pressed his hand into the wood. He deserved it. He was entirely to blame.

"The Nazis are saying they will not even be afforded the usual cattle-like transportation to Germany. I am sorry," she murmured. "And they are searching for you."

Kit lifted his chin and focused on the shed wall just above the dressmaker's head. His stomach swirled. Here he was, after a hearty breakfast. He should be the one who had been caught. He grimaced, and the dressmaker went on.

"However, you must remember that the Nazis deal in lies. This may not be the truth."

Kit nodded, but his lips curled. He could not speak. He could not find the words.

"The search party looking for you is large, and they may have put this story out in the hope that you will do something rash."

It could be lies. It *had to* be lies. And he would do everything he could to prove that this was the case. But he had been warned not to give the members of the underground too many details. Could he tell them that Charlie was his brother without putting him—or the crew—at risk? He would have to think this through. In the meantime, he would hang on to the dressmaker's last words.

"We shall go now," the dressmaker said.

Kit nodded, but his mind burned with questions. How was he supposed to stick to the original plan and let the underground guide him to Spain? He had no idea where to begin searching for his brother.

The dressmaker turned back to the door and the little girl held it open for them.

Kit was assailed with the memory of Charlie standing next to him in the latrines shaving, grinning at him in the mirror. If he could turn the clock back, he would have insisted that Charlie not come out on the mission that day. He and his brother looked similar, and yet they were so different. Charlie had followed him every step of the way. He had trusted him.

"I have told the dressmaker exactly when to pass through this street so that you time it when the German sentries on the roof nearby are having a break, just as I promised," the child said.

Kit laid a hand on the girl's shoulder as he passed through the door. "Au revoir. Merci," he said softly, suddenly overcome with emotion at the child's kindness.

"Good luck," her mother said.

"I shall never forget you," Kit said, meaning it. He followed the dressmaker out into the garden, and into the strange, beautiful country that was filled with nature's beauty, and yet enveloped in a darkness that hid his brother. Somewhere.

"You must pretend you cannot speak," the dressmaker said. She tucked her arm into Kit's. "Please leave the rest to me."

CHAPTER FOURTEEN

PARIS, SUMMER 1944

Louise

The room that has been reserved for Henri (I love the thought that it has been reserved as if he has a booking and is one of our special guests) is in a disused section of staff quarters. There is a hidden corridor in the hotel, tucked into the attic space, that the Nazis do not know about. Henri has a room in this silent, ghostly space. I have an alibi if I bump into some Nazi, and that is that I am taking food up to Arletty, as she is feeling unwell and requires my services. I have German food so that I will raise less suspicion among our German guests in the unlikely event that they decide to search me. Today Jean-Paul, the head chef, has given me pork, sauerkraut, carrots, and roasted potatoes. He has also supplied apple strudel and a carafe of wine, and there is a little touch from me, one of the hotel's wrapped bedtime chocolates, made in our patisserie. All of this is hidden away in my trolley among my buckets and cleaning products.

I sing a tune very softly in French and knock on Henri's door with a terribly complicated code I made up myself. I am rather proud of all of this.

Henri lets me in, and I look at his tiny room with satisfaction. It is sparkling clean and there is a silk cushion that I borrowed for him on the narrow bed, some of the very best gentleman's soaps, and a towel that I pinched from another suite.

"Good afternoon, Henri."

"Bonjour, Claudine." He smiles, and a dimple appears each side of his lips.

Once I have handed Henri his food, I do what I always do in the hotel rooms. I take a cleaning rag that I have tucked into the pocket of my skirt and begin dusting the already immaculate space, the wooden headboard, then the chair.

"You don't have to do that, you know," he says. "I have plenty of time to dust the room."

I pause with my cleaning cloth in the air. He is looking intently at his plate of food, and his expression is hard to read.

"I wish I could lend you a wireless," I say suddenly. "A wireless would be just the thing. I couldn't have got through without Louis and Ella in the early mornings. What is your preference when it comes to music?" I busy myself at my trolley.

"I'm more of a book person myself. F. Scott Fitzgerald and Hemingway."

I resume cleaning, whizzing around with my broom. "Well then. We can't keep their books in the library." I roll my eyes.

His eyes crinkle with warmth.

I think my cheeks have reddened, which will make my freckles stand out even more. So annoying.

He seems a little more relaxed now, and he starts eating his food.

"All our modern novels were removed and taken to Germany. We had first editions. Claude says it was a tragedy." I hesitate a moment. "Are you able to read in German or French as well as English?"

He lays his fork down on his plate. "As luck would have it, I read German. My German is not as good as your English, though. You have a real knack. No accent. Extraordinary."

"I can't tell you where I learned, you know. I could make up a story about it and tell you a whole lot of lies, but I don't want to do that with you." I begin sweeping again, brushing away imaginary specks of dirt from the wooden floorboards so that I can look down and not at him.

"I don't want to lie to you either," he says.

I pause, thrown by the soft tone of his voice.

"I wish I could tell you more. There are things..."

Something is stirring in my insides that is new and exciting. I don't know if he is feeling it too.

"Yes?"

But he shakes his head. "So, all the books that have remained in the hotel are in German?" he asks.

I hide my disappointment that he has put his barriers back up, even though I know this is what we need to do. "I shall sneak into the library and have a look." I flutter my hands about for a moment. "But I think so. Hitler's preferences are strident when it comes to literature. Tell me, is there anything in particular you would love to read? In German?" I look up from my broom under my eyelashes and grin at him.

He taps his fingers on his tray. "I'm already putting you at more than enough risk as it is. Isn't stealing books a huge crime when it comes to the Nazis?"

I shrug. "Since they have acquired half the country, I don't think they can complain." I pick up a duster and begin wiping over the small desk that sits beneath the curtained window.

"The truth is, I used to love the fairy tales."

I stop dusting. It is suddenly stifling in here, and I don't know why. All I know is that when I was a little girl, my father used to read me German fairy tales, and I have not thought about them for so long.

"Then I shall find fairy tales for you. And don't worry about me; I know how to avoid the Nazis." I turn back to face him, my duster clasped in front of my black dress. I don't want to leave, and there is an awkward silence for a moment.

"What do you want to do after the war, Claudine?" he asks. He frowns at my cleaning trolley.

"I...don't know, not exactly. I mean, I had plans before it all started, but they are gone now." We are quiet while he finishes his lunch. "And you?"

He smiles wistfully. "Most of my friends have simple ambitions. They want to marry a secretary, get an office job. Have a couple of children and settle down."

I bite my lip. "And that does not appeal to you?"

"I...don't know."

I laugh out loud. "Well, at least you're honest. I don't know either. Not about marriage, or children." I make a face.

"Listen, I hate the fact that I'm here drinking...whatever this fine wine is..."

"I had no trouble convincing Frank to give you the wine that is only reserved for the highest German officials. It is some of the best in the entire hotel."

He raises his glass in a salute. "In that case, you must bring up a second glass next time."

I raise a brow. If only I could bring my wireless up here. Wine and jazz at lunchtime between a mere maid and a downed pilot? The Nazis would be apoplectic.

I smooth down the counterpane on his bed. I am staring at his feet, and he wiggles his toes. "Stop it," I say, laughing.

"How about if I told you I want to be a bus driver, to drive buses around all day long?"

I laugh again, bringing my hand up to my mouth. His green eyes are full of mischief, and I realize that it has been a long time since I laughed or joked with someone my own age.

"And where would you drive your bus?"

He tilts his head to one side. "All the way to New York. Where would you drive yours?" he asks.

"To the Caribbean," I say. "A sun-drenched island, a cocktail, and nothing but beach. Nothing to clean."

"Perhaps when it is all over, I might tell you more?" he says.

I hold his gaze for a moment, not wanting to turn away.

He hands me his empty plate and drains his glass. "Thank you," he says. "I can't tell you how much I appreciate all of this."

"I shall come back in the morning with your breakfast," I say. "Sleep well tonight, Henri."

"Sleep well, Claudine," he says.

I hover in the doorway once I have hidden his empty plate and glass. And then, as quietly as I entered, I turn around and slip away.

The following day, I'm in Frank's office updating him on the situation with Sasha. Frank has secured me a selection of books from the library for Henri, and they are spread out on his desk. If anyone asks, we shall say they are for one of the guests.

"Sasha is spending an increasing amount of time away from the hotel. Last night, she came in very late, and I heard her yawning as she prepared for bed. We've hardly spoken since she warned me to be more discreet." I shake my head. "To be honest, I think she seems distracted."

"The only advantage is that she will sleep through your early-morning disappearances down here if she is not concentrating fully. If she stirs at all, do not leave the room."

I pick up a German copy of Remarque's masterpiece, *All Quiet on the Western Front.*

"Hitler greatly disapproves of that," Frank tells me. "It's my copy now. I managed to avail myself of the English version from the library before the Nazis arrived in the Ritz."

It is over ten years since the Nazis organized the first mass book burning ceremony, heaping "unacceptable" books into a pile opposite the University of Berlin and using the torches to set alight the books that were considered un-German—books by Thomas Mann, Heinrich Mann, Albert Einstein, Émile Zola, H. G. Wells, and Upton Sinclair.

"Hide it behind the Agnes Miegel and the Rudolf Binding," Frank says.

"Of course," I say. "But, Frank, this is all terribly serious. Henri needs something lighter. He mentioned fairy tales."

Frank raises a brow and chuckles. "How intriguing. But I cannot deny such an unusual request." He reaches into the bookshelf behind his desk. It is replete with volumes on wine and cocktails. But hidden among these is an old book that he pulls out with great reverence. "Give our dear English friend this." He hands me a copy of *Grimm's Fairy Tales*. It looks very old.

"Frank, this is a special book, no?"

"I hope its pages transport him far away from here, dear."

"Thank you. I know that Henri will appreciate it. I think it is you who are dear."

He smiles at me and waves me away. I am just walking to the door when it opens, unceremoniously, and Claude stumbles inside. He is followed by Jean-Paul, whose face is as white as his chef's clothing.

"Brace yourselves," Jean-Paul mumbles. He takes off his hat and throws it on the floor.

Jean-Paul can be dramatic, but I am still taken aback. I shake my head and pick up the hat, dusting it off and placing it on a chair.

Claude presses his hands into Frank's desk. His chest is heaving and, horribly, tears are coursing down his cheeks. His shoulders shake and now Jean-Paul is behind him, his hand on the older man's shoulder.

Frank and I stare, helpless.

"What is it?" I whisper. I begin to feel sick. Our managing director is pale with shock.

"Blanche has been taken," Jean-Paul says, his hand still pressed firmly on Claude's shoulder. "The Gestapo. They arrested her an hour ago."

Claude looks broken. Frank helps him to sit down.

He sobs openly, and Frank turns to the side table and pours him a large shot of brandy.

"She was having lunch at Maxim's," Jean-Paul explains. "She was with her good friend Lily Kharmayeff. They were celebrating D-Day and making plans."

"I cannot believe it, my darling Blanche..." Claude cries.

Frank's eyes dart toward me. "Louise, that's it. We cannot risk you."

I shake my head. *Not now,* I want to say to Frank. "But how was she betrayed?" Has Sasha done this? I bow my head. If the traitor who has reported her is sleeping in the same room as me, then how can I sleep there at night?

"I don't know," Claude whispers. "I managed to get to where she was taken. They have shackled her along with a dozen other men and women in ankle chains. They threw her in the back of a truck. They are taking her to Fresnes Prison."

I shudder and turn away. The newspapers are full of daily reports about prisoners being taken to Fresnes, the terrifying-looking institution on the outskirts of Paris, and it is well known that those who go there only stay there until they are transported to the German labor camps. I stare at the closed door to the bar. A loud bark of laughter comes through, and a German exclamation. The clink of glasses. I wrap my arms around my body.

"She will be beside herself," Claude mutters. He swigs the brandy. "She was so brave; you know my darling girl delivered microfilm with photographs of stolen documents showing German gun placements along the Atlantic coast to a French rail worker? Nothing scared her."

I did not know she had delivered documents as well as helped refugees escape from the Nazi regime.

"I fear for her life," Claude whispers. His lips are as white as Jean-Paul's face.

I reach for the coat that Frank always keeps hanging on the back of his door and place it over Claude's shoulders. Frank is scowling and pacing the room.

"She was pretending to be a Catholic," Claude sobbed. "We falsified her passport twenty years ago because she didn't want her Jewish identity to slow down my career!"

I catch Frank's eye, and he shakes his head. *Let him talk,* he mouths.

"She changed her last name to Ross, she changed the place of her birth for me, and all she has done is help others throughout this war. She is entirely selfless, and you know what the worst part of this is? You know what will break my heart the most, my dear friends?" Claude's voice rises into the room and swells.

We are silent. I bow my head. Claude's agony is too much to bear. I cannot look at the poor darling man. I begin praying for Blanche.

"I know that she will not budge under torture. They will try everything to get her to talk and my darling Blanche will not betray the Resistance. She will die rather than send her friends to a fate worse than death. And, because of this, I fear I will never see her again." His empty brandy glass falls to the ground and rolls across the carpet. "I am not nearly as brave as my wife."

I watch as a trickle of amber liquid slides along inside the glass excruciatingly slowly.

"You will get through this," I whisper. I lift my chin. I swipe my hand across my eyes. "And Blanche will survive."

But my dear trio of middle-aged men are all staring at the ground. Suddenly small and broken.

I look at them, and my heart contracts, but something determined and steely is rising within me as well. I need to step up. I must take on Blanche's mantle. I need to be brave and bold for my friend.

"I am not nearly as dashing as Blanche," I say, "but I shall do everything in my power to ensure that what she was doing continues while she is...not with us." I stumble on the last words, but with a surprisingly steady hand, I collect my trolley containing the books Frank has given me for Henri and move toward the door.

"Louise. No."

My hand freezes on the handle at the sound of Frank's voice.

But, surprisingly, it is Jean-Paul whose voice is clear in the room. "Blanche and Lily were arrested at Maxim's. It is still very much a place for the Nazis, Frank. And Louise belongs here. She will not raise suspicion."

Claude nods resignedly. "Let Louise carry on the work that dear Blanche cannot do. And, in the meantime, I shall insist that my darling is allowed to see her husband, like the other imprisoned wives."

Frank sends me a resigned sigh. He pulls a silver casket of cigarettes out of his waistcoat. "I understand the guards are open to bribes." He lights a cigarette and hands one to Claude.

Briefly, I hug Claude around his shoulders, and he holds my hand, his hand feeling bony and frail. "Thank you, my dear. You have much of her spirit."

I stare at the floor. "Please, look after yourself, Claude. This dreadful time will end and in the meantime we will fight on, and pray for Blanche."

The room is quiet. And I think we all feel the weight of this, as if a light has been extinguished in the hotel.

CHAPTER FIFTEEN

Kit

Kit followed the dressmaker along a narrow street that was lined with ramshackle shops clearly still trying to do business in the face of impossible odds. Nazis in uniforms strolled up and down the sidewalks, but barely noticed a man with a beret perched at an odd angle on his head. The long blue coat that he wore flapped along around him. Kit forced himself to focus on the dressmaker. She rode in a straight line on her bicycle, but she moved slowly enough for Kit to keep her in his sights.

He followed her into a narrow street lined with typical Parisian apartment buildings and shop fronts that were either blazing with swastikas or closed. She pulled her bike up outside an unmarked shop. There was a large window overlooking the street, and faded lettering in a curved hand told him it was a dressmaker's shop.

Kit slowed his pace until she had disappeared inside. When the street was clear, he knocked on the door and the dressmaker let him in, just as she had instructed.

"Welcome." She stepped aside for him.

There were neatly folded reams of fabric that sat on what looked like handmade shelves around the walls of the dim little room, and a dressmaker's model sat against the back wall, a white table next to it. A simple wooden chair sat against one wall, and in the corner, there was a curtained screen.

"Let me show you upstairs to the bathroom and your bedroom."

She led him up a narrow flight of stairs to a tiny landing, off which were two closed doors. She opened one of these and led him inside a bedroom with a single bed covered in a white counterpane. There was a vase containing three white roses on the bedside table, and next to this his eyes caught on the photo of a young girl. She was perhaps eighteen and looked directly out at the camera. The expression on her face was so intense that Kit found himself taken aback. Her long hair was blond, and she had a similar scattering of freckles across her nose as the dressmaker.

He turned to the dressmaker. "It's a beautiful room," he said simply.

She nodded but did not mention the fact that it must have once belonged to her daughter. "I am pleased. Come downstairs and we shall have lunch."

Kit gave her a warm smile. "I am so well fed by your countrymen that I don't know whether I need to eat for a week."

"Please, have a bath first; there is plenty of hot water," she said. "By the way, I shall be calling you Antoine, as that is what the underground have decided your name will be."

"*Antoine*. I shall practice it." Kit paused. The dressmaker was clearly practical and kind. Perhaps there might be some way he could make himself useful in her home. "If there is anything I can do to assist around the house, please let me know."

The dressmaker sighed and tidied her light blond hair. She folded her hands in front of her. "If you would like to help me measure fabric and cut material, there is plenty to be done."

That evening, Kit sat on the wooden chair at the table, a pair of shears in his hand, and a pattern on tracing paper in front of him, with a ream of sprint cotton fabric rolled up ready to be cut.

The dressmaker was working on another outfit she had pinned on her model. The blackout curtains were closed, and the room was lit by a couple of standard lamps. It felt companionable with the world outside shut away for a little while. There was a comfort in taking up an age-old skill like an artisan of years gone by.

Kit cleared his throat. "My brother...," he began.

The dressmaker lifted her head. Her expression was calm, and she waited.

"My brother was flying with me, but apparently has been captured by the Germans along with all of my crewmates." He cut a line straight down the middle of the fabric, taking care to follow the line. He turned the fabric over and placed the pattern atop it just like the dressmaker had shown him.

He couldn't begin to voice the guilt that cut into him at every waking moment. At night, he lay awake and prayed for Charlie's safety, along with that of his crewmates.

And then there was his mother. It broke his heart to think he might have to write a devastating letter to her. Would he be able to confess that it was he who had taken the dreadful risk that had caused Charlie to be caught behind enemy lines?

The dressmaker turned to him, her hands stilling on the model. "Antoine, you must keep faith. You must not lose hope that your brother will survive." She caught his gaze with an intensity that burned in its determination. "So many young people are burdened with guilt that is not theirs to bear."

But it is my responsibility.

She continued: "Guilt is what I have seen in all the people who have stayed here. I fear it is the cost to the heart and mind that is bearing down upon them with the greatest weight."

Kit concentrated on the pattern in front of him, his brows creased, and his hands steady, surprisingly so. How would forgiving himself bring Charlie back?

"I have learned the only way to get through this is to focus on what you can do, not what you can't," she said.

There was a silence. He could not bring himself to tell her of his burden. It was his alone to bear.

"We need to get you identity documents as soon as possible. Did you bring photographs?"

Kit nodded. "I have a collection of identity-card-sized photographs," he said. "I keep them in my pocket. There is one of me in a beret." He attempted a smile.

She raised an eyebrow. "I hope you look like a true Frenchman."

Kit lifted his face, and she was smiling at him. "Definitely," he said. They both laughed.

The following morning, Kit sat at the little table inside the kitchen out the back of the dressmaker's house. Next to him, the dressmaker was painstakingly tracing a red circle over his photograph. She had stuck the photograph onto a false *Kennkarten* and had taken an imprint of the eagle stamp in red and transferred this onto the forged document.

Kit focused on cutting fabric.

When there was a knock at the door, his hands froze.

"It is only my customer, here for her appointment. This is

a fitting for her dress." The dressmaker packed up the identity document and placed it in a kitchen drawer. "You must stay silent."

The dressmaker disappeared into the front room, and Kit was left sitting and staring at the kitchen drawer that held all the evidence that could incriminate him.

The women's conversation sounded harried. For the last two nights, the skies had been quiet. Kit knew this only meant the Allies were probably planning a bigger attack as they advanced southeast toward Paris. They would be carrying out reconnaissance missions to target storage facilities and aircraft bases, with an intention to destroy them. He only wished he could be a part of it all.

Half an hour later, the dressmaker was back, bent over her laborious detailed work to get Kit's identity card up to snuff. This time, when there was a knock at the door, the dressmaker sent him a worried look.

"Go upstairs," she whispered. She tidied away her work in progress and again placed it in the drawer of her kitchen dresser.

Upstairs, Kit rolled underneath the single bed. He lay still, alert for any indication of what might be going on downstairs. When the sound of footsteps coming up the staircase resonated into the bedroom, Kit remained stock-still exactly where he was.

"Antoine?" the dressmaker asked. The door had opened, and Kit was staring at the dressmaker's shoes, along with a pair of scuffed old boots that belonged to a pair of stocky legs.

Now feeling ridiculous, Kit eased himself out from underneath the bed. Even more ridiculously, he reached out his hand to shake the incoming stranger's.

"Antoine, this is the butcher."

"I thought a young man like you might need some extra

rations," the butcher said. He not only smiled but extended his hand to meet Kit's own.

Relief sweeping over him, Kit shook the butcher's hand vigorously, taking in his warm expression, his flushed cheeks, and the charming way he had not even attempted to control his head of slightly wild gray hair. Kit almost blurted out that he looked like a mad professor rather than a man who handled meat.

"You had me there for a moment. I thought this might be the end," Kit said.

"What a wonderful American accent." The butcher took off his glasses and wiped his eyes, reinforcing the impression of a professor.

"Is it as obvious as that?"

"I traveled widely in America when I was young. I was part of a band. A bass player, would you believe."

"The butcher is not only a bass player," the dressmaker said. "He is an accomplished player of the accordion and the guitar, no less."

"Perhaps one day I shall be able to play for you," the butcher said. "Look at this, all of us here talking about music." He lowered his voice. "You see, the Allies are coming, and we have much to look forward to. So, things are getting better."

Kit leaned on the side table and nodded. How could he argue, or bring up his worries, when these people, all they wanted was the freedom that the Allies would bring?

"The butcher has brought some information from my contacts," the dressmaker said.

Kit froze. *Let it be news that Charlie is safe.*

"The plans for you."

Kit heaved out a long sigh, and the sharp pain that had lodged between his ribs since he lost Charlie burned with a new intensity.

"You are no longer to go to Spain, but we are going to try to get you on a flight back to the United Kingdom." The dressmaker was watching him, her gaze intent.

He would have less time to find out the truth about Charlie and his crew...Unless British intelligence had any information.

"There are bands of local men hiding out in the forests of France," the dressmaker explained. "This has been the case since Hitler tried to arrange for our men to go and work in Germany in the factories in exchange for freeing prisoners of war and returning them to France."

Kit held the butcher's gaze. The Maquis. They were sabotaging German patrols as they passed through and detonating bombs on railway lines in advance of Nazi trains. There was information that these bands of men in the forests were also helping the Allied air force to land in occupied France, dropping Resistance members in the countryside.

"No self-respecting Frenchman would ever agree to go and make ammunition for the Germans," the butcher jeered. "They preferred to hide out in makeshift homes, deep in the forests."

Kit nodded. "I understand. And I'm fully prepared to do whatever you suggest. Do you want me to go and stay with the Maquis until a plane comes to collect me?"

The butcher turned to the dressmaker for confirmation, and she nodded. "I think this would be the best plan. We are waiting for confirmation from British intelligence."

As much as Kit hated to leave the country where he had lost trace of his brother, this was a sound plan.

The butcher reached out and patted him on the back. "Perhaps one day I shall come back to America, and we can sit in a jazz club together in New York."

"Both of you would be welcome in America."

The butcher glanced at the dressmaker, and she nodded. "Antoine, there is one thing I want to make clear. There are posters of you on every street corner and the Nazis are patrolling ruthlessly with the intent of capture. That is another reason we think you might be safer in the forests with the Maquis."

Outside the window, there was the sound of children calling out to each other. The beat of a ball game being played in the street. There was a hollow strangeness to the sounds, and an eeriness because they did not fit in with war.

Kit understood at once. "I will stay completely hidden and leave as soon as you are ready."

The butcher rested a hand on Kit's back.

CHAPTER SIXTEEN

PARIS, SUMMER 1944

Louise

Arletty spends her afternoons in a silk bathrobe. It breaks her heart to know that her beloved French audiences now hate her, but I understand why they do.

I begin busying myself in her bedroom.

Claude has not been allowed to visit Blanche in prison, and he sees this as an ominous sign. We do know that she has been placed in solitary confinement, and Frank thinks this is probably because she refused to cooperate and release any information. We know that she is being accused of harboring enemies of Germany and of aiding fugitives.

"Louise?" Arletty says, drawing me out of my reverie. She turns to me. The pain and torment in her eyes are genuine. They say luxury is a buffer against pain, but I am beginning to wonder if that is true. She picks up a folded newspaper from the coffee table that sits in front of her sofa. "They have murdered my friend Georges Mandel."

I bow my head. Georges Mandel was a long-term resident of the Ritz and a brave and vigorous opposer of the armistice that France had signed with Germany. He had been a government minister at the outset of the war. But he had then gone to North Africa to try to build opposition to France's collaboration with Germany. There, he had been arrested and sent by the French government to the Gestapo, who had interned him in Buchenwald camp in Germany.

"Pierre Laval, our own head of government, signed orders to bring him back to France," Arletty explains.

"That is awful."

"The French Gestapo took him out to the forest near Fontainebleau and shot him, before blowing up his car. This, they say, is a warning to the French Resistance."

I pick up a silver ornament from Arletty's dressing table, and, absently, I polish it with my cloth. Hans's words come back to haunt me. He implied the Germans will step up their efforts to quell the Resistance as the Allies make their way through northern France. And it does seem that the Allies are making progress. Towns are falling each day, and they are moving toward Paris even though we don't know how long it is going to take, nor what the Germans have planned for the liberating forces on their way.

"I am beginning to fear the French government far more than the Germans," Arletty says.

"This fretting will do you no good, madame."

She buries her head in her hands. "Things are becoming so distressing," she whispers.

"I am sorry," I say simply. I do not have the words. I remember her friend Georges. He was a warm and valiant person. A Jewish man.

Blanche is Jewish too. *When will this end?*

Arletty glances worriedly toward the door. She picks up a newspaper, *Je Suis Partout,* and hands it to me. I am certain that Hans has given it to her. I hate him right now. I read in horror that the French government are claiming that Georges had deserved death a thousand times. The most important thing, the article says, is that "the Jew" is dead.

"They shot him and then blew him up," she whispers. She seems to be stuck, repeating the horror of his death. "My poor friend."

I help her across the room and into her bed, where she sits, her face pale and tears running down her cheeks.

"Give me a few moments, and I shall be back."

I return minutes later with a pot of fresh coffee from the kitchen. I pour the coffee into a delicate porcelain cup and hand it to her.

She pats the bed, inviting me to sit down on its edge.

I hesitate. This is not something I should do.

But she looks at me and she whispers, "Pour yourself a cup of coffee. Please."

I pour myself some coffee and sit on the bed.

"Perhaps I was a fool," she says. Tears still run down her cheeks, and her beautiful eyes are puffed with grief for the death of her friend. "Perhaps I was a fool for believing that a man like Hans could truly love me for who I am." She holds her hand up to her chest. Her fingernails are still beautifully groomed. "I wanted to be loved," she says. "But look what has happened to poor Georges Mandel. How can I continue my affair with a man whose associates have carried out orders to murder my dear friend?"

You chose to be loved by a Nazi. And now you question it?

I stand up and move over to the window, and I stare out at the beautiful Rue Cambon.

A few days later, I am standing next to Arletty in the Passy Cemetery. We are under a long line of shady trees on a path that winds through the graves. There is a small gathering here to remember the life of Georges Mandel. I bow my head. The speaker talks in hushed tones, and my heart is somewhere out in the countryside near Fontainebleau where the ghost of him will remain. A rabbi should be reading these words over him.

"Georges Mandel was assassinated by French soldiers loyal to the Nazis," the man says. "He was shot sixteen times and assassinated by the enemies of France, he, a Resistance fighter who struggled to save France from being taken over by the Nazis but was gunned down for his efforts. On the night of July 7, 1944, he was shot by the French gestapo."

As we are invited to place a rose on Georges' coffin, Arletty leans heavily on my arm. And it is a slow procession that turns and heads to the line of waiting cars that will take us back to the hotel.

The car Arletty and I are in travels through the Paris streets. A line of black-clad SS Nazis parade along, their eyes focused straight ahead and their grim mouths turned down in cruel curves.

The afternoon has turned gray and the sky is loaded with clouds that feel as if they truly may rain down bullets over the most beautiful city in the world.

I wonder how many more Resistance members will be rounded up by the French Gestapo and murdered in the name of Nazism before the Allies liberate our country fully.

I notice that Arletty is pale and staring out the window. When she turns to me after a few moments, the expression in her eyes has changed. Gone is the raw sadness and the burning grief for Georges. What I see now is a steely determination that was missing from her before.

"I cannot leave Paris," she whispers, her eyes drifting to the driver, who stares straight ahead. "Today has made me realize I would rather cut off my head than leave my beloved France. What has happened here must change. And I cannot run away. Georges Mandel did not run away; he was not a coward, and I refuse to be one."

• • •

Back in the hotel, the lobby is swarming with departing German officers. Elderly staff, their faces as straight as rods, assist Nazis with their suitcases. The Germans stand around, their expressions grim. Gone are the self-satisfied smiles of the conquerors; instead, the mood is sober. This is a retreat.

Arletty stands with her hand over her mouth. "Mon Dieu," she says. "It is happening. The Germans are starting to see the outcome very plainly, Louise."

Claude approaches us with a note that he presses into Arletty's hand. "Officer Soehring would like to see you in your suite," he tells her. "He is on his way."

My heart goes out to Claude, and I can see the tiredness in his eyes.

Arletty tightens her grip on my arm. "I cannot bear to see Hans on my own," she whispers. "I may be persuaded into something that I should not do." She almost sobs the words. "I worry that I will be persuaded to go to Germany."

"I will come with you," I say.

Arletty moves toward the grand staircase, weaving her way through the milling Nazis with their neatly packed suitcases and their endless cigarettes. Upstairs, she rests her head against her bedroom door for one moment. "If there is one thing that I want you to know," she says, "it is that it was a genuine love affair, Louise."

"I see," I say. "I shall clean while you talk to him, and if at any point you want me to leave, just tell me so."

I hear her shaky intake of breath.

Ten minutes later, Arletty is pacing up and down the beautiful room when there is a soft knock on the door. Arletty's eyes shoot toward me, but with my head lowered, I go to let him in.

Hans Jürgen Soehring is hidden behind a bouquet of summer flowers and my heart sinks. When he lowers it, his dark hair is smoothed back on each side with an immaculate side parting as usual, but I see nervousness in his eyes.

I step aside for him to come into the room.

"Please," he says. "Some privacy."

Arletty turns from where she is standing by the window. It is a dramatic gesture, and I see the same pain reflected in her eyes as is reflected in his. "Louise must stay. I want her to be here, Hans."

I busy myself with the duster, even though I know there is nothing to brush away. The room is as pristine as a Nazi officer's boots. I have seen to it.

Hans drops to his knees. And to my horror, he pulls out a navy-blue velvet jewelry box. He flips it open and there is an exquisite solitaire diamond ring inside. "Marry me, my darling."

I wave my duster around as if I am swishing away the problems. I swipe imaginary specks of nothing. I will start singing in a moment if I must. The whole thing feels utterly absurd.

Arletty's voice is strained with tears. "My crime has been falling in love with an army officer who happens to be German."

"Darling..."

"I will love you until the day I die. But that does not mean I'm willing to leave Paris. I am not willing to go to Germany. How could I? How could you even begin to think I would?"

Hans shakes his head uncomprehendingly. "It was the *French* Gestapo who killed Georges Mandel. I know how upset you are. Please, my love, it is not safe for you to stay." He grinds out the words.

Arletty wraps her arms around her body.

He softens his voice. "I know Monsieur Mandel was your friend, and I do not for one moment think that he deserved death at the hands of the French. But I cannot stand by and leave you here to a similar fate."

A stream of expressions pass across Arletty's face.

My duster stills. The room is silent.

"The Gestapo," she points out, her voice as clear as a bell, "did not come out of France."

"I want to protect you," he says, his tone a little whiny now. "That is all I have ever wanted to do."

She kneels and takes his hands in her own. "How would I live with myself, running away? Falling in love is one thing; I could not control that. But abandoning my country is a decision I could never make."

Hans is weeping. Tears flow down his cheeks freely. He starts entreating her in German. They are words of love.

I turn away.

Later, I wheel my cleaning trolley toward Henri's hidden attic room. I knock with my code, and soon, I am facing Henri.

The skin on his cheeks was tanned when I first met him, but now it is pale, and his eyes are filled with telltale traces of red. I wonder if he is sleeping.

I hand him his food and busy myself with my duster on the windowsill.

"There are breaded pork chops dipped in buttermilk and flour and then fried until they are golden brown with a mushroom gravy sauce, German potato pancakes—"

"Claudine."

I wince at the sound of the unfamiliar name.

He walks over to me and gently removes the cloth from my hand. He opens a drawer in the little desk and pulls out one of my cleaning cloths. "I have done the work, so you can have a rest. Please, sit down. Talk to me while I eat." He places my cloth back on the trolley and then comes over and pulls out the wooden chair at the desk. "I insist," he says.

I feel close to tears. No one in a hotel room has asked me to sit and do nothing. Even when I am with Frank and Claude, I am working.

"What is it, this idea of rest?" I ask. I fold my hands together tightly. I am simply not sure what to do.

Henri pours a glass of wine and, incredibly, hands it to me. "Go on."

"I still have work to do." I glance at the closed door.

"Your work is simply to have lunch. Are you hungry? I'm very happy to share some of this with you."

I glance down at my hands. The idea of sharing lunch with anyone is wonderful, I must admit. But I shake my head.

"You must tell me how you learned to speak English so perfectly. You speak like a native, no accent. Where did you learn?" he asks.

"I've always loved languages. I love the way they dance and move, the way the words sound, and the way I see them on the page. I even enjoy grammar; it's a little like mathematics, don't you think?"

He smiles at me, his almond eyes crinkling. "You are not telling me you enjoy arithmetic as well?"

"Is there a reason that a lowly maid should not enjoy numbers and letters?" I know my eyes are lighting up while I talk.

"No reason at all. I think it's marvelous. Tell me, is English the only other language you speak?"

A sense of unease washes over me, but again, it is not altogether unpleasant. "Should I tell you? What if you're a German spy?" I send him a stern look.

"Good point. Would it help if I told you more about me?"

I eye him silently and take another sip of my wine. Henri is treading on dangerous ground, asking me personal questions. And yet I want to talk to him. I want to be able to open up about myself, and I want to know more about him. This strange attraction between us...Sometimes I wonder if it could lead to something more. Something lasting and real.

"The only thing is, I don't want to put you at risk," he says, his voice softening.

"I have survived four years under Nazi occupation. I know about risks." I bite my lip. That sounded abrupt. I take a deep breath and wait for him to speak.

"I respect that enormously. What you have been through, what you have survived." He pauses. "You know I love books?"

I nod.

"I worked in a bookshop in London before the war, until I absolutely had to join the armed forces." He places his knife and fork down on his plate for a moment. To my horror, he shakes his head and his face crumples.

"Henri!" In an instant, I am next to him, removing his tray and placing my hands on his shoulders, but he is staring downward, and he is shaking his head. "How can I help?" I ask. My voice comes out like a squeak.

And suddenly, he reaches out and takes my hand, holding it gently. "I cannot tell you," he whispers, but tears are falling down his cheeks openly now.

"Henri," I whisper. "You can tell me. It will never leave my lips."

He places a hand on my cheek for one moment, only to pull it back suddenly. "I'm sorry," and he buries his head in his hands again.

I pull the half-empty tray away and place it on the bedside table.

"I'm sorry," he murmurs again. "I won't waste the food; I will make the most of it. Grief and worry come at the most unexpected time."

"There is no need to apologize," I say. Goodness knows, the grief that I feel for my father and the worry that I have for my mother hit me when I least expect it. "But I want you to tell me," I murmur. "Please. It is safe with me. Whatever it is."

Slowly, he raises his head, and his eyes meet mine.

"Oh, Claudine. There are things that I can't talk of. Secrets that I never want to repeat."

I take in a deep breath. I am not the only one.

CHAPTER SEVENTEEN

PRESENT DAY

Nicole

Mariah, Arielle, and I sit in the office of the archives of the Ritz. Outside the room, the sounds of cutlery clinking and conversation from the restaurant fill the corridor. I am still overwhelmed by the luxury and grandeur of the hotel. Aunt Mariah is perfectly at home. She folds her manicured hands on the lap of her pale blue silk dress and crosses her legs at the ankles, her feet encased in their high-heeled pumps.

"My search has been interesting." Arielle takes a pair of black-rimmed glasses and places them on her nose. She folds her hands on her desk.

Silently, I scan Arielle's face for signs that she knows anything. For signs that she has found any evidence about my granny Louise.

"There was no guest by the name of Louise Bassett in the hotel in the summer of 1944. However, I have found there was a maid."

I glance across at Aunt Mariah.

"That can't be right," Mariah says. "What is your evidence?"

Arielle slips a photocopied page across the desk. It is an inventory of tasks dated June 21, 1944. Clearly, it states that Louise Bassett will be cleaning the room of Arletty, a film star I vaguely remember hearing about.

"My mother never mentioned that she knew Arletty. Surely she would have if that was the case." My aunt shakes the piece of paper as if doing so will wipe away the words.

"Granny would not have seen the fact that this woman was a film star as important," I say. If only my aunt understood her mother as well as I did.

Mariah lays the piece of paper down and glares at me. She removes her own glasses and waves them so close to my face that I have to lean back. "My mother was domestically useless, hated cleaning. This is simply impossible." She slides the piece of paper back across the desk. "You have the wrong woman."

I catch Mariah's eye and raise my brow. "So, I am guessing this clears up any misunderstanding that Granny could have been the woman in the photograph outside the hotel. It puts paid to any suggestion that she was a Nazi collaborator, Aunt Mariah."

Aunt Mariah places her hands on her knees, but she is ruffled. Two pink spots have appeared on her cheeks.

But before Aunt Mariah can reply, or I can hammer the point home, Arielle clears her throat.

"The woman in the photograph outside the hotel was identified as Louise Bassett," Arielle says carefully.

You could hear a butterfly's wings in the silence that envelops the room.

I sit back in my chair. "I am sorry? I don't follow."

Arielle leans forward in her seat and clasps her hands on her desk. "I looked at the records, and it is documented that a maid working in the hotel named Louise Bassett was captured by the French and accused of being a Nazi collaborator." Arielle's voice is neutral. "I'm sorry to give you this difficult news, but it is definitely her. We don't know what happened to her afterward."

I shake my head. "No," I whisper. I can hear Mariah's heavy breathing next to me, but all I am aware of is this picture of my grandmother as a young girl inhabiting these very rooms, cleaning the suites, looking after Nazis. Yet I cannot believe that she could ever have given them favors.

"I know that nobody wants to hear those sorts of things about people they love," Arielle concedes.

"She is not here to defend herself," I murmur. I feel as if my grandmother has been accused of being a murderer, or a thief. "How will we ever find out the truth? I don't for one moment believe we should leave this here."

Mariah flutters her hands uselessly.

"I know this has been very upsetting. I'm afraid we do not have any more information or answers for you."

I can hardly speak, but my aunt is already collecting her patent leather handbag. She places it over her arm and stands up as if to leave the room. "I do not accept that my mother was some maid."

I roll my eyes and wait until she has disappeared.

Arielle begins tidying her papers.

"I have a question."

Arielle looks over the top of her glasses directly at me.

I decide to be direct. "Why were you so rattled when you first saw the photograph? It seemed that it was affecting you in a way that went beyond what we are discussing here. Was there something you are not telling me?"

She stands up. "Please. I have another meeting."

The archivist is suddenly curt. The difference in her behavior is perplexing. She is hiding something. There is more to this story, and I am certain she knows what it is.

Outside her office, I accidentally go the wrong way down the corridor and end up in a magnificent hallway lined with glass cabinets filled with designer French handbags, exquisite silk scarves, glittering diamonds, and exotic perfumes. Two couples are peering into the cabinets. They look at me oddly, not bothering to hide their disdain.

And that's when it is clear to me. Granny Louise would have been much more likely to have worked at the Ritz rather than stay at the hotel. That part of the story makes perfect sense. But why did she never talk about her early life in France? Why the secrecy?

CHAPTER EIGHTEEN

SUMMER 1944

Kit

A few days later, the butcher sat at the dressmaker's table, his forearms resting on the white tablecloth. The plates were polished clean. No one would dare to leave anything of the meal that they had been lucky enough to enjoy. Kit would never take good food for granted again.

"There is a reason for my visit today," the butcher said. "I am not just here for the wonderful cooking." He sent a glance toward the dressmaker.

If Kit was not mistaken, he saw a faint blush gracing her cheeks.

"The butcher has relayed news that British intelligence has decided it is time for you to leave here, Antoine," the dressmaker said. "But there is another change of plan."

Kit waited.

"You will no longer be flown to the United Kingdom; instead, we are going to get you to Paris. That way, you will be there when the Allies arrive. You see, we are hoping this will happen within two weeks. I trust that is good news for you."

"Of course." He would get in touch with British intelligence once he was in Paris; he would find out what had happened to Charlie.

The dressmaker began collecting plates. She moved to the kitchen sink and then commenced preparing the ersatz coffee.

"I will be accompanying you on your journey to Paris. According to your new *Kennkarten,* you are my son," the dressmaker said.

Kit shook his head. "That is too dangerous; surely I should go alone?" The stories about what had happened to members of the French underground were stark. Fresnes Prison outside Paris. Transportation to Germany to a labor camp. Almost certain death. He shuddered.

"The dressmaker is one of the most important Resistance leaders in this area. You could not be in safer hands," the butcher reassured him.

Kit looked over at her. He had become fond of her during the time they'd been living together. She wiped her hands on a clean cloth and came back to sit down at the table.

"In the morning, early in the morning, at precisely eight o'clock, two gendarmes will come to arrest us both," she explained.

"We are certain this is the safest way to get to Paris. No German will take a second glance at a Frenchman being arrested. It is something that they simply expect to see. The gendarmes will throw us in the back of a plain car. These men are Resistance members, two of our most trusted couriers in the underground." She spoke in a low, determined voice.

Two men dressed as false police officers. There was so much that could go wrong. "I don't want to put anyone else at risk." *Not again.*

But the dressmaker continued. "They may handle us roughly, so please do not be surprised if this happens. From here, they will take us to Versailles."

"What about the dressmaker's reputation among her neighbors? Surely, they can simply just arrest me and leave her alone."

The dressmaker shook her head. "I want you to be prepared, dressed, and ready for departure at eight o'clock in the morning."

She stood and crossed to the kitchen, retrieving a large cake.

"Made with our black-market shortening and flour." She sent the butcher a sidelong glance.

The butcher grinned in return.

"Coming to Paris with you is not negotiable, Antoine." She toyed with the moist, plain cake for a moment. Her brow creased. "The fact is I can't not come with you."

She glanced toward the butcher, and he nodded at her.

She lowered her voice. "The war has taught me to become a strong judge of character. So, I shall tell you: I am coming with you for a reason.

"My daughter is in Paris. And, you see, I must get her to safety. I believe she could be in danger."

Kit held his fork poised over the cake.

"She may not be safe in Paris when the Allies come through."

Kit frowned. "I am afraid I don't understand..."

"My daughter has been working in the Ritz Hotel since the German occupation. Serving the Germans. Looking after them."

The butcher cleared his throat. And with a slow, steady gesture, he reached out and placed his hand atop the dressmaker's.

"I miss her terribly," she managed. "At night, my dreams are haunted with worry that I will never see her again."

"That will not be the case." The butcher was firm. "She is a brave girl. I do not believe that she would be compromised in any way."

"I have been too scared to contact her," the dressmaker went on. Her voice was filled with urgency, and in this moment it felt like the calm woman Kit had come to know had gone. "She has been writing to me and I've had to destroy all her letters. If I was caught in my Resistance activities, then the Nazis would go for her. She is surrounded by them in that hotel. Such an easy target. Defenseless. It has been impossible for me to have any communication with her throughout the war and this, I know, would have broken her heart." She wiped her hands over her eyes now and pressed her forearms into the table. Her plate of cake sat untouched. "I need to go to her. As soon as the Allies reach Paris, I must reach her too. I must find my daughter, and, Antoine, taking you there is the perfect reason."

The dressmaker gathered herself. She sat up and took in a deep breath.

"We must prepare for the morning."

She pushed back her chair and began clearing the table.

Kit's eyes followed her across the room, but his heart was leaden. They had been warned in the UK that the remaining Nazis in France were being ruthless. How would they be behaving now that the occupation was under serious threat? And what of the French Gestapo and their crackdown on the Resistance?

The chance of the dressmaker, a leading underground figure, making it safely through the Nazi barricades to Paris with an Allied pilot in tow and a daughter in the Nazi stronghold that was the Ritz was going to be nigh impossible.

The following morning, Kit glanced around the little home that had been his sanctuary since he had come to France. The dressmaker stood by the front door, with no luggage, because if she were genuinely arrested, she would not be carrying a suitcase on her way to prison.

They stood in silence. When there was a rap at the door, his eyes jolted to the dressmaker's. In a split second, she reached out and grabbed his hand.

"Prepare yourself."

But every fear that Kit had experienced since landing on French soil came back to haunt him a thousand times again. If he were to be seen even in a gendarme's car, he would be exposed. He had no doubt that, were he caught, he would be shot on sight.

The dressmaker leaned forward and opened the door. She stepped aside while two large burly men in their sixties, dressed in faded uniforms of the gendarmerie of France, burst through the door and grabbed Kit, one holding his arms behind him, while they clipped on a pair of rusted handcuffs and jerked him forward by the scruff of his neck.

Kit's eyes darted toward the dressmaker, his protective instincts kicking in as the other gendarme roughly handled her. He grumbled away in some indecipherable French while grabbing her arms, handcuffing her, and pushing her out to the waiting car. Kit had to force himself not to reach to steady her as she was shoved into the car alongside him.

The car was black, just like the black uniforms of Hitler's SS officers. Kit felt as if he was about to be sick.

The car sputtered into action, and they began rolling down the cobbled street that Kit had first walked along when he was following the dressmaker to her little home. He gasped when he caught sight of a barricade at the end of the narrow street that intersected with the main road.

One of the men swore under his breath.

"Jean-Claude?" the dressmaker asked, her voice hitching.

The driver thumped his hand on the steering wheel. "I did not expect this."

In front of them, a line of black-clad Nazis had blocked off the street and there was no turning back. Turning back would be an admission, a disaster, a one-way ticket. Kit shuddered.

A pair of black boots appeared right outside Kit's window. It was the Gestapo.

CHAPTER NINETEEN

PARIS, SUMMER 1944

Louise

"I cannot tell you. It would put you at too much risk." Henri places his empty plate on the bedside table. He leans forward, resting his hands between his knees, and he looks at me. "Look what has happened to Blanche."

"If the Nazis knew what I had done already, I would have been arrested a thousand times. You can trust me. I know how to keep a secret."

But he shakes his head. "We all know how the Nazis extract information. I don't want you to have any information from me that could incriminate you."

I sigh and sit down on the end of his bed. "Sometimes, being a maid is difficult. No one notices you. No one cares. But at other times not being noticed is a huge advantage. I can help."

This has been my mantra throughout the war. Hide away. Do not be seen. I find it hard to imagine a time when I might be free of this. And I am starting to feel that I want to imagine this.

For the first time in an age. And I am certain that Henri has something to do with this.

"Talk to me," I say.

Henri rakes a hand through his hair. He has kept it clean, and he always smells of shampoo and soap. "I don't want you taking any more risks for me."

"There is someone here in the hotel who has extensive contacts in the underground network. He has been like a father to me. I would trust him with my life, and I know he will help you."

Henri sits up and leans a little closer to me. He reaches out and rests his hand on my arm. Our eyes meet and linger a moment.

"I hate this situation," he says. "If circumstances were different..."

"But they aren't, not for us."

Us. The word hangs in the air.

Henri tilts his head to one side and the expression on his face is so warm and so moving that I almost draw closer to him, but instead he reaches out and takes hold of both of my hands.

"My brother was the pilot in the aircraft crash. It is killing me not knowing whether he is safe, whether he is alive."

I take in a ragged breath. I know what it is like not knowing whether your loved ones are alive. "You must tell me his name."

"Kit Harrington." But he entreats me with his eyes. "Please, there is no need for you to risk anything."

"Harrington," I whisper. "It has a nice sound to it. I like your name."

"I'm glad to hear that."

I realize he is still holding my hand, and I hastily remove it and move across to my trolley, curling my fingers instead around the handle. But it feels cold after the warmth of Henri's hand.

"I will ask my contact to do what he can to search for your brother. Leave it with me, Henri Harrington."

He grins at me, a wide smile that breaks through the pale worry that is clearly haunting him every hour of the night and the day. "It's a good name for a bus driver, don't you think? Mr. Harrington taking you all the way to New York?"

I chuckle, and there is a tinge of sadness to my laughter. "Until next time, bus driver."

He tips an imaginary cap at me, and I rattle out with my trolley full of cleaning things and Henri's empty plate.

But once I'm in the silent corridors, my senses are on full alert. I catch a glimpse of a blond girl ducking into a stairwell on the floor right below the attics. There is the slam of a door. Sasha.

I abandon my trolley and run. I trot down the hallway, the soles of my shoes silent on the plush carpet that has borne the tread of so many treacherous feet. When I get to the door that leads to the staff staircase, I throw it open. I trip down the stairs at a steady clip. I know this hotel. I understand the rhythm of the staircase and I am faster than Sasha. My hand glides down the banister like a gull on the wing.

"Stop."

She is almost at the bottom of the staircase, but she does stop. And slowly, she turns to face me.

In one second, I am down there next to her. I'm not proud of this, but I grab her collar and push her against the wall. "Why are you following me?" I grind the words out. "What are you doing? Give me an honest answer. You are in my room, in my shadow; you owe me an explanation. Although your sort seem to think you can step in and take what you want."

"I am not going to betray you." Sasha's sapphire-blue eyes burn into mine, and her chest is heaving underneath one of her fashionable dresses.

"I am not important." I laugh as I state the obvious. "So why are you following me, instead of working for your master?"

"Let go of me," she murmurs. She holds strong and lifts her chin. "I promise you this, Louise. I will never betray you."

I release my grip, and she presses her hands to my shoulders and looks into my eyes.

"Listen. I cannot tell you all that I would like to tell you. Yet. But all I can ask you to do is trust me. Please. I am not here to hurt you."

"Then why follow me? Why not betray me?" My anger makes me brazen. My voice echoes in the stairwell. And my hands shake. We stare at each other for a moment in silence, locked in an impossible battle that neither of us can win.

There is a silence, and it seems endlessly drawn out.

"The answer is in the language you speak."

And only then do I realize my terrible mistake.

We are speaking in German. I am speaking German. Something I must never do.

I shouted at her in her own tongue.

We stand there, and the only sound is the intake of our breath.

She knows I am half German. Therefore, she knows who I am. She knows that the reason I speak her language so well is because my father spoke it at home to me when I was young. She knows that one reason I have hidden away here in this hotel throughout the war is because I am too ashamed to step outside into the streets of Paris, when it is my father's countrymen who have occupied the country of my birth. My mother's country. I have no idea where I fit in. Sasha knows this because she is a Nazi. Because they know everything and there is no privacy for anyone living under their regime.

But I have kept this secret from Frank, from Arletty, from every single darned person I have met since moving to Paris. It was when Hitler came to power in Germany that my father started drinking, and that was when his soul turned hopelessly dark.

Sasha presses her hand to my arm for one moment, and then turns around and slips away.

If I'm being protected by the Germans, then what happens when the Allies come?

I slip into bed at the end of my long shift and turn my face toward the wall. Sasha's bed is empty. While this should comfort me, it unnerves me. Sasha's words that she will not betray me only serve to unsettle me, because they see me as one of them.

I made it through the rest of my shift automatically, and then I went and asked Frank to investigate the whereabouts of a pilot named Kit Harrington. He told me he would do what he could, but he wasn't sure whether he would be able to get a clear line of communication through the Resistance networks because they were taking to the streets, building barricades, and preparing to take up arms. They were preparing to fight. Frank warned me that if Henri's brother was an Allied pilot, he had most likely been murdered by the Nazis.

I stare at the blank wall by my bed. The lines have been so clear the past four years. The Germans were in control. The French had no choices, and now the sands are shifting and none of us know exactly what the next tide will bring in. The French government betrayed us. The French Gestapo are killing their own citizens. Who will look after the citizens of this country now?

And what does this change mean when it comes to Sasha, and what she clearly knows about me?

Most of the German residents in the Ritz have left Paris. Göring has left. Hans has left, a broken man. I watched through one of the windows while he climbed into a taxi and was escorted to the railway station back to Berlin. I went to check on Arletty late this afternoon. But she was staring out the window, dressed in black.

The door opens softly and Sasha steps inside. I lean up on my elbow and our eyes lock.

"I know that you are working with Claude Auzello and the barman Frank Meier, translating codes. I know that you are hiding a downed Allied pilot in the closed-off wing of servants' quarters in the hotel."

I am shaking. Every inch of my body quakes, and my hands flutter about uselessly.

She removes the light trench coat she is wearing, sits down on her bed, and takes off her shoes.

My heart races and bile courses up through my throat, but I say nothing. It is what Frank has taught me to do. His words burn into my mind. *Do not trust anyone. Not a soul.*

Sasha reaches out and lays her palm on my hand. "You can trust me," she says. "I will not tell a soul. Never. You have my word."

CHAPTER TWENTY

PARIS, PRESENT DAY

Nicole

I can see Mariah's formidable figure disappearing through Place Vendôme. She is still in a mood because Arielle told us that Louise was a maid. I need to break through that because I need to try to get Mariah on my side.

I chase her in the high-heeled pumps that I put on for our visit to the Ritz. I keep my focus trained on my aunt's silk dress, which shimmers in the sunlight streaking through the gray clouds overhead. I wave my umbrella in the air like Mary Poppins, and I call to her, but she marches full steam ahead. What I don't want to do is lose her to the Metro. Once she is in that labyrinth, I will have no way of finding her again.

"Mariah!" I yell at the top of my voice, not caring that the sophisticated pedestrians in this beautiful part of Paris are turning to stare at me, a mad Englishwoman in the heart of the fashion district.

She stops, and I heave a sigh of relief, pressing my hands to my knees and bending down to catch my breath. My aunt turns and places her hands on her hips. In full view of everyone, she shrugs and throws her hands in the air. I rise, and soon we are standing face-to-face.

"Mariah," I whisper, trying to get my breath back. I place my hand over my belly. "Sorry, little one," I add.

"What are you doing now?" she demands. She sends a simpering smile toward a middle-aged couple who are staring at us openly and clearly looking down their noses at me with my red face and my umbrella.

But I always carry an umbrella. I don't like the rain.

"My mother was not honest with us and she did not tell us the truth. She was a maid who clearly collaborated horizontally with some Nazi? The entire situation is beyond me, Nicole. There is nothing more to say. The matter is over. It was over long ago."

The couple drift away, and I am left facing my aunt. "Don't you care?"

The words ring between us and a flock of pigeons take flight from the cobblestones.

Mariah lets out a rough laugh. "I don't want to know any more."

But I take a step closer to her. "She loved you, and we owe it to her to prove that the story that photograph is telling us is wrong. I think Arielle's story is wrong."

Mariah glares at me. "I fail to see anything except the fact that I want to go home and leave the past behind. It was a mistake to delve into my mother's history. I do not know why I bothered. She showed no interest in sharing her story with me."

"But Arielle is hiding something. The last time I met with her she was pale with shock at the sight of the photograph. This time, she wrapped the story up neatly with a bow. She wanted to get rid of us and I want to know why."

Mariah starts walking again. "Put it to rest and go home. Don't you have a little husband waiting for you in *Wimbledon* or somewhere?"

I beat down my annoyance at the way Mariah is belittling me. "You have no interest in who your mother really was?"

She stops again at the edge of the square. The boulevard spreads in front of us. It is a one-way street.

I reach out and grasp my aunt's arm, taking advantage of her momentary hesitation. "I know that your relationship with Granny Louise was difficult. But if you don't come to some form of understanding about her, and about who she truly was, then you are never going to find peace."

"The only peace I want is to be free of your incessant chatter." She glares at me.

I am determined not to give this up. For Granny. For me. For my child. "You have a history in this country, and more importantly, you have a family. You had a mother who loved you. You deserve to know who she really was. You deserve to know who you are."

Mariah's jaw is set, her lips run in a straight line, and her arms remain folded across her body. "What are you going to do, Nicole?"

"Go back to Arielle. Find out the truth. But we must do so together." Perhaps it is the fact that I am expecting a baby, but I would like to have women relatives in my life.

Finally, finally, she takes in an audible breath and her arms fall to hang at her sides.

I take her arm. "Come on, let's work out how to approach her."

And I walk with her out of the square where my grandmother was paraded as a woman of shame over seventy-five years ago.

CHAPTER TWENTY-ONE

PARIS, SUMMER 1944

Louise

It is Bastille Day, and one hundred thousand Parisians have turned out to face down the panzer tanks of the military government of France. Outside, they have closed off the streets and here in the hotel we can hear gunshots, while wisps of smoke from the bonfires rise into the hot summer air.

In the room I am cleaning, the acrid, sickly smell of smoke wafts in through the open window from Place Vendôme. I am scrubbing the bathroom of one of the rooms that was inhabited by a high-ranking Nazi officer. As I place a wrapped bar of beautifully scented soap on the edge of the enormous porcelain bath, I wonder who will next stay in this room.

The newspapers are saying that the liberation of Paris is near. The British and Canadian armies have smashed the Germans in Falaise and Caen, and it is reported that the mighty American forces will sweep on toward Versailles. Frank says that under the noses of the Gestapo, the underground is properly starting to arm, and that fifty thousand French Resistance fighters are also ready for the battle for Paris.

The Resistance movement is starting to come out into the open, after four years of existing on faith, whispers in cafés, nods at the entrance to the Metro, or meetings in shuttered houses.

For four years, Parisians have been outlaws. Now, the Nazis are the outlaws of France.

I hear the rattle of gunfire. Resistance fighters are waiting with guns in the windows of the buildings on the grand boulevards. They have sandbagged suburban streets, and now many of them openly wear the white Resistance armbands that would have led to instant death before the underground took to the streets in such numbers.

I turn to clean the vanity, and as I look at my harried reflection in the mirror, the vase of flowers on the basin shakes. The rattle of machine-gun fire is accompanied by the sound of the deep throttle of tanks. I hear the scream and thud of a bomb.

Yesterday, I smuggled a newspaper up to Henri, and he devoured it in what he calls his schoolboy French. Our conversations have turned to the Allied advances and to the books I loaned him. Sometimes he has one of them open on a page because he has become stuck as to the meaning of one of the words. I translate them for him quickly and efficiently, and he seems delighted by this. Genuinely so.

We carry on with our jokes about driving buses but nothing more serious. Planning for the future seems impossible...

Last night, the announcer on Frank's wireless talked of members of the Red Cross coming out waving flags between the constant scuffles in Paris's streets. Of how they would carry out stretchers and collect those Resistance men who had been wounded. There is no organization, no government. The people of Paris have taken things into their own hands, but there is no word of Blanche. Nor has Frank been able to secure any information about Henri's brother, Kit.

There is an explosion nearby, and the entire hotel shakes. I press my hands against the vanity, then rush to the window to look out at the square below. A vehicle—a German vehicle—is exploding and flames burst from it. I see the figures of four charred bodies and a black cap strewn in the middle of the square.

My hands shake, the building shakes, and the battle for Paris thunders, unheeding of the fact another four men have just died too young.

There is more gunfire, and another vehicle sweeps into the square as the squalling fire flares from the burning vehicle like the flames from a dragon's mouth. But I refuse to leave the vacated suite unless it is perfect. Working is one thing I can do no matter what. I know my mother feels the same way when it comes to her dressmaking. She used to tell me that it was important to have something that no one could ever take away. And yet, I do not know if she is alive or dead. I have heard nothing. Still, I write.

I stay in the beautiful suite for as long as I can. When there is absolutely nothing left to do, I finally slip out of the room into the corridor of the Place Vendôme side of the hotel. I almost fall over backward when I walk straight into Sasha and her boss, Carl-Heinrich von Stülpnagel. Given that most of the Germans have left, it seems surprising they remain. And yet, their presence is a reminder that the war is not over yet.

He walks straight past me, dodging my trolley, and pounds on down the corridor. But Sasha grabs my arm and I freeze.

Von Stülpnagel disappears behind another closed door, and Sasha lowers her voice. "Meet me in ten minutes back here," she says. "Please. We are in the midst of the battle for Paris. I need to tell you the truth."

CHAPTER TWENTY-TWO

PARIS, PRESENT DAY

Nicole

Pandora lets me into her apartment. Once again, she looks effortlessly put together. Her long blond hair glides down her back, and she is wearing a soft black cashmere sweater with a pair of matching silky capri pants. Diamonds sparkle at her ears. Patterns and fabrics are sprawled all over the dining room table, and there are racks of little clothes lined up underneath the window. She has invited me for dinner. After I managed to convince Mariah not to accept Arielle's story about my grandmother. Just...

"I'm in the middle of designing a new collection. Do excuse the mess."

"When did you start designing and sewing?"

"You know, I always thought that I was only good at one thing. That I was defined by this." She sweeps her hands down her long, lean body. "But when I was pregnant, I fell in love with children's clothes, and I saw that it might be somewhere I could contribute. Designing is something in which I can lose myself."

"That's fantastic," I say, meaning it.

In the kitchen, we are met by the smells of beautiful cooking. Pandora's husband, Thierry, is squatting down by the open oven, shaking out a roasting pan of perfectly browned gnocchi, and my taste buds dance at the thought of the pillowy, chewy interior. There are also roasted peppers with minced garlic, and fresh basil is sitting on the marble bench.

"Nicole!" Thierry comes forward and kisses me on both cheeks, just as Pandora did. His brown eyes are warm, and his dark hair is slightly tousled.

I'm a little starstruck; he is a famous fashion photographer who shoots for the top magazines, and we have not yet met as he came on the scene after Granny died.

"Let me get you a drink," he says.

"Just water or something soft."

He doesn't miss a beat and goes straight to the fridge. "Lemonade, orange juice?"

"Orange juice would be great."

Pandora looks down at my belly. "When were you going to tell me the news?"

"I was going to tell you this evening."

"Mia will have a cousin!"

"I would love them to be able to get to know one another."

We hover in the kitchen, leaning against the benches and chatting about Thierry's work, my work, Andrew and me, and our expected baby.

"You seem happy, Nicole," Pandora says suddenly when Thierry sends us to the kitchen table to sit down while he arranges the gnocchi on huge plates.

"I am."

"I'm pleased to hear that," she says, squeezing my hand.

It's not until we are sitting at the table, the gorgeous food in front of us, that I raise the topic of our grandmother and her French past.

"It's going to be incredibly difficult to find out where she was born," Thierry says. "But not impossible. She didn't tell you anything at all?"

I smile at Thierry, glad to have someone who is not dismissing me, who seems to want to encourage me.

"She'd change the subject if you asked anything about herself."

"Mum told me that you think the archivist at the Ritz knows more than she is letting on." Pandora hands me a bowl of crisp salad leaves tossed in French dressing.

"I'm sure of it," I say. I chew on my lip for a moment, but then I decide the question must be asked. "Why do you think Aunt Mariah has the feelings that she has toward Granny?"

The glamorous couple are quiet, but I let the silence linger as I help myself to salad and a baguette.

Eventually, Pandora speaks. "I don't think she felt accepted. I think she always felt there was some distance that was not there between your mother and Grandmother."

I wince at the way she calls Granny Louise Grandmother.

I sigh. "I understand that. It can happen. But was there anything specific that really pulled them apart?"

"Grandmother hadn't kept anything from her past."

I pause from eating the delicious food and glance at Pandora, confused.

Pandora glances at Thierry and then lowers her voice. "My understanding is that the real fallout happened when my mother became a young woman and was interested in who she was, and in her family. She started asking questions of Grandmother about her younger years, and one day, my mother came home from university to find Grandmother had thrown out everything that pertained to her life before she met Grandfather."

But she missed one book. A book of fairy tales...why? I stay quiet, but an unsettled feeling begins to lodge in the depths of my stomach.

"The way Mum tells it is that Grandmother had cleared out the entire attic of the house in Sussex. There was a bonfire and Mum never knew what had been destroyed, just that there was nothing left."

"I see." My voice is small. "So, this was Granny's reaction to Mariah asking about her past?"

Pandora nods, and Thierry reaches out and takes her hand, stroking it gently.

I gesture at my food. "This is a beautiful dinner," I say. "The gnocchi is perfect."

"I'm so glad you like it," Thierry says, and he sends me a warm smile.

Like me, with my darling Andrew, Pandora has married happily.

I choose my words carefully. "Now that I think about it, my mother was a little more off in her own world. She loved literature and she adored singing. I wonder if she was simply escaping. She had such a different personality to Aunt Mariah. I don't think my mum was really interested in the realities of the past."

"I think as sisters they grew apart," Pandora says.

We eat quietly for a while, and chat about Paris and Thierry's decision to branch out from fashion photography into interiors. He tells me that he designed the interiors in this house.

It's not until I'm at the door about to leave that Pandora brings up Granny again.

"I think we need to clear this up," she says to me quietly. "But I think that my mum's refusal to accept the news that Grandmother may have been a maid is a cover-up for her hurt at the fact that Grandmother never told her or trusted her with the information of who she truly was."

The baby wakes, and for the first time since I arrived here at eight o'clock for dinner, the sounds of the next generation roar through the air. I can't help but think that this is Mia Louise telling us she is here. She has a voice. She needs to be heard.

I shake my head. "Sorry," I murmur. I think what I have realized is that we all make up our own interpretations of things. We all make up our own stories about our lives, and sometimes it is difficult to know where the truth lies and what is real.

Granny decided to hide her story. She went so far as to burn it to the ground. It must be incredibly difficult for Mariah to understand why Granny shut her out.

"Don't be sorry," Pandora says.

She looks back into the apartment, where Thierry is standing in the hallway, cradling baby Mia in his arms. He is murmuring to her softly.

"But I think," Pandora continues, "it's time to put out the flames that have split our family."

"I hadn't thought of it like that," I whisper back. "But in my own way, it's what I want too."

Pandora hugs me, and I hug my cousin back.

I clutch my umbrella and my bag, and I go out into the darkness of the Paris night.

CHAPTER TWENTY-THREE

PARIS, SUMMER 1944

Louise

I am hovering outside von Stülpnagel's suite. My instinct is to run to Frank, but Sasha has stuck to her word not to expose me, Frank, or Claude. She must have had countless opportunities to report us, and yet we are still safe, even though I feel as though I am living under the blade of the guillotine.

"Louise." Sasha is behind me, and I whirl around to face her.

My heart is beating wildly. I search her face, then glance toward the end of the corridor. In case I need to escape.

"Please. Come in with me, and we shall talk." She takes the key and leads me inside.

"You are allowed to be here?" I glance around the magnificent hotel suite.

She looks down at the thickly carpeted floor. "There is a reason I am not going to turn you in. And it is time for me to tell you what that is."

She moves across to the window. A siren wails, and I don't know whether it is the Red Cross or the Nazis, come to clean up their own blood.

"I was sent here to find you by someone who holds you very dear."

I am silent. The Nazis play all sorts of tricks to get you to speak. This seems like one of the lowest to me.

Sasha turns around to face me. I can see genuine feeling there and I am taken aback. "He told me I would need to bring something to prove myself."

And then, to my astonishment, Sasha holds out a small, smooth stone. It is in the shape of a heart. I would know it anywhere.

My hand flies to my mouth. I gasp. I am back at the beach, eight years old. My father and I are bent over, buckets in our hands, while we scour the tidal sands for precious pearly shells and the very smoothest stones. Our soft murmurs are the only sound in the clear Atlantic air. I can smell the salt of the sea, feel the sand between my toes, and I remember my fingers rubbing over the stone in Sasha's hand.

It is in the shape of a heart, and I show my father what a beautiful treasure I have found.

His face lights up and his handsome features crinkle into a warm smile. He presses the little heart-shaped stone into the palm of my hand, and he tells me that every time I hold it, I must remember how much he will always love me. I throw my arms around him, squeezing my eyes shut and squeezing his shoulders hard. I never want this feeling to end.

I have not felt it since he left.

Things became bad as the situation in Germany deteriorated further under the Nazis. Every night became a terrifying night. He would go drinking at the local hotel, then come in drunk, yelling at my mother and me, shouting at us as we tried to sleep, words we did not understand, and swearing foully as he raged around the house.

Lamps fell to the ground, chairs clattered across the floor, glass broke, and wine bottles pooled and scattered across the kitchen floor. We knew he would not remember any of it in the morning, and we knew that before I went to school, there would be a dreadful mess to clean up.

I cannot breathe, my heart is constricted, and the words I want to utter will simply not come out. My mother never spoke of these occasions. In the mornings, she would quietly sweep up the mess, the broken glass, and the sticky remains of the alcohol on the floor. In silence, she would right the fallen chairs.

"Where did you get this?"

Sasha moves closer, and in the frighteningly exact same way that my father did with me, she presses the little stone into the palm of my hand and closes my fingers over it. "He gave it to me, to return to you, and he told me that the message I was to give you was the same one he gave you on the beach. He says it is eternal; he says his love for you will never die. He says that it crosses boundaries, languages, and barriers. He says you must always remember that."

I am unable to look at her. I am tongue-tied, and I cannot find the words that need to come out from my lips. I thought I knew my father. I had given up on him.

"Louise." Her eyes search my face, and I swallow, but all I can taste is the thick sea air and the saltiness of the ocean.

Don't make me change the story I had accepted about him.

It is as if I am listening inside a shell. I am transported. I have gone back.

But the dark memories I have of him ever since that day only threaten to swell, like equally strong waves lapping against the beach, as the deep yearnings of hope that he loved me and loved my mother try to break free from the place where I have locked them away.

"Your father gave it to me himself."

I wheel around and lean on the pristine, golden-covered bed.

"No." This means he must be a high-ranking Nazi if he

was working with or knew von Stülpnagel! I don't want to believe it. Papa hated Hitler. Hated what he was doing to Germany, especially after the devastation of the Great War. Is my own father one of Hitler's henchmen?

"I promised him I would pass it on to you. I must do that now in case it is not safe for me to remain in France. It may not be, Louise. Safe for me. I don't know what I'm going to do."

My lips tighten and I loosen my grip on the stone, letting it sit on the smooth counterpane. It might be smoothed into the shape of a love heart. But some love is treacherous. Some you cannot trust. And at the end of the day, my father left. So why should I believe the girl standing opposite me now? My breathing is coming in fast gasps.

Down in the square, there are sounds of men shouting where the burned vehicle is being cleaned up. Sasha is right. She certainly may not be safe. As one of the last remaining Nazis in Paris, I doubt the Allies will show any mercy, young girl or not. There are stories of the French facing down those who have collaborated with the Nazis. The Allies are moving through the towns of northern France, and I have seen pictures in the papers of women being hauled up onto the back of trucks and paraded through the liberated towns while people jeer at them.

I curl my hand around the little stone, closing my eyes for a second and reveling in the familiar feel of it.

Sasha speaks. "Your father sent me to work with von Stülpnagel."

I close my eyes. "In that case, I do not wish to know anything more."

"Please," she whispers, "do not judge him for that."

"Do not judge him?" I echo. I turn to face her. "You are telling me he is a Nazi. And you are telling me not to judge?" I place the little stone down on the bedside table. My lip is curled in disdain. "Why is he not here in France? His wife and daughter, we mean nothing to him?"

Sasha moves toward me. "Louise. You must listen to me. He knows that he was not behaving well. He knows that he was not safe. And that is why he had to leave you."

But my head is shaking, my hands are shaking, and my legs want to collapse and buckle to the ground. "I don't believe you. You have just told me that he is a Nazi." I place my hand on my heart.

"I am telling you he is German."

"I knew that!" My cheeks burn, and tears want to explode from me now. "How do you think I have felt, having to keep my nationality a secret for the past four years!"

"He had to go back home and work out what was wrong. Why he was behaving the way he was. Why it was only drink that could bathe his wounds, and why he needed to forget. It wasn't your fault. It was not your mother's fault." Her eyes move out toward the window again. "His demons were due to the war. His war. The previous war."

Our eyes lock. "He never spoke of that," I whisper. And yet the Great War had hovered over France like a damaged bird when I was at school. I still remember sitting in shock when our teacher told us that more than sixteen million people died; an entire generation of young men were lost.

I remember learning about the unspeakable horrors of life at the front in the trenches in my own country, in disbelief.

We are quiet and the past seems to hang between us.

"This is our war," she says. "I only hope it will not break us as the last one broke your father."

I am silent. My mother used to say there was an explanation for everything. This war has come to test that belief for me, but I am certain of one thing. What Sasha is saying about my father's behavior after Hitler came to power in Germany makes sense. He must have been terrified about the prospect of another war.

"He fought in a place called Passchendaele," Sasha confirms.

I nod silently. I have heard that the battle there was horrific. A bloodbath. I had no idea my father was there.

"The men he killed were Frenchmen. And then having to live among them with your mother, as if he were their brother. As if he deserved a place among them as their kin." Sasha shakes her head.

I swallow.

Sasha continues. "He never felt he was worthy of you. Nor your French mother. He simply could not cope."

My heart aches for him, but still there is pain there, pain over what he did, and pain over who he is.

Sasha lowers her voice to barely a whisper. "I am your cousin. I am working for your father. For you. Not for anyone else. I came here to protect you."

"No." I take a step back and sit down with a thump on the golden bed. The landing is soft, but the beating in my chest is rhythmic and hard. "That is impossible," I say.

But Sasha's voice rolls on. "I have told the authorities repeatedly that there is nothing to worry about when it comes to you, that I am sharing a room with you, and that you go about your day as any normal maid would."

I am shaking my head. My arms are wrapped tightly around my frame. I want to sink into the bed, bury my head in the pillow, and make this all go away. I would do so if the bed was not being slept in by a Nazi.

I come to as if out of a dream. I stand up and stare unseeing at the bed.

"Uncle Joachim could not give me a letter. It was too dangerous. So, instead, he asked me to sing you a song."

She begins singing the words to "Die Gedanken Sind Frei," the song my father used to sing to me when I was a little girl. Her voice is soft. Softer than Papa's. His voice was rich and mellow, and it used to resonate throughout the room when he sang me to sleep at night. And I can't help it. Sasha's voice transports me, and I am back home at the farm, and he is sitting on the edge of my bed.

All thoughts are free,
Who can ever guess them;
They fleetingly pass
Like the night's shadows.
No man can know them
No hunter can shoot them;
It will always be:
All thoughts are free.

I think what I will
And what brings me joy,
But all in privacy
And how it behooves me.
My wishes and yearning
Are no man's condemning.
It will always be:
All thoughts are free.

And if they lock me up
In a dark dungeon,
Those are purely
Efforts in vain;
For my own thoughts
Tear down the barriers
And walls that be:
All thoughts are free.

That's why I forever
Cast off all worries
And nevermore will

Let whims plague me.
Then in his own heart one
Has laughter and much fun
And thereby see:
All thoughts are free.

She takes in a shuddering breath.

"Now you must listen to me. Please. If anything happens to me, go to Heidelberg and find him. For that is where he is living now." Sasha lowers her voice. "Your father is involved in the German Resistance."

I am quiet. These revelations have shocked me, but the realization that my father is not a Nazi but a Resistance fighter like me takes me aback.

"It seems that rebellion against the Nazis runs in the family," she says.

More memories flood back; the stories my father used to tell me of the fairy-tale city where he grew up, with its old town, overlooked by two leafy hills with a magical castle high above the town walls, and cobbled streets that lined the Neckar River, with baroque buildings that spoke of a Germany of long ago.

When Sasha told me she had come from there, I was so tainted with Heidelberg's recent strong association with the Nazi Party that I forgot about how magical the city is.

"Your father was working with Hermann Ludwig Maas, the Protestant pastor in Heidelberg who was helping the Jewish community escape persecution from the Nazis," Sasha explains.

I sit down on the bed. This is all too much to take in. I have held on to negative thoughts and expectations of my father for so long, but now that I am being told the opposite, it is as if a great curtain has been swept aside on a closed stage, and, finally, I can see the play for what it truly is.

"Hermann Maas was a friend to the Heidelberg Jewish community, no matter who they were, from apprentices to professors.

Many of them were rounded up and sent to a concentration camp in France. But Hermann was able to get some of them released. Your father, who is an excellent translator..."

My hand covers my mouth. *He is a translator?*

"He provided them with immigration papers to the United Kingdom and raised money to help them through his friends in the parish community. Together, your father and Hermann found foster homes for some of the young Jewish people in England. They found jobs there for adults and produced legal visas and work permits for them. They arranged transportation for these refugees. They visited and cared for the elderly Jewish community who remained in Heidelberg."

I look down at the stone in my other hand.

"Hermann Ludwig Maas has been described as the de facto rabbi of Heidelberg." Sasha smiles at me. "Your father worked alongside him in great faith."

"You are talking as if this happened in the past," I whisper. "Where is the pastor now?"

Sasha shakes her head. "Helping Jews is a crime in Germany. Hermann was under constant scrutiny by the Gestapo, but he had strong support within the community of the Holy Spirit Church. They stood beside him, many of them prominent Nazis themselves. On top of that, Ludwig was recognized internationally and so the Gestapo were cautious about mistreating him, a man who was widely known in England as well as Germany. However, just last year, the police finally arrested him. He was sent to hard labor in France and is in a camp here."

"I am sorry," I say.

"Your father is carrying on the pastor's work."

"Then he is in great danger."

Sasha nods. "He seems undaunted by the risk he is taking, although, sadly, there are not many Jewish people left in Heidelberg. So, your father—my uncle—who was living with us, taught me to help those who are less fortunate than I am. Louise, your father is truly a good man. He hasn't drunk alcohol for over five years."

I sit quietly for a moment. My eyes sweep the floor that I have swept for the past few years. Endless repetition is what has gotten me through. Skirting over the surfaces of things, making them clean. This is what I could control. But I know I have never gotten to the heart of what has left me broken. I realize now I have never even tried to understand. If understanding is what I need to do now to find peace, then I will do that, because I think that understanding is what is required to forgive.

In a way that I have not done since I was a little girl, I reach out with unbridled spontaneity, and I hug the girl standing opposite me. And I hold her close.

CHAPTER TWENTY-FOUR

Kit

The Nazi guards waved the car through the barricade as if they were any ordinary traffic police directing the car down any ordinary street. Next to Kit, the dressmaker slumped back in her seat with relief. He glanced over, frowning at the sight of sweat beading on her forehead, while the hand she rested on the hot vinyl seat between them was shaking visibly.

In the front seat, the two men dressed as gendarmes carried out a quiet conversation in rapid-fire French. The dressmaker was quiet and pensive, and Kit took the opportunity to look out the window at the passing countryside. The vista that lined the straight road was lush with rich green trees. Summer was at its full height in France, and he allowed himself a moment to tip his head back, close his eyes, and let the sunlight fall on his cheeks.

The two men began singing, their voices ringing through the air with a sense of hope that seemed to be intertwined between the future and, somehow, the past. They were songs that spoke of generations, and of traditions that came with those generations being able to be together, which only served to heighten in Kit the feeling that this was not home. These years of impossible loss and heartbreak over Europe and throughout the world had taught him one thing: To appreciate simplicity and stability. And family. Kit only hoped that the dressmaker would find her daughter and that he would see Charlie again.

When the car slowed, and the gendarme in the driver's seat swore softly, Kit sat forward, suddenly on alert.

"You are going to have to get out of the car and run for it," the gendarme in the passenger seat said. He turned and patted the dressmaker on the knee. She had been sleeping.

Kit's heart began to beat wildly in his chest.

The driver pulled into a bank of trees. "There is another barricade ahead," he said. "We got lucky once today, but these Nazis manning the countryside are ruthless. We will all be taken."

Kit risked a glance ahead, his eyes landing on a formidable black line of Nazis standing across the country road. Cars were lined up, and every driver was being questioned. Some cars had already been taken off to the side, their occupants marched away into a makeshift tent.

Kit shuddered. Heaven help them now. Evading the Nazis on his own, with his training, was one thing, but trying to keep both himself and the dressmaker safe in the forests was something he had never been prepared for.

"Quickly," he whispered to the dressmaker. Fortunately, the gendarmes had removed their handcuffs.

The dressmaker took in the line of Nazis and slid across the seat, following Kit out the door. As quietly as he could, Kit closed the car door behind them. He bent down double, told the dressmaker to follow him, and, hauling his knapsack onto his back, he ran into the forest that lined the road.

• • •

Later, Kit leaned his head back against a tree, the dressmaker next to him. The forest was silent apart from the calls of birds and the rustle of leaves. He adjusted his position on the hard earth upon which they had come to rest. France needed rain. The clouds needed to burst open, and so did this war.

At the sound of footsteps, Kit sat up on high alert. He rested a hand on the dressmaker's shoulder, cautioning her. But he need not have warned her. She was sitting silently and not moving an inch.

Kit eased himself up and quietly reached out his hand for the dressmaker. He helped her up and they started moving, their bodies half bent, through the undergrowth.

But with every step they took, the sound of footsteps only became louder. They were being followed by more than one pursuer. Their chances of evading capture were slim, almost nonexistent.

When the dressmaker stopped, doubled over, and wrapped her arms around her waist, her face was puce. "Go on without me," she whispered, her voice raspy. "I am not trained for this."

Kit glanced around. There was nowhere to hide.

When three men burst through the trees and came upon them, Kit automatically stood in front of the dressmaker. He held up his hands and told them to stay back. The tallest of the men, and the oldest by far, came with a face streaked with dirt, his dark hair shoulder-length. His white shirt hung loosely from his broad-shouldered frame. He had the bearing of the sort of good-looking rogue that any woman might fall in love with, and in the split second that Kit appraised him, he knew one thing for certain: The man standing opposite him was French. He was flanked by two boys; they looked like twins and were probably only around sixteen years old.

"Maquisards," the dressmaker whispered.

Kit only hoped so. If they were in luck, the men standing opposite them were three of the renegades living in the forest.

The leader glanced around and indicated that they follow him. "You can come with us."

Kit glanced at the dressmaker.

"You are the American pilot," the leader said. "I am aware that you were trying to make your way to Paris today. The butcher told me. I go into the local village regularly, and I have seen posters of you. I recognized your face. Come with us. We will take you to our camp."

He handed Kit and the dressmaker canteens of water.

It was all Kit could do to nod.

They walked, a silent party, their boots crunching on the forest floor the only sound apart from the singing of the birds in the dying day.

Later, Kit sat in the total darkness outside the makeshift hut that the Maquis had built in a clearing in the forest. The leader, who called himself Michel, had told them their food and ammunition were delivered at great risk by the butcher.

The two young men were local twins who had been called up to go to Germany and work in the factories. The Nazis were getting desperate, and the men being called out were getting younger and younger. These boys' faces still held the early flush of youth. They introduced themselves as Jacques and Guillaume and insisted on giving up their stretchers for Kit and the dressmaker.

"We need to take down the Nazi barricade that is blocking the road to Paris." Michel lowered his voice and glanced at Kit.

"You have military training. You can teach us how to use the weapons that we have stored here. We have done some basic things, you know, like tripping up motorcycles and messengers. But the fact is, the boys do not know how to use a gun. They have no military training. I am a pacifist. But I see my feelings are useless in the face of this war. We need to afford the Allies a safe passage through to Paris. If you can help us devise a plan to take down the Nazi barricade, at least we will feel we have done something worthwhile." He eyed Kit. "All of us."

Kit grimaced. He sensed that handing these three weapons would be far more risk than it was worth. And what of the dressmaker's safety in the struggle that would ensue if they blew up the barricade?

But as if she were reading his thoughts, the dressmaker turned to him, her expression serious, and she nodded.

She was giving him the go-ahead.

The following morning, Kit stood in the clearing opposite the makeshift target he had set up for the men. They had spent the morning cleaning out the barrels of their rifles, while Kit had given his three students basic instructions on the firing of the guns. Sending these two young boys out to battle against a team of sophisticated Nazis with ammunition, patrol cars, and a swath of motorbikes, and with the potential to call for armored vehicles, would be like sending a bunch of children out to battle a siege.

But the boys were determined. Their leader was determined. And the dressmaker herself was standing next to him, holding a gun.

Kit frowned as he watched Jacques pointing a loaded gun at the flap of material he had set up with a target painted in the middle of it. Already, Michel had shot through it with his silenced rifle, and it sported a gaping hole.

He spoke softly to the young boys, whispering instructions. And after a few practice rounds, they were proving to be good shots.

At lunchtime, Michel made a soup out of wild rabbit and vegetables.

When Michel and the boys stretched out on the ground

for their afternoon rest, Kit started at the sound of someone approaching. He sensed Michel stirring next to him, and, slowly, Kit reached for his gun.

The undergrowth parted, and a woman stepped toward them. She was dressed in civilian clothes, and with her was their old friend the butcher.

The dressmaker stood up from where she had been sitting on a log.

"Bonjour," she whispered. She walked forward, and the butcher pulled her into his arms.

"I am glad you are safe," he said. "I had a message that your drivers had to abandon their mission. We will get you out of here, and I have brought someone to help."

The butcher turned to the woman standing beside him. She was of diminutive stature, but she stood with her hands on her hips and there was such an air of authority to her that Kit stood back a little.

"This is Pauline. She is not military, and this is her code name. She is running all the Maquisard groups in this part of France and has been sent here by British intelligence."

The butcher moved over to stand near Jacques and Guillaume. "Michel sent a message last night that you plan to blow up the barricade. Antoine will train you all in the use of grenades and hand weapons. But Pauline will teach you unarmed combat. She has undergone nine months of extensive military and espionage training in Britain, and she has been working here in France for two years."

"It is not how hard you strike someone," Pauline said. She stood, her dark hair tied back in a French roll and her brown eyes serious. "You must know where to strike them. That is what counts." Pauline turned to the dressmaker. "We value you. You must not show your face in the skirmish, so I think the best plan is for you to hide here. I understand you want to go to Paris?"

The dressmaker nodded.

"Very well. We shall accommodate that. You have been an indefatigable member of the underground. However, you place yourself at great risk being here in the forest. If the mission is not successful, then they will come and they will hunt you out. You are placing much faith in these Maquisards, and in this air force man."

"Yes," the dressmaker said simply.

Kit raised a brow and folded his arms.

"Very well, you can come with me. Continue training your comrades, Flight Lieutenant."

Kit watched the dressmaker disappear with Pauline, his heart in his throat.

CHAPTER TWENTY-FIVE

PARIS, SUMMER 1944

Louise

I am fast asleep when Sasha wakes me in the middle of the night. She holds a finger to her lips, and I sit up. She is dressed in a pleated skirt, a long top, and a pair of striped stockings; her blond hair is all brushed out. Her eyes are shining with excitement. I can smell the telltale scent of some beautiful cologne. Perfumes are things that sit enticingly in bottles in Temptation Corridor, and such luxuries are not something I have come to associate with my life as a maid.

"Louise?" she whispers. She takes my hands in hers and holds them. "Don't question me. We are going out."

"What?" I say helplessly. In my half-awake state, I wonder if this is my comeuppance for believing everything she told me today.

Her lips are painted ruby red, and her nails are painted red as well. Her hair is flowing in waves down her shoulders. As my eyes graze her face, I see a striking similarity to my own features and it is as if I am looking into a mirror.

We stayed up talking until I became sleepy, and she told me that her mother is my father's younger sister, and that my father and her mother grew up together and were close as children. My father returned to my aunt Carol in Heidelberg before the war started when he knew he needed help. Gradually, after we had talked for hours, I began to feel a closeness to Sasha, and this was not something I had experienced with another young woman, not since Papa left, and definitely not since the start of the war.

She turns back to her bed and picks up an outfit almost identical to the one she is wearing. "Put this on."

Sasha has dragged me half out of bed. Sleepily I'm standing there, my mouth opening and closing while she holds up a bright red-and-black-pleated skirt and a sweater in red.

"Here are your boots," she says. "And here," she adds, holding up a brand-new lipstick, "this is for you."

My eyes widen. I remember hearing about rebellious young girls and young men earlier in the war. *Zazous,* they were called. The girls were famous for their blond hair, red lipstick, pleated skirts exactly like the one Sasha is wearing, and rolltop sweaters. The boys wore checked jackets, and their passion was for English-style umbrellas and multicolored scarves.

"Quickly," she says. "Our timing must be perfect. We must get through the Paris streets."

I hesitate, uncertain, my eyes on the outrageous outfit. This is not something I do—go out late at night. But the clothes are enticing, and Frank has told me that I've missed out on so much.

"I haven't been out of this hotel for months...Except to a funeral."

Sasha grips my arm. "No funerals tonight," she says. "I have had more than enough for an entire lifetime. You are twenty-two years old, and we are going out dancing. You have no idea how I live to dance."

I stare at the outfit.

Sasha passes me the sweater. "You know you want to put it on."

I bite my lip, and, before I can think how dangerous this could be, I grab the sweater and start pulling it over my head.

Four years of caution, one night of recklessness?

How bad could it be?

The streets of Paris, wild and out-of-control, snipers on the balconies of the grand mansions outside this hotel. Despite the recall of Nazis to Germany, there are still people locked away in prisons—Blanche—and the Nazis still have military bases on the outskirts of Paris. Armored vehicles are lined up ready to attack the advancing Allies, and the Germans have air bases around France. Most of the country remains under Hitler's control, and there are armaments in Paris itself that remain guarded. The Vichy government is bearing down upon the Resistance...and that means me.

And yet as I pull on the black boots, the pleated checked skirt, and the roll-neck sweater, and as I brush out my own long blond hair and paint my lips with the lipstick that Sasha hands to me, I start humming the jazz tunes that I love to listen to on the wireless, and somehow I'm asking myself, could it be that Sasha's arrival has brought a new light into my world? Could it be that all those mornings spent secretly listening to Ella Fitzgerald might be about to burst into life? I had no idea the Zazous still existed. I had no idea that the spirit of dancing among our generation had not stopped.

Ten minutes later, we are out in the corridor. Hilariously, we both hold black umbrellas. But, out of caution, Sasha has organized two pale blue overcoats for us to wear over our outlandish clothes. I remember learning how the Zazous operated, rebelling against the Nazis in France right under the noses of the Vichy regime. But the Zazous, who used to openly strut around Paris, were rounded up by the Nazis in bars, and beaten on the street by the fascist youth organizations, who, armed with hair clippers, attacked them, scalped them, then arrested them and sent them away to the camps. My umbrella is the only weapon of defense that I have!

Sasha seems to sense my hesitation as we approach the end of the corridor and the double doors that lead out to the main part of the hotel. She grips my arm. "The Resistance will not stop us, and if there are any Nazis, I shall tell them that I work for the military governor. They will not *dare* to question me."

I am not used to operating on the powerful side of things.

We sneak out into the warm summer night. It is quiet, and moonlight pools over the cobblestones in the beautiful old Place Vendôme. We walk down the Rue de Castiglione toward the Tuileries Garden. The lawns spread out in front of us.

"Here we go," Sasha says.

She takes my other hand and begins to run. We run like two girls in pigtails, our heads down. Our blue coats fly behind us, and soon we are standing looking out at the dark mysterious waters of the river Seine.

"Across we go."

I can hardly believe Sasha's confidence out here. It is as if Paris is her domain, while all I feel is trepidation in the face of my own city, in my own country.

As we hurry through the dark narrow streets of the Left Bank, I rush to keep up with my cousin. We are running through quiet cobbled laneways, until we come to a stop outside a closed door. It is dark, silent, eerie, and I cannot help but whip my head around every five seconds to check that we are not about to be ambushed. But the door in front of us opens like a miracle when Sasha knocks in a code, and we are face-to-face with a young man around our age, his long hair slicked back, wearing the checked jacket and thin trousers of the Zazou. My nerves tingle with anticipation and I follow Sasha through the door once she has given a volley of passwords in English.

Sasha leads me down a narrow staircase to a basement and I am assailed by the sounds of jazz. It is the music I love! Young women and men my age are sliding around, their feet shuffling across the floor before they spin, their footwork intricate and their bodies jiving around the room. The sounds of Cab Calloway's classic song "Zaz Zuh Zaz" tells everybody there is no need to be blue. For the first time in an age, I feel lifted from the shackles of occupation and work.

Sasha pulls me into the middle of the dancers, grabs my hands, and begins to jive. The excitement is infectious, and, despite everything, my face lights up and I am dancing, freely. I can't help it. This feels like freedom.

On the stage of the dim nightclub that must be a remnant from the 1920s and Paris's wonderful jazz age, a group of girls are floating around in elaborate feathered costumes. Behind the dancing girls, there's a motley jazz band of grinning musicians, their eyes catching one another's as their fingers move to the intricate syncopated rhythms of the music.

For this moment, I am dancing, and it is as if nothing else matters but the music, and this night.

The girls parade off the stage and into the crowd of dancers. They waft among us with their feathers, waving them and dancing slowly as if they're walking on air. A pair of young men come to join Sasha and me, and one of their handsome faces lights up in a boyish grin. He takes my hand and twirls me around the dance floor, and, before I realize it, we are moving in a slow dance. When the band strikes up something faster, we speed up and my new dance partner spins me around in a wild set of turns.

My chest is thumping, and I am grinning. After a few

dances, I collapse against him, and he takes my hand and leads me to a table in the corner where Sasha is sitting with a group of girls and men all dressed in this radical, beautiful way.

I think of Henri, and how much he would love to be here. I wish he could be.

My dance partner pulls out a chair for me, turns one around for himself, and rests his elbows against the back of it, running his hand through his collar-length black hair. "Where have you sprung from?"

My insides quail at the honest implications of this question, and despite the joy I'm feeling, I hesitate, not wanting to give away anything about myself. "Around and about," I say.

"Smart girl," he says.

I shrug.

"You speak English without any accent at all. It's perfect," he remarks. "I'm guessing you grew up in London, were educated at Oxford, and were dabbling in Paris when the war broke out, leaving you stuck here ever since."

I chuckle. "I'll never tell."

My unnamed companion grins at me and another boy brings a carafe of white wine. He pours out glasses for us all. I sip the drink, and it is delicious.

"I'm serious," he says. "You speak English like a native. I presume you must have grown up there."

"I am French," I say simply.

"Then I take it you are a translator." He places his wine glass down onto the table and turns to me. "Or you should be."

I stare at him. And slowly, my mouth widens into a grin. "A translator, you say?"

Then I sit back in my chair. The musicians turn quiet and suddenly all I can hear are words spinning around the room, young words, in what language it doesn't matter. The main thing is that people are communicating happily.

I turn to him.

I swallow; tears want to fall down my cheeks, but I don't let them. It is too momentous; my father is a translator. This has come together. Being a translator would be something I would love to do after the war!

He grins at me. "Let's go and dance again," he says. The band has struck up another round of fabulous music, and he stands up and holds out his hand, and I take it, and he leads me out to the floor.

Later, much later, a group of us are sitting around on a couple of sofas. Cigarette smoke filters through the air, and girls are chatting animatedly, the sorts of conversations that my generation have been forbidden to have. They talk of the future, they talk of freedom, and they talk of their plans for travel, for the books they want to read, for the lives they want to live now that we have some hope of being freed from the restrictions of the Nazi regime.

When it is very late, or very early—I hardly know the difference, and after years of living under curfews, I honestly don't care—a couple of boys oversee the entrance to the little club and begin letting us out in groups of one or two, instructing us to disperse immediately, to keep our heads down, and not to draw any attention to ourselves.

The boy who danced with me takes my hand, and I imagine I might never see him again. "It was a pleasure to meet you," he says.

And just like that, he disappears out into the warm Paris night.

Sasha takes a different route back to the hotel. The early-morning summer sun is dawning over the most beautiful city in the world. We walk beside the river Seine, our arms linked and our shoes clicking along the cobblestones like two girls in the Paris that I hope will be restored one day. We pass a couple of Nazi soldiers patrolling the streets. They stare at us with barely disguised interest, but they do not stop us. Perhaps Sasha's confidence intimidates them.

I automatically go toward the servant stairs in the Ritz, my mind already in preparation for the cleaning rounds I must do today and on everything I want to tell Henri.

But Sasha holds me back. "Come with me a moment."

I glance up at the clock on the wall. "I can't..."

She links her arm through mine, just as she did last night before we went out. Again, I am following her, and again, I feel a sense of anticipation. It is as if my cousin is bringing me back to life.

A couple of minutes later, we are walking into the hotel kitchens. I hesitate, but Sasha strides confidently in.

"Bonjour," one of the chefs says, and Sasha smiles at him.

We come to a stop at the end of the long line of chefs in the *brigade de cuisine* adding the final touches to the breakfast platters.

"Sasha, and Louise," the sous-chef says. He leads us into a small larder off the main kitchen. On the benches, three covered baskets sit, and my senses are assailed with the smell of fresh baking coming from the ovens. "Here we are."

"Take a basket, Louise," Sasha says. "Come with me and I'll show you what they are for."

I pick up one of the covered baskets. The smell of fresh baguettes and croissants causes my appetite to stir, and I follow Sasha back out into what is now a glorious Paris summer morning.

We walk away from the wealthy square, back along the Seine, and turn up a narrow street, this time on the Right Bank, where the elegant lampposts are covered in spiderwebs.

Sasha knocks precisely five times on a peeling door and then waits.

A middle-aged woman answers. Her face is grimy with dirt, and yet she holds her head high. "Bless you," she says.

Sasha responds in hesitant French, and we follow the woman up a narrow staircase to a flat in the attic of the building. Three children sit expectantly at a wooden table, and the mother wipes a hand across her tired forehead.

"Please, sit a moment," she says. She goes to her kettle, which sits atop an old wood-burning stove.

Out of one of the baskets, Sasha pulls some firewood and newspapers, old copies of *Je Suis Partout.* She strikes a match on the neatly piled kindling in the old stove. Children's clothes and other washing hang from a line across the top of the kitchen. Tucked away in one corner there is a single mattress. Achingly, there is a teddy bear sitting up on the pillow. Clearly, all four of them are sleeping together in one bed.

The woman fills the kettle from a bucket on the bench. When the kettle starts whistling, she makes three cups of ersatz coffee from the contents of the glass jar that Sasha has pulled from the other basket. We set up the selection of croissants and fresh bread for the children, who wait politely until their mother serves them all.

I watch my cousin, this German girl in a foreign country, and I sink down into the wooden chair that the mother offers me. I cup my hands around the mug of ersatz coffee and accept a small piece of bread that Sasha has spread with preserves from the hotel.

When one of the children tentatively shows me a drawing of a stick figure, a garden, and a house with two front windows set atop a red front door, my heart almost explodes with tenderness.

Sasha takes a fresh pile of newspapers, expertly twisting and knotting them to maximize the time they will take to burn in the stove. And I catch a glimpse of the face of Pierre Laval, the leader of Vichy France, staring up from the paper.

I turn back to the child's simple drawing and tell her it is wonderful. Perhaps there is hope that it is nearly over, for all our sakes.

CHAPTER TWENTY-SIX

Kit

Kit glanced at the pond that was filled with muddy water at the edge of the clearing. He was the only one awake, and he was about to get ready to send two young boys out to blow up the Nazi barricade.

When Guillaume eased himself up on his elbow and sent Kit a lazy grin, Kit's heart only contracted further.

"My shooting is improving. Don't you think?" Guillaume moved across to the small fire, pulled the black kettle from where it hung above the flames, and filled it from the tank of water that was replenished by Michel. He struck a match from the stores and set a nice blaze going.

Soon, he was joined by Jacques and Michel. Only the dressmaker slept on.

Michel came and stood next to Kit. He stretched, lifting his arms above his head and sighing. "Pauline wants no further delays. The longer we stay out here shooting at targets, the more we risk being exposed. We are taking down the barricade tonight."

"The orders have come from the SOE?"

"Pauline has the authority to give orders, given she is officially the head of the Maquis in this part of France."

Kit looked at the two young boys, joking around like a normal pair of youths. The boys reminded him of himself and Charlie, and Kit felt a pang for his brother. The sooner the barricade was removed, the better. Once he was in Paris, he would be able to search in earnest for Charlie.

Kit walked around behind the hut with Michel, where he had set up a makeshift storage depot, and inspected their paltry supply. They had a selection of old rifles and two boxes of hand grenades.

He squatted down by the equipment, picked up a stick, and drew a rough outline of the barricade in the dirt. "How many personnel do you expect to be there tonight? What is the intelligence on numbers?"

"Three, maybe four. They are just straight-down-the-line Nazis. No special training."

"Ideally, we'd throw grenades from either side of the barricade, but we can't do that," Kit murmured. "We'll have to attack from this side of the forest. I can't risk sending the boys over the road." Kit stared at his rudimentary sketch in the dirt. "We will need to spread out, but we need to be able to hear each other." He lowered his voice. The boys were sitting nearby around the campfire having breakfast. "If we are too close together, we risk all being destroyed by rifle fire or return bombs."

Kit scowled at the ammunition and muttered something not altogether supportive of the Resistance, those who had sent orders to his new friends.

It was a very dark night, and there was no chance of seeing anything unless the moon were to break between the clouds. The wooden chest that contained the boxes of grenades and the tin of igniter sets lay open in the hut, and the only thing that remained to do to arm the pineapple-shaped bombs was to unscrew the base plug and insert the detonator assembly. They would have to do this undercover and ahead of time.

Kit had no choice but to rely on the boys to concentrate. If they let their attention wander and made one false move with these bombs, they would all be history. He'd warned everyone that noise from return German machine-gun fire would be unbearable, but the noise would be the least of their problems. The dangers of the indiscriminate bullets would be immense.

In the best-case scenario, they were going to have to send the grenades over the tops of the trees and wish them the best of luck. Then, they would have their rifles ready to meet any Nazis who sought them out.

Kit handed two grenades to everyone.

The dressmaker's expression was impossible to read. She had to come; he couldn't risk leaving her here alone. And the boys were excited, but behind their flushed faces, Kit could sense their nerves.

As they whispered their way through the undergrowth, the unavoidable crackling of dry leaves under their feet was the only hint that they were there. When they came to the line of trees that edged the road, Kit indicated to everybody to crouch down.

The plan was for him to throw the first grenade as far forward as possible. Behind him, the dressmaker was his carrier, and behind her were Jacques and Guillaume. Michel was at the rear, assisting the boys and tasked with the gruesome responsibility of taking over if any of the others became a casualty.

Kit turned to the dressmaker, took the prepared grenade, and hurled it. In perfect synchronicity, the boys started throwing bombs over the trees, and then, the mayhem began.

Kit winced as the body of a German was propelled up above the trees and splintered into tiny pieces. But there was no time to dwell. He reached out to the dressmaker for his second grenade and hurled it as hard as he could.

The pepper of machine-gun fire rattled the air, but Kit and the boys threw their grenades until flames shot up into the sky. When it seemed there was no one left, he and his comrades in arms stared at each other and then cheered.

The fight for a free passage to Paris on this road was won.

They looked at the burning mess that was once the barricade and ran. The same two gendarmes who had tried to get Kit and the dressmaker to Versailles were waiting at the campsite, and, wordlessly, the whole group followed them.

The following morning, Kit woke in a barn. He and the dressmaker had been dropped off on the land of a farmer who was an underground member and they'd said a quick farewell to the Maquisards.

Kit's throat was parched when a woman appeared with two rough pieces of bread and a carafe of wine.

"Thank you," he said. He tore off a piece of bread and took a good slug of the wine.

The woman lingered at the door of the barn. Her blond hair fell down her back, and there was a strange sensation of her looking like an angel with a halo around her in the morning sun.

Kit finished half of the bread and left the rest of it for the dressmaker.

"Is there any news of our departure?" he asked. "I don't want to burden you for too long."

The woman bowed her head.

Kit stilled. Slowly, he stood up and moved toward her. "You have news."

She nodded and remained looking at the ground. "I'm sorry; it's not good news. The butcher was taken by the Gestapo late last night after your mission to destroy the barricade. They came for him and raided his store. Took all his supplies, left a dreadful mess, smashed all the windows, and arrested him."

Kit bent forward, his hands resting just above his knees. His stomach folded in on itself.

The woman's voice was soft and strained. "I am sorry. We all liked him. The problem is...They are now after the dressmaker. They are after you."

Kit lifted his head, and a flurry of birds flew through the blue sky just outside the barn and landed on one of the trees in the field. Kit found himself staring at a blackbird, its head moving in jerky movements this way and that.

The woman folded her arms across her old summer dress, worn at the elbows, faded and with clear darning marks. "You will have to move on. Today."

The dressmaker sat up and opened her eyes. Kit did not know where to begin.

CHAPTER TWENTY-SEVEN

PARIS, SUMMER 1944

Louise

Sasha and I are sitting in the tea gardens of the Ritz Hotel, even though we are not supposed to be here. It is strange to think how César Ritz, the owner of the hotel, was confused by the British tradition of taking tea in the afternoon, but soon this gorgeous terrace became one of the most fashionable places in Paris to do just that.

Our legs are stretched out in front of us after another night of dancing. We found a swirl of other partners who were happy to twirl us around the room. Tonight's underground venue was on the Right Bank, near Montmartre, the center of the Belle Époque.

Sasha procured a cigarette from a couple of late-night stragglers who were still sitting at the bar when we came home to the hotel. Now, the sky above the terrace is lit up in glorious shades of pinks and yellows. Dawn is coming to Paris. We could almost be forgiven for thinking there is not a war.

But then the sound of aircraft flying over the city threatens to deafen us.

Sasha tips her head back. "The Allies are starting to bomb

German military targets closer to the city." She looks at me, her eyes narrowed through the smoke and her beautiful blond hair hanging straight down her back. She rubs out her cigarette in the silver ashtray and leans forward, her chin cupped in her hand. "It won't be long until they liberate Paris now."

We look at each other, two cousins separated by nationality. Two cousins who are supposed to be at war. We have not discussed what happens when the Allies arrive. It is something that hangs between us but seems too painful to contemplate. I cannot imagine life without her now. And my feelings about my father remain complex, but the more I have thought about it, the more I am coming to a deeper understanding of how he felt. I only wish he had opened up and spoken to my mother, because I think she would've understood and helped him. But then, it is a little too late for that now.

I sigh and lean forward to rest my forearms on the table. "Sasha," I say, "have you thought about what you want to do after the war?"

The expression in her blue eyes is thoughtful. The sound of the aircraft is receding into the distance. "I would love to be a pilot. I'd love to fly planes all over the world. I wonder whether that will be possible for a girl like me?" She chuckles. "It is hard to imagine the world without all the restrictions we have faced. To be able to travel freely, to be able to fly, sail, or drive wherever we would like to. You know, when I was a little girl, I wanted to see every inch of the world. And you?" she asks.

I bite my lip. "I would like to be a translator," I say. It doesn't sound half as exciting or daring as wanting to be a pilot. "Maybe I could be a passenger in your plane, and we could travel the world together, me as a linguist and you as a pilot." I smile at her. "Maybe you and I could make a difference. That is not something I have ever contemplated before."

She reaches her hand out. "Of course we shall."

I squeeze her hand. "Let's make a pact."

Her face lights up. "I am all for it."

Henri chuckles as I translate the words of the famous fairy tales into English for him. He nudges me where we are sitting together on his bed. I'm incredibly proud of him for putting up with the confines of this room, and every day I try to give him an update as to how close the Allies are coming to Paris.

"What happens when they do come?" I ask.

He looks at me, and we are sitting so close that I would imagine I would be able to read his expression, but I cannot, and my nerves tingle at how close his hand is to mine, but they do not touch. "I go back to England," he says gently. "And then perhaps to America, where my mother is, along with the rest of my extended family."

The book of fairy tales sits open on my lap. Fairy tales where love reigns triumphant, and people end up together and happy. I want to find happiness after this war ends.

"Sasha and I made a pact," I say.

Henri has been intrigued about her, and I've told him how she and I have become close, how we have shared confidences across the borderlines of two countries that have pitted two sides of the family into a bitter war. And I have told him about my father, and the secret I have kept all these years, of my heritage.

He looks down at my hand and then back up at me, and his eyes seem to search mine in a way that makes me think he does know what I want, that he does want to understand me. There is a determination and a strong yearning in his expression.

"Sasha would like to be a pilot after the war. She's always had a wanderlust for travel."

"I hope I get to meet her."

"I hope so too."

There it is, that silence again. I take in a breath.

"And you? What is it that you'd like to do, Louise?"

I love the way he says my name. His American accent lends a certain grace to it, and his voice is deep and resonant. It is a safe voice. I feel safe with him.

"I'm already doing what I want to do." Our eyes meet, and there is a melting warmth in his expression.

"I'm glad," he whispers.

"I want to continue to translate." I screw up my nose. "But not codes. I want to translate novels." I turn the page and trace my hands down the words. "Sasha and I, we have promised each other that we will do these things together perhaps. It seems like a dream."

"Getting to stay in the Ritz Hotel, with you...It's been like a fairy tale."

I look down at the book and feel my cheeks flush.

"London, you know, would be a wonderful place to study to be a translator...So would New York."

I nod, and in the most natural way ever, I lean my head against his shoulder, and he places an arm around me, and we sit quietly together, two young people who have been kept safe in the embrace of a magical place.

It's funny, for so long I had seen myself as remaining in the Ritz after the war, with Frank and Claude and Blanche. But now I feel that this is going to be time to spread my wings and leave this safe little nest behind. I can see a future now.

But when I pass by the open hallway that leads to the lobby I come to a dreadful and sudden halt. SS men are swarming the Ritz. Their black uniforms are raven-like under the chandeliers. Black boots gleam, and their pristine, razor-short haircuts are set in precise, implacable lines against their collars.

I almost dry-retch. *Frank. Claude.*

The SS are storming the hotel.

I step back and crouch down in the shadows. Blindly, I make my way through the back corridors toward the bar. Inside Frank's bar, the black-clad beetles are turning up tables, pulling out glassware, emptying out precious bottles of spirits. The room is thick with cigarette smoke, and this only serves to cloud the scene in front of my eyes. Orders are barked, and men are yelling. Here is the chaos that only the Nazis can invoke.

I beat my way through the throng. There is no one in here except SS. The underground conspirators, the drinkers, the talkers, they have all fled, they have all slipped away.

A gun goes off across the room near the bar, right where Frank normally stands, and I fall to the floor. I drop under one of the banquettes, gripping the seat. The SS are all crowded around the bar, and I can see a clear path to Frank's office. I crawl toward it like a crab.

I manage to ease the door to Frank's office open. Inside, my intake of breath is sharp. Frank is standing behind his desk, and next to him Claude is sitting in Frank's chair, his head in his hands on the desk.

It will be seconds, not minutes, before the SS are in here.

"Frank?" I want to slap him into action. They are just here doing nothing.

I grip onto the sharp corner of his desk and send him a look that is worthy of a wildcat. "Please. Get out of here. Run!"

"We must act as if nothing is wrong or abnormal," Frank says. He closes a filing cabinet and turns around.

A new round of shouts erupts from the bar.

"What about Henri? I should go and get him out!"

But Frank's voice is steady and even. "There has been an attempt on Hitler's life."

"An assassination attempt? Oh, tell me it has been successful!"

Frank glances toward the door. "Everyone thought it was, but the bomb detonated too far away from Hitler in his private rooms, and he survives. That is all we know at present. That he is alive."

"So, it was carried out by high-ranking Nazis who turned against him, if they had access to his private rooms?"

Frank nods. "Here lies the problem for us. One of the main suspects is living in this hotel. And now we will be punished."

"What?"

"Carl-Heinrich von Stülpnagel arrested all the Gestapo and SS in Paris after the news of the assassination attempt came through. But he was unable to convince Field Marshal von Kluge to support the uprising and has been forced to release his prisoners."

Sasha. Sasha's boss was in on the assassination attempt.

I shake my head, taking in this information and trying to process it as quickly as possible. Sasha came here with von Stülpnagel. She was working for him.

"My understanding is that von Stülpnagel decided that Hitler was going too far." Frank sighs. "I'm afraid his chance of survival is nil."

Sasha was working for him because he was *not* loyal to Hitler. Now, it all makes sense.

"Where is von Stülpnagel?" My voice is shaking.

Where is Sasha?

The question forms on my lips and yet I dare not utter it; I can barely think it. Pictures of her being arrested flash in front of my eyes. I have only just found her. I cannot lose her. She is the only family I have.

"Carl-Heinrich von Stülpnagel was ordered back to Berlin." Frank almost whispers his words. There is a clatter and shouting outside in the bar. Claude stares straight ahead at the wall. "He attempted suicide on the road out of Paris but was stopped and is now in the hands of the Gestapo."

My stomach lurches, and I focus on the patterns in the woodgrain on Frank's desk.

"The SS are here searching for evidence of the plot. Any Germans that remained here have fled."

And what of Sasha? Has she fled?

Frank goes and stands by the closed door. "While we were only hearing filtered rumors of an attempt on Hitler's life, von Stülpnagel was acting as if it had been a success. That is why he went ahead and arrested the Gestapo in Paris. He was starting to take control; he was starting to take control out of the hands of the Gestapo. Everybody connected with the plot is wanted by the Gestapo. It is going to be brutal."

"Frank, I must go, I don't know what's happened to Sasha! His assistant. My friend. My cousin!" I can hardly think straight I am in such turmoil.

"Louise?"

I sense Claude whipping his head around.

But I wrench open the door, not caring for one second that I am about to push through a roomful of murderers dressed in black. My pulse is beating in my mouth. I taste the acrid salt of my own bile, my hands are clenched like two steel vises, and I am running through the bar.

Nobody notices or cares who I am. But I care about Sasha. I love her. It all makes terrible sense. Why Sasha was sneaking out all the time when she first arrived and I thought she was after me. They were planning the insurgence that would follow the attempt on Hitler's life.

And then, as I rush through the corridors of the hotel, another thought flings itself in my direction and I am nearly winded. Papa? What if he was part of this too?

I have only just come to understand him.

I navigate the fastest route up to our room as if my fingers are tracing an imaginary line on a map. I move through the complex labyrinth of the building to find my cousin. She came here to ensure I was safe. But it is I who must keep her safe now.

I swipe the hot tears that sting my eyes at the thought of what the Gestapo did to Georges Mandel. Shot in the forest, and he never attempted to harm Hitler. Frank is right. They will be merciless.

We have all seen far too much in this war. We need redemption, we need goodness and good people, and Sasha and my father were two of those.

I strike a door open, and it is the wrong door leading to the wrong corridor. Sobs escape from my throat. I cannot lose her. I hardly bore losing my father.

I open and close doors that I should not be opening and closing. I need to slow down. I cannot slow down.

I arrive back in the lobby, but it is deadly quiet. Hitler's henchmen have spread like a plague through the wings of the hotel. The sound of jackboots beats on the upper stairs.

Tears stream down my face, and it is all I can do to pray wildly that Sasha is somewhere far from here. Then something swells in me. Terror. I lean against one of the walls. If they already have her, they will murder her.

I turn around and run, coming to a shuddering halt in Temptation Corridor on my way back to the Rue Cambon side of the hotel. I am surrounded by the mocking luxuries of the Nazi regime gleaming in cabinets: fine perfumes, leather handbags, gorgeous shoes. How I hate them all.

I continue on to the door that leads to the servants' quarters. Finally, finally. My heart is beating so wildly that I can hardly reach forward and grab the handle of the door. My fingers slip; my feet want to buckle underneath me. Somehow, my hopelessly slick fingers slide the handle open.

I fix my eyes on our closed bedroom door.

And with my head held high, I walk toward it, desperate to find Sasha, but dreading what I may discover.

CHAPTER TWENTY-EIGHT

PARIS, PRESENT DAY

Nicole

I have called a meeting with Aunt Mariah and Pandora, because we need to work out how to get through to Arielle. Opposite the park bench where we sit like a row of three birds, children play on the equipment in the oldest square in Paris, the Place des Vosges. It is one of my favorite squares in the city, surrounded by charming old buildings and a stone's throw from Pandora's home. Mariah clutches the take-out coffee I convinced her to have in her hands. I wanted her to have something to do with them, a distraction while we discuss what to do next. I know that this journey is still painful for Mariah. While she has agreed to stick with me, just, Pandora worries that the memory of Granny Louise burning her past still haunts Mariah to this day.

"The answer lies not in what Arielle is telling us; it lies in the gaps. I think the truth is in the things we can't see, slipped in between the things that people say."

Two women balance their toddlers on the seesaw and begin pushing them up and down.

Mariah hands her empty coffee cup to Pandora and rests her head in her hands. "I'm sorry I have been so difficult about this."

"Don't be," Pandora says. She rubs her mother's back.

I take in a sharp breath. Was the perfumed armor she's been wearing for so long simply a method of protection rather than intimidation? I have been reading her all wrong. And now, I am no longer intimidated by these glamorous relatives who always seemed to operate in a glittering world that was beyond me.

"I think I know where the problem is," I say, sitting up and speaking with conviction.

Mariah's shoulders shake. I catch Pandora's eye, and she nods at me.

"But I need to go and see Arielle again. Mariah, I want to go with your blessing. Louise was your mother. Our grandmother. You deserve to know the truth."

Mariah sits up, her face reddened and blotched. Pandora hands her a tissue and she blows her nose noisily.

I bite my lip and we all laugh.

"You are extremely persuasive, Nicole," Mariah says.

"Yes." I chuckle again.

"I hate to think what you are going to find out."

I stand up. "No more hiding; no more lies."

"You think that is the answer? Honesty?" Mariah looks up at me, and I smile down at her.

"I think it is what you have been seeking all along. Yes?" I raise my brow and smile.

She lets out a long breath. "Honesty was something I never got from her."

We will see about that.

For a short moment, probably as long as she can bear, I lay a hand on my troubled aunt's shoulder. I feel now as if I am doing this for her, although I don't think she can quite see that yet.

CHAPTER TWENTY-NINE

PARIS, SUMMER 1944

Louise

As the SS storm the building, I open the door to my bedroom and take in the room. I have no idea what I will find. Everything is as Sasha left it, so I tear through her drawers, searching wildly for any incriminating evidence, rifling through every single piece of her clothing. My fingers are sure as I run them along the sides of the drawers looking for hidden openings. Under her bed, where there is not a speck of dust because I clean it, I bark out a nervous laugh as I pull out her leather suitcase, but it is empty. I sob as my hands flutter over a single white handkerchief, embroidered with the letter S. It is the sort of thing my mother would sew.

I pull back her bedsheets, and my heart hammers. The sound of a German barking orders rings through this floor of the hotel. I run my hands over her mattress, nothing, nothing, nothing. No strange bumps in the fabric, nothing hidden underneath it or in it as far as I can see. Finally, I wrench open the wardrobe, but all that stares back at me are her few dresses, and I check the pockets, linings, all the places that a conspirator might hide documents, notes, or any other evidence. But still, nothing.

The beat of men's footsteps rings this way and I slip out of the room. My feet working nimbly now as if I am a ballerina dancing a pirouette on the stage, I move toward the other door at the end of the corridor, and silently I swing it open and disappear into the depths of the hotel.

I realize this is my skill: hiding away, being discreet.

Henri is waiting right by his door. He lets me in immediately, as soon as I knock out our code.

"Darling," he murmurs, and he pulls me into his arms. "I heard shouts. They are here. Tell me..." He talks into my hair, his whispers close and soft and comforting, and it would be so tempting never to walk away from here. "If they come to you, I will shield you. They can kill me, take me. Climb out of the window, get out of here. You must protect yourself."

Sobs are racking my chest. "It is not me they are seeking, not Frank, nor Claude. If it was me, I would never be up here with you. Risking you."

I lift my face to meet his, and he strokes a tendril of hair behind my ear. In an instant, he pulls off my restrictive maid's cap, letting my hair flow down my back, and he holds my face in the palm of his hands.

"Tell me what I can do to help." He searches my face, and my heart wants to salve the deep concern I can see in them.

"Henri, there has been an assassination attempt on Hitler's life. My cousin..." I cannot hold back my sobs.

He places his hands on my shoulders. "Sasha?"

"Sasha has been working undercover for the military governor of France on the assassination of Hitler."

"Von Stülpnagel?" Henri shakes his head.

"It seems that he has had enough of Hitler, and he rounded up all the Gestapo and the SS who remained in Paris, because he assumed the assassination attempt that was carried out in Germany had been successful."

"And it wasn't." Henri's voice is flat.

I shake my head. Tears stream down my face. "But I have just found her, and she has disappeared. Von Stülpnagel has been deported to Germany. I don't know where she is." My voice is shaking.

His fingers trace my lips.

"But there is also my father. He is active in the German resistance. If Hitler finds him, there is already enough that he has been doing to indict him, but this will mean instant..."

Henri pulls away, his hand drawing across his mouth. He goes to stand by his desk and frowns down at it.

I stand tall, my chin up, but I cannot contain the wobble in my voice. "I am not proud of my heritage. I can do nothing about it. But I love Sasha and my father, and I cannot sit here while they are in danger. I have to do something. I am the only person who can."

He lifts his head slowly. "So, what will you do?" he whispers.

"I have to find my father."

"No..."

I lift my chin. I have hidden away long enough, and now Sasha's and my father's lives are on the line. "He has been safe working in the sanctity of the church in Heidelberg as a volunteer. I need to go back to Germany, Henri. I need to go back to my roots because he is the only person who can protect Sasha and he will know what to do. And, goodness knows, I need to do everything I can to protect them both."

I move toward him, and I reach up to stroke his cheek with the back of my hand.

"You can't do this. Please."

My touch is soft, and I trace the smoothness of his skin. "And when I am back, I shall come and tell you everything. But I need to warn Papa that they have Sasha. Please, I need you to understand."

"It is too dangerous."

"It may be my last chance to see my father, and it's the only chance I have to find out where Sasha is."

He takes my chin in his gentle fingers. And I close my eyes and I am in heaven.

Perhaps I shall get to come back here before too long.

Back in the bar, tables have been turned over, every bottle emptied, and glass is smashed all over the floor.

I barge my way into Frank's office.

Frank is there; Claude is gone.

I shut the door and lean against it. My hands are pressed into the soft wood and my heart is beating wildly. My breaths are coming in tiny gasps. It is as if I have run a marathon.

But my real marathon has only just begun.

Frank looks up from the devastation that was his office. Drawers are open. Papers all over the floor. The contents of his desk look as if they have been swept aside by a baton.

I gasp silently at the sight of Frank's swollen eye. There is a savage cut running from his mouth down to his chin. And his hands are covered in blood. He is holding a white handkerchief up to his face.

"Frank!" I say, rushing toward him.

But he holds up a hand. Incredibly, he stands up to acknowledge me. "I am fine. Please, dearest Louise. They are not after me." He barks out a strangled laugh.

I help Frank down into his seat, go out to the bar, and get some warm water. I reach for the medicine cabinet that I know is in one of the lower cupboards. There is liniment and a plaster to cover his eye. Back in his office, I hand him the bowl of warm water and a towel from the neat little rack, along with the liniment. My hands are working fast. My mind is working double speed.

"Where is Claude?"

Something I cannot fathom passes across Frank's face. "They marched him back to his office. I have no idea..."

I pick up a paperweight and place it gently back down on his desk. As quickly as possible, I move to his filing cabinet and begin sorting papers. There aren't very many. Frank is good at hiding his tracks.

"Louise."

I cannot stop. I must do something.

I close the filing cabinet gently and turn back to Frank. "Is there any more news of the people involved in the assassination attempt?"

"It happened in East Prussia at an important meeting of several high-ranking Nazi officials. Among them was one official who placed a suitcase containing a bomb right next to Hitler's seat. However, when he went outside on the pretext of taking a phone call, someone else moved the suitcase, and the bomb went off on the other side of the table near a sturdy table leg."

I close my eyes.

Frank holds the towel up over his cut lip for a moment. "Apparently the plan was to activate the bomb in a cement bunker, where the meeting was supposed to be held. But due to the hot weather, the meeting was changed to a more open upstairs room. It was bigger, and apparently instead of two bombs, the conspirators only let off one due to a hitch."

I keep tidying. I'm picking up books and placing them back on the shelves behind Frank's desk. Beautiful books.

"The idea was twofold. Some of the conspirators, I imagine, could see that Germany was not going to win this war. They wanted to install a new military government. Others, I suspect, had had enough of Hitler. Perhaps they had found their consciences at last. I think this was the case with von Stülpnagel, as it is well known that he had rebelled against Hitler before the war."

"I did not know that."

"Hitler is well used to assassination attempts." Frank shakes his head. "He is being typically clinical and cruel in his retaliation for these crimes. I've heard through the underground networks that Hitler has organized the immediate murder of all the conspirators, and talk is that he is going to watch a film of some of them slowly being tortured to death in prison in Berlin for his enjoyment."

"He is a sadist," I whisper. My hands shake but I keep tidying, wiping up the mess. It is all I can do to get through, for now. "And for those who might be associated with people who were involved in the assassination?" I ask. I pause, my hand over an ornament of a small white bird.

Frank places the towel down. His lip is swollen, his eye has turned red and is beginning to bulge. "The repercussions will be enormous."

My heart is hammering and aching at the same time. It is all I can do not to collapse and crumple onto the floor. "I am going to get you some ice for that." I bustle back out to the bar, my forehead creased in a frown. My hands moving quickly, I wrap ice cubes in one of Frank's tea towels and rush back into the room. "I would get you a brandy if it had not all been spilled."

He accepts the ice wrap and holds it to his bulging red eye.

I return to my tidying.

Frank is watching me.

"Frank," I say finally. The room is back in order. I will need to clean the carpets, but for the moment this must wait. "I have something I need to ask you." I pause, but then I plow on. "I am concerned about von Stülpnagel's assistant." I come and stand near the desk. "Sasha."

Frank watches me with one eye. He is silent.

"Is there any intelligence about what happened to her?"

"Claude and I are aware..." He sighs heavily and places his hand down on the table. "Louise, I have reason to believe that she has also been deported to Germany. But I am not certain. At present, we are unclear."

I take in a shuddering breath.

Frank is silent.

"Sasha is my cousin. My father is German. In Germany—"

"You shouted this at me the last time you were in my room. Louise—"

"I have reason to think that Papa also may have been involved in the assassination attempt. I know he sent Sasha here to protect me from the Nazis."

Frank places the towel that has been over his eye on the desk. His expression is set. "I knew that you two were going out together, sneaking out of the hotel late at night." He sighs. "I thought that was a good thing. I thought...I thought you had taken my advice. To live."

I hold in the tears that are stinging the backs of my eyes. "I have wanted to be safe, and the Ritz seemed safe for so long to me. But since I have met Sasha, and seen the way she lives her life, so bravely, so freely...she, who has come out of Germany that is living under a terrible regime..."

Frank's jaw is set. He stares straight ahead at nothing.

"I am going to go to Heidelberg." My voice is shaky. "I need to ask my father to find Sasha. He sent my cousin to look after me. He will be able to help."

Frank flinches. That strong line appears between his eyes and does not move.

I close my eyes. "I need you to help me get to Germany. I will work with the underground. I will take any disguise you want to give me. I will also need a new *Kennkarten,* with an address listed in Heidelberg." I open my eyes again. "And I need it quickly."

Frank just stares at me.

"I shall travel by train out of Paris, and I shall cross the border in disguise. I shall go as a maid. You see, the thing about this is that no one will notice me."

Frank speaks in low tones. "Heidelberg is one of the strongholds of the Nazis in Germany."

"Yes."

"Louise, the entire town is loyal to the Reich. They will know you are French."

"Being surrounded by high-ranking Nazis? I know something of that."

"There will be no protection in Germany."

"My father is there." My voice is gently soft. "And you are forgetting, I am half German." My secret is my only chance.

Frank lets out a shaky sigh.

I rush toward him, and I pull him into a hug.

CHAPTER THIRTY

Kit

Ever since the news of the butcher's capture had come through, the dressmaker had retreated into herself. Kit only wished he could produce some fabric and a sewing machine so that she could forget her worries and concentrate on something productive. But the only news that was filtering through was coming from the elderly farmer and his daughter.

"Two pieces of news for your journey," the old farmer who had brought them some lunch, a simple soup, said. "First, there has been an attempt on Hitler's life."

Kit stood up, and opened his mouth, but couldn't find the words.

"It failed." The old man held up a hand as if in precaution. "All the conspirators have been sentenced to death. Apparently, the scheme was cooked up by some of Hitler's top-ranking officers. But the news that it had failed didn't get out fast enough. The military governor of Paris, thinking the plan to plant a bomb under Hitler had been successful, decided to arrest the Gestapo in the city. He has been deported back to Germany."

"It's not over yet," Kit said quietly.

"No, and the Nazis will punish Paris for this. Now, for the second part of my news." He lowered his voice. "We finally have a car to take you to Versailles. We have not yet found a safe harbor for you in Paris. The situation in the capital is unstable, but two drivers are coming for you at 4 p.m. this afternoon. I believe you are acquainted with them. They are a pair of gendarmes."

Kit smiled, despite the worrying circumstances, but his smile was short-lived. "She is worried about the butcher," he said, looking toward the dressmaker. She sat on a hay bale, her hands folded neatly. She had refused food today.

"He may survive, you know." The old man was quiet for a moment. "He just may survive."

"Thank you," Kit said, meaning it.

The old man nodded and moved slowly back to his farmhouse.

At 4 p.m. precisely, they were standing hidden on the road that led out of the farm toward Versailles. When the sound of a car engine came rumbling along, Kit turned to the dressmaker and placed a hand on her shoulder.

The dressmaker's face was a picture of sadness and worry. He knew how hard this was for her, stepping back into the real world while the pain of grief encircled her. He walked with her toward the car.

Inside, the gendarmes greeted them with one simple word. "Bonjour."

They drove down toward Louis XIV's grand palace set in the beautiful town of Versailles. Kit felt relief wash over him as the dressmaker began peering out the window, her hand resting on the car door.

"There it is," one of the gendarmes said in a gruff voice. On the left, the grand courtyard of the palace spread before them.

Two Nazi guards stood to attention at the gates, and others in uniform chatted.

The gendarmes sat in the front, their expressions implacable, as they wound their way through the streets of the beautiful old town. Nothing could sully its glory, but the atmosphere was loaded and quiet. Overhead, a single German plane flew, the sound of its engine the only noise to break the quiet in the streets. Kit shuddered. Memories of the day he'd failed his brother swooped down on him like a flock of ravens.

When the gendarmes pulled up outside a typical French town house on a quiet street not far from the palace walls, the dressmaker turned to Kit. "It is as if the town is waiting. We are walking into the lull before the storm."

One of the gendarmes looked at her kindly. "Let's hope the storm is nearly over," he said.

"Amen to that," the dressmaker whispered.

"Thank you," Kit said to their two drivers.

The car drove away, and he and the dressmaker were standing outside a closed front door.

That evening, after a long bath, which their hosts, a middle-aged woman and her husband, had insisted Kit take for as long as he wished, he sat at their dining table.

The couple who had rescued them kept a neat and quiet apartment. Kit was to sleep in the bedroom that had once belonged to their son, who had been killed in Normandy during the Allied landings. The couple were still in a state of shock, and the bed where he would be sleeping was next to a little shrine devoted to the son of these brave underground workers.

The dressmaker was chatting with the boy's mother, Bernadette.

Bernadette was talking softly of her daughter, in whose bedroom the dressmaker was to sleep. Bernadette's daughter was working in a munitions factory north of Paris, and Bernadette's face was creased with worry for her because of the Allied bombings.

"You were an Allied airman," Bernadette's husband, Alain, said.

Kit nodded. "I'm afraid I detest the fact that we have to use the past tense."

"I think we are going to see some action around the outskirts of Paris closer to here in the coming days." Alain stood up. He adjusted his brown sweater and smoothed his hands down his linen trousers. "Come with me, Antoine."

Kit followed the gray-haired man upstairs. Alain stopped at the window at the top of the landing of the narrow flight of stairs. Still, it was light. Nightfall would not happen for another two hours.

"The height of summer," Kit said. "And we have to all remain indoors."

"The blackouts have been one of the worst things, almost impossible to bear for the average Frenchman." Alain sighed heavily. "Take a look out there."

Kit frowned; in front of him spread a vast military airfield. Banks of German bombers, from the light bombers to the medium planes to rows of heavy aircraft with large capacities for dive-bombing using glide bombs as well as carrying out long-range missions, were all ready to be put into action once the Allies started approaching Paris.

"Oh dear," Kit breathed. He turned to Alain. The man's face was pale with grief.

"The base popped up here two weeks ago, and I reported it immediately to the underground authorities. I have not had any response." Alain shook his head sadly.

The airfield looked menacing, an opportunity for the Nazis to destroy Paris before they left. Kit followed his host back downstairs, his heart heavy with worry.

• • •

Kit sat in the evenings with Alain and listened to the reports on the wireless of the progress of the Allied troops through northern France. The reporters on the Yankee Doodle station were optimistic that by the end of August all of northern France would be liberated, and the invading forces would be reorganized for the drive to Germany, where they would eventually unite with Soviet forces from the east to bring an end to the Third Reich.

Kit was glued to the news that was coming in about the German retreat. While the Allies were focusing on destroying all the bridges across the river Seine, the Germans were improvising pontoons and ferries to hold off the Allied advance. There was news that Hitler must soon recognize the inevitable and give permission for a withdrawal from Normandy. But the only route of escape the Germans would have was through a gap between the converging American and British spearheads at Falaise.

The wireless was full of reports of the Resistance forces in Paris arming to revolt against what remained of the German garrison there.

"I suppose you are frustrated," Alain said to Kit.

Kit nodded. "When I first crash-landed in France, I was told that I would be finding an escape route to Spain, then I would be flown back to the United Kingdom to be reunited with my group." He lowered his head. "I've been hidden by your kind countrymen for too long. I'll do everything I can to help liberate Paris when the time comes. I think it will be soon."

CHAPTER THIRTY-ONE

PARIS, SUMMER 1944

Louise

I wake, make my bed, tidy my room, and put on the freshly ironed and laundered maid's uniform that I laid out last night on Sasha's bed. I look at myself in the chipped mirror that sits on the chest of drawers between our beds. Frank has called me to his office, as he has made progress, albeit reluctantly, so that I can go to Germany. The worry I feel for Sasha's safety is almost numb, it hurts so much. I wish I had been able to protect her, as she protected me. I wish I had given her half as much as she gave me in the short time we had to get to know each other. And I wish I had known why she was really here, so that I could have done something to help and so that we would have had more time. But guilt is useless now. She has been taken to Germany, and I must entreat my father to start up a search.

I walk downstairs, taking the servants' quarters staircase, and carefully avoid the wing of the hotel where Henri is hiding. This is in case I decide to turn around, run away, and hide like I have ever since this war began.

In his office, Frank pulls out a ream of papers from underneath his desk. There is a new *Kennkarten* with an address in Germany, and he has even updated my passport and included an address in Heidelberg.

"This is a miracle." I bite back tears.

A range of emotions pass across his face. I can't read them, but he stands up, comes toward me, and holds me in a hug.

I hold him tight and breathe in the familiarity of his cologne. It is impossible to imagine not having him around. I hate to admit to myself that it is terrifying. He has been my rock.

"Au revoir," he whispers. "Until we meet again."

But then, in a magnificent sweep, the door to Frank's office opens, and a vision is standing there.

"Arletty?"

There she is, a fox fur thrown around her shoulders and a deep-red dress complementing her long, dark, wavy hair. I take a step back. Every time I have gone into her room since Hans left, she has been silent as if in mourning. Now, she looks like the glamorous film star of days gone by.

She lifts her chin and raises one of her perfectly arched brows. "I heard you needed to go to Germany. So, here I am. Isn't it funny. I would like to go to Germany too. And, as the lover of a high-ranking German Nazi officer, I will be able to get a safe and secure passage, and it is most reasonable that I would want to travel with my maid, is it not?"

I stare at her, then turn my gaze back to Frank.

"You can't live in the Ritz," he says, with a twinkle in his eye, "and then expect to travel third class. Everything is arranged, Louise. Arletty will accompany you to Heidelberg. The Nazis would not dare touch her because of her status, which they will respect."

"My lover's credentials are impeccable. He is entirely loyal to Hitler. They will treat me with the utmost care."

I run my hands down my black costume. My white apron is pristine.

"You have been there for me. I have no qualms about being there for you," Arletty says.

I stand there, hesitant. All I can hear is that Hans was entirely loyal to Hitler. It revolts me to be traveling under these circumstances, even if they are a pretense.

"Louise," she says, her beautiful rose-red lips widening in a smile, "I understand what it is to receive a helping hand."

I look from Arletty to Frank, but he simply nods at me.

"I shall be listening for news on the grapevine." Frank sighs. And then he opens another drawer in his desk. "Here is the address you need in Heidelberg. I hope you find him safe and well," he adds.

He presses the paper into my hand and covers it with his other hand. The look between us says more than words ever could. He has gotten me through. But I must carry this out without him. I am leaving one father figure to find my real father. Somewhere along the line, perhaps I will find a sense of peace about the past, but my first priority is Sasha.

Arletty places a little felt hat on her head. "To the train station," she says.

And for one wild moment, I feel like I am in one of her films as one of her co-stars, but the stakes for me are horrendously real.

At the Gare de l'Est station, Arletty marches straight to the platform for the train to Heidelberg. Frank has thought of everything. Arletty is holding our tickets, and a porter walks behind us carrying her small bag. People recognize her and they stand aside, leaving a parting in the crowd for her to make her majestic way through.

I keep my head down and scuttle along behind her in my maid's uniform. My old leather suitcase bumps against my knees and I avoid looking right or left.

Arletty senses my discomfort, and she slows her pace. She

turns to me, with a kind yet knowing expression on her face. "The best way to be disregarded is to be a woman who is both single and poor. My dear, no one will notice you."

I nod, but she takes my arm and marches me on.

"I know this is true," she says, "because I have been there myself."

"How anyone could ever ignore you, madame," I murmur, "is beyond me."

"Artistry goes a long way to hide things we don't want others to see," she replies. "I know I will prove a distraction for you on the train. That is the way it is with men." She sighs. "I put on my best war paint for you today."

We are approaching the guard who will allow us to embark on the train.

"Stay quiet," Arletty whispers.

Her porter rushes along behind us. He is almost comical, but my heart beats in time with the pounding of his feet on the platform, and I'm finding it impossible to control the shaking in my limbs.

We come to the middle-aged guard, and he stands back, appraising Arletty as if she is a prime cut of meat.

I stand behind her.

Slowly, exquisitely slowly, he reaches out to take her passport. He spends what almost amounts to minutes flipping through the pages, and then he asks for her *Kennkarten.* She hands this over with a sweet smile.

Finally, the guard hands back her papers.

She waits for me while I pass mine to the guard.

I stare at the ground, and then slowly lift my head as I realize the guard is scrutinizing my face, to check that my features match those on my *Kennkarten.*

"A German maid," he says. He sends a lazy glance down my body.

I want to throttle him. I only wish I could.

But then the guard calls out for everyone to board and hands my papers back to me. I struggle to calm my nerves because I want to rush to get on board before he changes his mind, and I must keep my calm.

Our cabin is plush, and we are sharing with four uniformed Nazi officers. I cannot stop the curl of my lip. This was not a situation I had prepared for or wanted. If I had traveled third class as I had expected, I would have avoided this.

I have no idea what to do, or say, or even how to sit. I am like a bird on a perch, my head swiveling from here to there. In the end, Arletty places her magnanimous hand on mine to calm me. She seems the picture of composure and I wonder whether she truly is, or whether this is the acting performance of her lifetime.

Two of the Nazis are middle-aged, and one of them leans forward and offers Arletty a cigarette from his silver case. She reaches out and accepts it, thanking him in German. He nods and smiles indulgently.

He asks whether she is spending a long time in his country.

She says she does not know. She says that she adores Germany. She tells him how she wishes to see Bavaria and sets him off on a long rant about Munich, and Hitler's headquarters there. He then starts to tell her how important it is to Hitler that people see Germany as welcoming.

I lean back in my seat and watch the landscape outside the train. We are heading east toward Strasbourg, and because we are on an official transport of the Reich, we pass by without any stops. This train is going straight through to Heidelberg. After that, it is continuing directly to Berlin. This is the route the Germans have taken throughout the occupation, using Paris as their playground, and coming from Berlin for weekends of indulgence in a city where its residents starve and fear for their very existence.

Outside, the French landscape is unspoiled. We are going through the country of champagne grapes. Vineyards line the railroad tracks, and overhead, the sky shines on the lush green vines.

None of this helps me contain my growing nerves.

The real price of war starts to show its hand when we pass through the towns. My stomach turns at the sight of children on the edges of the railway tracks, scrounging around in the bushes for food scraps that may have been thrown off the train. Their bellies are distended, and their faces grimed with mud. The Nazis don't seem to notice or care, as they laugh and joke as if they are on holiday. I close my eyes to block them out.

I manage to fall asleep and waken when we arrive in Strasbourg, because now we are going to wind our way up through Germany.

In a few hours, I will be at my father's house.

The slip of paper in my pocket with his address burns my fingers.

So many times I have questioned this decision. But there is no turning back.

CHAPTER THIRTY-TWO

Louise

It is said that going back to the place of your ancestors should make you feel immediately at home, but all I feel is a sense of loss. I enter the old square at the center of the city through a set of majestic, medieval gates, and it is all I can do not to imagine my father walking in this very place.

Arletty is sitting at the train station, waiting for her return ride to Paris. She never intended to stay in Germany. She kissed me briefly on the cheek, wished me well, and insisted she would be perfectly fine having coffee in the railway station café before returning safely to the Ritz. I feel even more conflicted by her than I ever have. She is the woman who fell in love and received privilege from the Nazis but who has also now aided me. I wonder if I will see her again.

In front of me is the pinkish-red Church of the Holy Spirit, which I have learned has been home to both Catholic and Protestant congregations over the centuries. Outside, a group of Nazi officers linger like beetles that have crawled out from the town pipes.

The castle looms high on the hill above the city, and the Neckar River flows as it has done for centuries, while the hills are studded with lush green trees. Seeing nature sitting so serenely in the face of all this human failure is something I can hardly bear.

The people of this city walk by with their heads down and their eyes averted to the ground. There are tables set up for a café in the center of the square. The only patrons are Nazis in uniforms. I'm walking among a nation that has been cowed.

I take tentative steps around the church, the coat I brought to wear over my maid's uniform lending me a sense of inconspicuousness, for which I am appreciative.

The address that Frank gave me takes me to a blue-painted building with white-framed windows. Every building that lines the square is exquisite.

I stand for a moment, my stomach pinching. Is this the place where my father grew up? I do not know, and it seems inconceivable to me that I may be about to find out.

The church looms like a long-lost friend, a benevolent shape looking kindly over the square. I remind myself that it has seen much history, much sadness, that cruelty is a human failing indeed, but the opposite of it is kindness, and strength.

Nevertheless, I am tentative as I reach up to knock on the front door. I have no idea how my father will receive me. I knock three times, and then stand back.

There is no answer. I close my eyes. I had not imagined this.

I turn away from the door, only to hear a tentative creak behind me, at which I turn around, swift on my feet, and I come face-to-face with a middle-aged woman, whose expression bears the fear I have come to see on the faces of the citizens of Heidelberg.

"Yes?" she asks me. She glances nervously around the square. She is wearing a simple yellow dress, and her hands rub and rub in front of her. Her hair is waved and curled and is streaked with layers of gray.

I press my lips together, take a step forward, and state my case. "I am looking for Joachim Bauer," I say. Thank goodness, my mother had the foresight to change our names to her maiden name of Bassett when the war broke out.

The woman narrows her eyes and glances around nervously. "He is not here," she whispers. She begins to close the door.

I think of Arletty, and something kicks in. Like a man in a movie, I stick my foot in the door so that the woman cannot push me out. We are locked, our gazes tied together. I can feel the terror emanating from her. But I have not come all this way for nothing.

"Please," I say. The woman is shaking now. I open my mouth, then close it. "I am not a Nazi," I whisper. I glance down to the curved back of the church. The men are still lingering.

One yell from this woman, and I could be arrested on the spot.

She is trying to push the door closed.

"He is my father," I whisper, in the same terrified tone that she has used. "I need to see him."

She brings her hand to her mouth and gasps.

"My name is Louise Bauer," I say, using my German surname for the first time since the war began when I adopted my mother's French name. "I have come all the way from Paris. I need to talk to him urgently."

The woman's mouth is trembling, and her delicately painted lips are pursed in what looks like disdain. She shakes her head. "No," she whispers. "This is not possible. He is not here."

Something, grief, swells up in my throat. I stumble backward, my hands reaching, and I fall hard on the cobblestones.

The woman slams the door in my face.

CHAPTER THIRTY-THREE

VERSAILLES, SUMMER 1944

Kit

The dressmaker had gone to the markets with Bernadette. Kit was listening to the wireless with Alain, glued to the debate between Eisenhower and de Gaulle, not, as one would expect, as to who would liberate Paris, but about whether Paris was worth liberating at all!

Kit scratched his head at the sentiments of Eisenhower. The idea that Paris would be too much of a distraction on the important route to Germany was unthinkable. Leaving Paris's starving citizens as they were was a strategic flaw in the plan of the Americans that Kit could not reconcile.

At the same time, however, General de Gaulle was insisting that Paris must be liberated by the French first. He was arguing that whoever liberated the city would gain a great strategic advantage in postwar Europe.

Alain was sitting quietly, but Kit was nervous, and every now and then he would glance out the window, hoping to see the dressmaker returning home safely.

The butcher's arrest had shaken him. Until it had happened,

the strength of the Resistance had seemed formidable. And the fact that the Allies were circling around Paris had rendered the underground almost invincible, but every now and then, there were still terrible reminders that they were not living in liberated France.

The soft click of the door opening signaled the dressmaker's arrival, along with Bernadette.

Kit pushed back his chair and went down the stairs to greet them. He needed to make sure they were safe.

The women had made the most of the sparse pickings at the market and had come back with a slab of goat cheese, some lettuce, and a small basket of strawberries.

"I will show you how to make our goat cheese salad," the dressmaker said cheerfully to Kit. "We shall have it for lunch."

Kit carried the shopping bag upstairs for her, only pleased to see some spark of life in her again. Being here with Bernadette was clearly good for her.

"It should be quite a party," the dressmaker said, a little sparkle in her soft blue eyes. She turned to Kit and laid her hand on his arm. "I have come to realize," she said softly, "that I may as well enjoy the life I do have, as there are so many things that I can do nothing about."

"I'm relieved."

Kit placed her shopping bags on the kitchen bench. Bernadette was busying herself opening cupboards and getting out mixing bowls. The color of the beautiful produce was striking and summery. She went to fetch the kettle and place it on the stove. As she did so, she started singing a tune, a folk song perhaps, and Alain turned the constant news on the radio off.

The dressmaker took out four perfect rounds of goat cheese. She showed Kit how to slice them in half, before coating one with thick breadcrumbs from the loaf that Bernadette had baked two days ago. Soon, Kit was slicing the rounds expertly in half, his knife easing beautifully through the soft, succulent cheese.

Working deftly, he started shaping the delicious morsels, then coating them in crumbs.

The dressmaker took four plates and laid out some fresh lettuce and a few slices of tomato from their visit to the market earlier in the week. Next, she took a jar and shook some vinegar and olive oil together to make a dressing.

Bernadette set the table with a carafe of white wine and a jug of water. The smell of ersatz coffee filtered through the air. She polished her silver cutlery and laid it out on the pale blue tablecloth. She produced a vase of summer flowers and placed this as a centerpiece for them all.

"Now we shall toast the pine nuts," the dressmaker said. "Bernadette has a friend who managed to get a few for us today."

"One certainly learns who one's friends are during war," Bernadette said. "I shall never forget those who have found tiny delicacies for us. Sometimes, it is the little things that make all the difference."

Alain sent her a smile filled with love and turned the radio to a music station. And while they cooked, as if it were any Sunday morning, Schubert played from the wireless, and they were transported to another time, another place, when there was no war against the great countries of the composers, and when Europe was at peace.

"Now, we can cook the cheese." The dressmaker showed Kit how to quickly fry the morsels of cheese in the pan, turning them once in olive oil until they were golden. "You don't want them to be overcooked and soggy, and you don't want melted cheese oozing all through your salad," the dressmaker said, standing next to him and watching Kit while he cooked. "You are becoming quite the Frenchman, you know."

Kit laughed. "My mother would love to hear you say that."

Bernadette set the plates out on the table, all decorated with the pretty green, jewel-like lettuce, lush red tomatoes, and golden goat cheese. The sprinkling of pine nuts was a treat.

Alain poured out the wine, and everyone took their seats.

Kit had become so settled here. In just a few days, he had his own chair at the kitchen table and was being treated like family.

"You are close to your mother?" Bernadette asked.

Kit placed his glass of wine on the table. He looked at the beautiful meal. "I haven't seen her since the war broke out. I worry about her and how she must be feeling now that her sons are missing." He caught the dressmaker's eye and she smiled sympathetically at him.

"Well, I think she has done a fine job of turning you into a gentleman. I am a good judge of character," Bernadette said. "She will be so proud of you when you go home. And I hope your brother will go safely with you."

Kit looked down at his food. He was grateful for being here but also abashed. Hopefully, Charlie had been half as lucky.

A shadow passed across Bernadette's face, and she placed her knife and fork down. Alain reached out and placed his hand on his wife's.

"Our son will never have any such chance...," she whispered.

The following morning, Kit woke to the sound of Bernadette's sewing machine whirring through the apartment. He stretched and moved across the bedroom to open the blackout blinds, letting in the dazzling sun that promised another beautiful, French summer day. He smiled to himself; the dressmaker had decided to sew him a set of new shirts. Along with the produce that she'd been getting at local markets, she had been buying cotton in pale blue and white—so he didn't disgrace her when they arrived in Paris and so he looked suitably French, she said.

Kit, intrigued, had asked her where she had learned to tailor shirts. The dressmaker had admitted that she made all her husband's shirts for him, and then, with downcast eyes, she had set the sewing machine going again and closed the conversation.

Kit had not pushed things. *But what of her husband?*

He pulled on a pair of trousers and a shirt, went to the bathroom, washed, and went down to the kitchen, where Bernadette was sitting reading a novel at the table, while the dressmaker's sewing machine trundled away in the background.

"Here we are," the dressmaker said. She held up what looked like a perfectly tailored shirt in Kit's size. "Go and try it on. Please," she urged, handing him the almost-complete shirt.

Kit went back to his bedroom and, in front of the mirror, eased his arms into the perfectly cut shirt. He took it off and wandered back into the kitchen, handing it to the dressmaker for completion. "It's perfect," he said.

Bernadette handed him a cup of coffee and offered him a plate of fresh bread and preserves.

Kit sat down, frowning. "I don't suppose there is any news of when we might be moving on?" He winced at his words, knowing that he should be incredibly grateful for everything he had. But they were getting too settled. The old drive to contribute and do something was back, tenfold. "That is not to say that I couldn't stay here forever."

Bernadette smiled. "It is a matter of getting a trusted driver," she said. "And being able to secure a safe passage out of Versailles, given that the Germans who remain in France are setting up more barricades and taking more Resistance prisoners. We have heard terrible tales of the Nazis interrogating those who they catch at gunpoint, while the underground members are forced to kneel, a rifle poised between their eyes, and their heads bowed to the ground."

Bernadette went to stand by the window, gazing out at the Nazi military base just beyond the bank of trees. At night, Kit was often woken by the sounds of German airplanes flying overhead.

The dressmaker returned to her sewing machine, her fingers and foot moving deftly as if in a coordinated dance.

"Thank you for my breakfast," Kit said. He finished his

coffee, took his plate over to the sink and washed it, and moved upstairs to the salon.

He leaned heavily on the windowsill. Outside, there were at least one hundred black German planes. They could do a huge amount of damage, not only to the Allied airmen, but to the French citizens living on the ground.

The Nazis would not show any mercy in their air attacks. Ever since France had been occupied, German pilots had been known to fly low over people trying to escape the city and bomb them while they ran.

There was no doubt that was going to happen in the last days of the war, just as it had happened in the early days when Germany invaded France. The world had been horrified by reports of children being chased by German airplanes and gunned down to the ground with their mothers.

Kit stood alone, frowning down at the rows of aircraft. Ready and waiting.

CHAPTER THIRTY-FOUR

HEIDELBERG, SUMMER 1944

Louise

I stand up and realize how impossible this situation is. My coat is covered in dust from the cobblestones outside the blue-and-white-painted house. My disappointment is renewed. Perhaps I hadn't realized it, but the prospect of seeing my father and believing him to be a good man had given me hope. I cannot begin to imagine why, now, I am here. Was this story that Sasha told me a fabrication? If she was lying about my father, then that would mean she was possibly lying altogether, and that is something I do not want to contemplate. But is my father the same destructive man he was when he was living in France? They say people do not change, after all.

In the absence of a better plan, I walk toward the church.

Inside, high arches soar toward the ceiling. The stained-glass windows are exquisite, and I am certain that they tell stories from long ago. I slip into a pew for a moment. It is impossible not to be awed in here, and being inside this quiet building for a few moments is an opportunity to plan what to do next.

Here are my options: I have very few.

I could go back and try to engage this woman once more. But that seems futile, impossible. She was clearly terrified and will not let me inside.

I could ask around the church and see if anybody knows my father.

I shudder. Living under a government you cannot trust to help you with the most basic of human rights has made a mockery of Europe.

Right then, I feel somebody come and kneel beside me. I sense them before I see them, and, slowly, I turn my head around.

"You are the dressmaker's daughter?"

I turn to see a girl of perhaps eighteen years old next to me. She is wearing a scarf, but it is clear to me that her features are like Sasha's, except soft auburn tendrils of hair escape around her cheeks.

"My mother is your aunt Carol," the girl says. "And I am your cousin Mathilda. My older sister, Sasha, has sent coded messages to us praising you, and your father. He...carried a photograph of you."

Carried. Past tense.

My eyes dart around the inside of the quiet church. There are a couple of worshippers a little farther up toward the altar, but otherwise it is empty. There are no Nazis in sight.

"Have you any news of either of them? Please." I am almost begging, but a sort of wild relief is washing over me that Sasha was telling me the truth.

"Your father was captured by the Gestapo as soon as Hitler started rounding up his suspects in the assassination plot."

My spine presses into the hard-backed pew.

There is a soft hand on my shoulder. "The last thing he asked me," she whispers, "was to find my aunt Violette and my cousin Louise, and to tell you both that he loved you, and that he regretted everything very much."

I take in a shuddering breath. I stare up, try to look at the ceiling, to focus on the dual bright colors of the windows. But everything is blurred, and nothing seems clear. I am a pool of conflicting emotions.

"And Sasha?"

"We have no news. My mother is beside herself."

I swallow. Of course. That explains her behavior toward me this morning. It is as if everything that had woken up inside me in the last few weeks has frozen solid again.

"Louise," Mathilda whispers simply. "I am about to walk home. Please, follow me a few minutes later. Walk past the blue house with the white-painted windows and go to the end of the row. There, turn left, and you will find a lane that runs behind the buildings. Please, walk down the lane, and I shall leave the back door open. Come in, and you will see a narrow tall staircase. Come up to the second floor, and knock five times, softly, on the door."

I nod, but there is only one thought in my mind: *I will never get to see Papa again.*

I am back out in the stark sunlight. The Nazis are milling around the square. I walk past the blue-painted house, past the fairy-tale gingerbread houses that line the square. I turn into the narrow lane that runs behind. There is a door open. I take a tentative step inside, go up the stairs, and knock on the door.

Mathilda lets me in quickly, then closes the door behind me with a click.

"Welcome, Louise," she says.

My aunt Carol is standing with her back to me. She is staring out the window, and she does not move. Her feet are planted implacably on the wooden floor. There is a large wireless in the corner of the room, a rug patterned and faded in deep blues and reds, a sofa, and two armchairs. Through a door, I glimpse a kitchen, and there is a large table. For a family, in better times.

My eyes linger on a photo of my father on the mantelpiece. He is young. He is wearing an open-necked shirt, and his hair is flickering, as if there is a breeze. There is water behind him, the sea perhaps. He is smiling, the way he used to do when he sang.

"*Papa.*" I cannot help it.

"Your father is my brother." Carol's voice seems to haunt the room. She still uses the present tense. She turns around slowly to face me. Her eyes, which I notice are a startling green, flicker toward the front door, and she speaks in low, urgent tones. "They came to take him away in the dead of night. He could not even pack a bag. They searched every drawer and every cupboard in the apartment. If he is alive, I..."

I bite my lip and wait. Carol rushes on as if she is urgently trying to get every word out.

The woman turns those hurt eyes toward me. "The Nazis pushed him down the stairs so that he rolled to the bottom like a sack of potatoes. I no longer sleep at night. He is a good man. He was troubled, but he only ever tried to do right by his daughter and his wife." She turns back to face the window and leans on it heavily.

I have no idea what to say to her.

"Mother." Mathilda's voice is soft behind me.

Carol remains perfectly still. I have a blurred view of her face reflected in the windowpane. Tears roll silently down her cheeks. "I have no idea what has happened to my daughter. As soon as I heard about the failed plot to assassinate Hitler and von Stülpnagel's actions in Paris, I knew Sasha would be in trouble." Carol sinks down into a chair by the window. "My family."

"I will make coffee," Mathilda says. "Please, sit down, Louise."

I sit down and face my aunt.

"I am sorry," I murmur. Sometimes, there is nothing else to say.

She nods and folds her hands tightly in her lap.

• • •

Mathilda and I wash the dishes after dinner, and Schubert is playing on the radio.

"Louise, would you care to go for a walk with me before curfew?"

"Please," I say. I am devastated for my aunt and for my cousin, but I need to get out of this apartment and think, even if this means encountering Nazis.

Outside, the rose-colored church is bathed in the pink setting sun, and it casts long shadows across the old town square. We turn in silence toward the medieval gate that leads to the river.

There is a secluded park bench under a tree, and as if in silent agreement, we sit down opposite the river. I wish I could have gotten Papa safely to Paris. Frank would have looked after him; he could have joined the underground.

"As *Mutti* said," Mathilda remarks, "we must wait; it is all we can do."

I am aware that we need to be careful what we say out here. I feel that the very air is alive with eyes and ears, but the river is moving slowly and consistently at its own pace.

"Who can help me get a message to Paris?" I whisper, not looking at Mathilda.

She stirs next to me, and, slowly and surely, she places a hand atop mine.

"There is someone."

The café is on one of the narrow streets a few blocks from the main square of Heidelberg. The dress I have borrowed from Mathilda is the color of clementines. Outside, the sky is overcast. Rain has fallen the past two days. We have spent most of our time inside, helping my aunt sort out her collection of wool for the winter, trying to divert ourselves from the fears we have and failing.

The river is bathed in a mantle of gray. I have ordered two small cups of coffee—ersatz coffee, of course—one for me and one for the man who I am expecting to join me in precisely five minutes' time. The café is busy, and for that I am thankful. I have ordered coffee in perfect German and have aroused no interest from the staff.

Right on cue, a man fitting the description Mathilda gave me slips in the door. I place the white glove that Mathilda has lent to me on the table. My companion is a man in his sixties; he is dressed in a cream shirt and a pair of pressed brown trousers. His sandy hair is flecked with streaks of gray. He is wearing tortoiseshell glasses, and he leans down and kisses the top of my head. He murmurs an endearment, leaves his arm resting on my shoulder for a minute, and with his other hand passes me a slip of paper, which I in turn place in my cousin's black patent leather handbag.

He takes my hands in his. "You are well?" my companion asks.

"Very well."

The sky bursts open and rain begins to splash on the cobblestones.

"We have wet weather forecast for the next few days."

"Indeed, we do." I nod at the man.

"And I was able to purchase apples this morning. Would you like some?" He peers inside a brown paper bag and shows me the apples. Another piece of paper is nestled inside.

I feign an expression of delight and take the bag. "Oh, thank you, *Vati,*" I murmur, wincing at the pain I feel in saying this word.

He nods and chats on about the rain.

After fifteen minutes, I stand up, and he waits for me to walk first outside the café. Outside, I put up the umbrella that I thought I should carry and march to the apartment, thanking goodness for the anonymity of the rain.

CHAPTER THIRTY-FIVE

VERSAILLES, SUMMER 1944

Kit

It was early afternoon, and humidity hung over Versailles. The gray clouds were laden with unshed rain. Alain was reading the newspaper in the wingback chair by the blacked-out window, and Kit frowned at the tiny print in the novel that he was attempting to read. Charlie was the one who could read in French, not Kit.

While Alain pressed on with the newspapers, Kit had turned to books after they had all read in horror a news story about a liberated labor camp in Poland called Majdanek, along with photographs of the tragedy that had been going on behind the barbed-wire fence. The world was in shock at images of gas chambers, and of stories of thousands of innocent people the Germans had imprisoned being murdered.

Kit turned a page in his book, not taking it in. The dressmaker and Bernadette had gone out for a picnic, and they were due back any minute now.

When the whole room flashed, a violent cornucopia of color, as if lightning had struck in red, gold, and purple all at once, Kit shot out of his seat like a rocket. The electricity faltered and shivered, and the standard lamp flickered and finally died out.

Then, the roar of airplanes ripped the town in two.

It was happening. The Allies were finally attacking the nearby Nazi airbase.

The noise was deafening. Airplanes whirred and screamed overhead. The earth shuddered and thundered beneath them, and it was as if the house was about to cave into the ground.

Kit hurled himself toward Alain, gripping the old man and pulling him toward the wall, where he sank down onto the floor in the absence of any better choice.

"Bernadette!" Alain shouted above the din outside.

The dressmaker. They were both out there. The room exploded in another kaleidoscope of color, and the sweep of airplanes hurling around outside in the sky was accompanied by the boom and thud of continuous, heavy bombing and the rattle of artillery fire.

Kit hauled himself up to the window and glanced above the treetops. Black smoke billowed from the German aircraft base.

It felt as if the building was about to explode. Soon, Kit's head began to pound in time with the noise. He slid back down and stuck his thumbs in his ears to drown out the deafening roar.

Alain was sitting with his head bowed and his knees pulled in to his chest. His entire body shook as he said, "My darling, she is out there."

The wail of air-raid sirens started up. Next to him, Alain was sobbing silently into his hands. Kit put his arm around the older man, helped him up, and led him down to the basement.

When, after what seemed like hours, the planes soared away, Kit took Alain's hand.

"Wait here. I shall go out and look for Bernadette and the dressmaker. I won't come home without them."

Alain did not respond. He was curled up in a ball like a child, his hands covering his ears. The ground still felt shaky and murderous.

"I will return soon," Kit whispered to Alain.

His friend attempted to sit up. "I'll come with you," he said. But the face that he turned up to Kit was pale and haunted, and his eyes were bloodshot.

Kit simply responded by shaking his head.

He went into his bedroom and reached for the gun he had kept after he left the Maquisards.

Kit strode through the streets of Versailles, with all the confidence of a man who was not a wanted target, to the open countryside where he knew the dressmaker and Bernadette had been strolling this afternoon. Outside, there was an eerie silence. The sky was bilious; the air filled with the smell of smoke. Blinds were drawn in houses, and nobody was in the streets.

Kit moved toward the edge of the gardens of Versailles. This wilder end of the property was miles away from the palace, and well beyond the great fountains and formal gardens that the Germans had availed themselves of during the war. Here was the open countryside where Marie Antoinette had ridden and played at escaping court life with her friends.

Kit traced the pathway that curled through the trees. He was following a brook and the water seemed to shimmer and shine in the strange semidark air. It lay still and tranquil, unaware of the fighting that had just taken place. The air was thick with the lingering smell of smoke.

Kit stopped at the sound of voices and looked up to see three figures ahead of him.

They were wearing the black uniforms of the Gestapo. Guns were slung over their shoulders, and they were laughing at something.

Kit slunk into the trees that lined the path and looked over again to the laughing men.

Laid out in front of the Gestapo officers was a body. The brown dress, the stockings, the sensible shoes, and the hair slightly graying and speckled with spots of blood. And blood pooling on her chest.

Bernadette was curled up on the grass like a little girl.

A neat bullet wound went straight through her heart.

Kit buckled down against a tree. He stuffed his knuckle inside his mouth.

The dressmaker was nowhere in sight.

Kit reached for his gun.

It took Kit only three shots to kill the Gestapo. Soon there were four bodies lying in the clearing. They were murderers, and Kit had to make a tough decision in the face of war. Clearly, they would have seen the dressmaker. No doubt, she would be their next target, unless they had shot Bernadette instead of her. Bernadette had simply been going for a walk; she had been going for a walk in the park near her home.

He ran over to look at the body. Every fiber within his being yearned to close Bernadette's eyes, so he did. He laid a hand on her temple for a moment. This forest that had seen so much history, and so much bloodshed, revolutions, wars, and yet, it seemed the number of innocent victims only continued to grow. And now kind, cheerful, generous Bernadette was one of them.

It wasn't fair. May she rest in peace. May she have died and gone to a kinder place to be reunited with her son.

Kit held in his tears.

CHAPTER THIRTY-SIX

Louise

The walk from the café to my aunt's house seems interminable. My ears are beating and pounding with the sound of my shoes on the cobblestones. The window boxes, which Carol tells me are usually filled with red geraniums in the summer, are empty, as they have been ever since the war began.

I fumble with the lock and my key until, finally, I push the door open, climb the stairs, and burst into the sun-filled living room.

Carol and Mathilda are sitting listening to the wireless, but we are only receiving scant information about the Allied bombing attacks on Germany. Whispers of more reliable news relay that the Allies are targeting German fuel supplies. They are also hitting railway lines, to hold up the transport of troops. On top of that, the Allies are carpet-bombing German troops in advance of the land invasion. The bombing of German cities continues.

We all know that the worst is yet to come. So far, Heidelberg has been spared.

I take out the two precious notes. Carol and Mathilda are by my side in an instant.

"Papa is in Tegel military prison, just outside Berlin," I read out loud, my eyes scanning the note.

My aunt leans down heavily on a table, her head bowed. "He is in the hands of God."

I swallow. "I shall not give up hope," I whisper. "I simply cannot."

Carefully, I unfold the second piece of paper. It is coded, and I reach for the notepad and pen that sits on the table, my eyes scanning the numbers, my fingers working quickly with the pen.

Mathilda is standing behind her mother, her hands on Carol's shoulders.

I look at what I have written. "The defender escaped. Back at work."

Carol gasps. "Sasha, the defender. I named her well."

"Thank goodness," I say with relief.

I push back my chair and go to stand by the window. The beautiful old church shines pink in the sunshine, and the blue sky overhead is untainted with clouds. My time in Heidelberg is ending. I am going to have to leave my father's homeland. It is my fate to go back to Paris, to Sasha, to Henri, to Frank and Claude.

Families come in all sorts of guises.

I turn back to face these two women, who are also my family. Relief for her daughter, and fear for her brother, are etched all over my aunt Carol's face. Impulsively, I move toward her and hug her.

"I will never give up waiting for Papa," I promise. "And I will never, ever give up hope."

CHAPTER THIRTY-SEVEN

VERSAILLES, SUMMER 1944

Kit

Kit approached the lane behind Alain's house, and as he climbed the staircase toward the apartment that had been home to him for the last few days, Kit forced himself to take deep breaths. Even as the gun in his jacket pocket still felt as if it smoked.

He turned the handle of the door. Inside, the sound of low, urgent voices came from the kitchen. Kit closed the door quietly behind him using his back, leaned against it, and closed his eyes.

In the great gaping void that was this room, this home, Kit finally opened his eyes and came face-to-face with Alain, and the haunted expression of a man who had lost his wife. Behind him, the dressmaker stood with her head bowed. Kit slumped against the wall. She was alive. She had escaped, but Bernadette...

Alain's expression clouded over and he turned away, clutching onto the kitchen table for support.

"There is a car coming to take us to Paris any moment," the dressmaker whispered. "It is all seen to. I have told Alain everything that happened. They ambushed us, and they shot the wrong woman."

The dressmaker had been their target, then. But the truth was, the butcher and Bernadette had both been protecting him, Kit. How many more kind souls would the Nazis murder trying to get to him?

Kit moved across the kitchen and pulled Alain into a rough hug. "I am so, so sorry, Alain."

Sirens wailed through Versailles. Thick black smoke lingered like a haze over the town, and the smell of burning was acrid. Kit's ears rang with the drone of airplanes, and his head pounded with the thud of bombs. His eyes flashed with the yellows and reds of the burning sky. He felt as if his entire body belonged to the war.

Alain kissed Kit on both cheeks in the tradition of a true Frenchman. His bravery was almost unbearable. "I shall never forget you." Alain grasped Kit's hands. "There is nothing you could have done."

"I was picking berries; I was a few feet away," the dressmaker said. "They wanted me. Alain, I am terribly sorry."

It seemed an even greater tragedy to be this close to the end of the war and yet for the Nazis to remain such a threat to their lives, to kill another innocent soul.

An hour later, Kit sat in the back of another car with the dressmaker. It wasn't until they were well clear of Versailles that one of the two strangers who were driving spoke.

"There is something that I can tell you," the burly man said. "We have word that the butcher is in Fresnes Prison. Our understanding, which comes from a released prisoner, is that he is being tortured daily to make him reveal the names of the underground network that has been operating in Saint-Germain-en-Laye."

The dressmaker sat perfectly still.

"We understand that the butcher has lost one eye for refusing to confirm where the dressmaker was."

Kit glowered out at the passing landscape.

"We are led to believe that some Resistance members in Paris have been planning to storm the prisons and the forts where the Nazis are still holding members of the underground. They are terrified that the prisoners will all be murdered prior to the Allied liberation of Paris. However, the underground network has refused permission for this."

Kit reached out and placed a hand over the dressmaker's. Her face was white.

"It would be reckless, as the underground network is largely only armed with rough weapons, and no training."

Kit had thought as much about the Maquisards, but they had come through in the end.

"The men and women of the underground, while brave, are also half starving, and therefore we have decided to wait until the armed forces liberate Paris before the prisoners are freed."

"Have the Americans and French decided who is going to have the honor of liberating the city?" Kit asked.

"I believe it is going to be the French." The two men in the front seat exchanged glances. The driver caught Kit's eye in the rearview mirror. "But I'm sure the Americans won't be far behind."

That evening, the sun burned low in the sky, still blue in the summer evening, and yet, they were far enough away from Versailles to be clear of the rank smell of decay that must still linger over the old town that had once held France's glittering royal court. The whole way here, Kit had worried about how Alain was coping with the shock of his loss and the sudden onset of grief.

They had pulled into a gas station. Kit and the dressmaker climbed out of the car and hopped immediately onto the back of waiting motorcycles. Soon, they were winding their way through the narrow streets of Paris.

They passed by groups of Resistance members, hanging

around street corners bearing makeshift weapons. At one point, they approached a homemade barricade at the end of a narrow suburban street. Trash-bin lids had been arranged alongside old chairs and planks of wood. There was even a long, low table at which snipers could attempt to hold off any Nazi threat. Kit gave these barricades three seconds against a panzer tank.

The motorbike rider placed his foot down on the ground and turned the bike around again, choosing an alternative route. The dressmaker sat upright on the back of the bike in front of Kit. She had been given a helmet and her hair was tucked inside, hidden out of sight.

Soon, the rider pulled up outside a nondescript building. Next door there was a bar, and a few elderly gentlemen sat on tables outside on the narrow sidewalk.

Kit slipped off the bike. He couldn't help equating this place with the street where the dressmaker lived. If he imagined hard enough, he could picture the butcher walking up to him, his hair in disarray. He could imagine the dressmaker patiently sewing the dresses that all her clientele so loved.

"Thank you," Kit murmured and stood with the dressmaker on the sidewalk.

"The green door will be unlocked," the driver replied, indicating the plain house next to the bar.

Kit took a sidelong glance at the elderly men sitting outside on the sidewalk. One of them raised his coffee cup and the other nodded at him with the slightest, almost imperceptible movement.

Kit adjusted the bag on his back, opened the door, and stepped inside, his hand shielding the dressmaker, despite the fact that he was certain they were safe.

A woman wearing a blue apron over a violet-colored dress was standing at the top of the stairs. Her dark hair was neatly waved. Another person putting her life at risk for him.

Kit took in a deep breath, almost tempted to turn around and walk away. But the dressmaker gave him a little push.

"I am Josephine. Please, come upstairs, and welcome to my and my husband Lucien's home. We are proud to have you here," the woman said.

"Thank you. I am Antoine, and this is the dressmaker," Kit said.

"My husband is very keen to meet you," Josephine said. She led them up a narrow flight of stairs to her apartment. Once they were inside, Josephine closed the door to the living room, which was painted light green and furnished simply. Off this, there was a narrow corridor leading off to one side with what Kit presumed were bedrooms.

"He and his friends down in the bar below have been following the news of the Allied air force strikes with great interest. Lucien fancies himself an expert on aircraft."

Kit grinned at her. "I was forced to become an expert, but I will be interested to talk with your husband."

Josephine rolled her eyes. "My husband owns the bar downstairs, and he takes great delight in talking. I'm not sure that his actions ever quite match his words."

Kit glanced over at the dressmaker, but she was standing looking a little lost. He couldn't wait for her to be reunited with her daughter, and he suspected that being away from home and not working with the underground, not keeping herself busy, was taking a toll on her.

"Thank you for your hospitality," Kit said to Josephine. "I only hope that we will not have to trespass on your kindness for too long."

Josephine nodded briskly and turned to lead them down the hallway.

CHAPTER THIRTY-EIGHT

PARIS, SUMMER 1944

Louise

The atmosphere in Paris is strange. Barricades block the narrow streets, and snipers sit behind them, chatting and laughing with their comrades. The Resistance is armed and waiting, but the Nazis still patrol the streets. Outside the buildings that are still Nazi-controlled, uniformed Gestapo stand to attention like guards, and the threat of the looming action hovers over the city in the same way as the leaden skies.

I enter the Place Vendôme, and the Ritz is there, the doorman standing outside lending a sense of normality in this strange, intense situation. It is like coming home after a journey in which I missed Arletty's determined presence while staying as discreet as possible. I try not to obviously pick up my pace as I feel a burst of new energy at the thought of seeing Sasha again.

The doorman nods at me as I pass him by, and I head to the staff entrance to the hotel. Inside, I rush up the back stairs, whipping off my white gloves, my small suitcase dangling in my right hand.

I hope she will be there, but the room is empty. I throw my

bag down on my bed, pull my wardrobe open, and take out one of my two maid's uniforms. The other one is missing. Of course, Sasha has assumed my identity and is carrying out my work in my name. My hands move quickly, and I put on my other uniform.

Five minutes later, I am in Frank's bar. He sees me the minute I walk in. It is still early, and he is polishing glasses behind the counter.

I walk over to him, and as usual we express no emotion on seeing each other. Instead, he leads me into his office and closes the door. Only then does he draw me into a hug, and I close my eyes against his shoulder.

"Papa is in prison. Tegel Prison. I am so pleased to see you. Thank you for looking after Sasha," I blurt out.

"She is still out visiting the ill and infirm. Why don't you go and find her, surprise her?" He catches my eye. "She has false identity papers in your name."

I nod. "Of course."

"Go," he says.

I rush through the Paris streets, toward the exact location where Sasha looks after our Parisian friends. The river Seine glitters in the morning sunlight, and the shadows in the water reflect the pink sky.

Sasha is coming out of one of the houses. She is dressed in my uniform and, from a distance, looks exactly like me.

Our eyes meet, and she drops her basket to the ground. She holds her arms out wide, and I move toward her, suddenly not caring that someone might see us, hear us, or glean information about us that I do not want them to know. I simply want to see my cousin, and I want to live in a world where I'm free to embrace her without scrutiny, without anyone watching me.

I have almost reached her side when something stirs from one of the buildings, the building right next door to the one Sasha just came out of. A swarm of Gestapo are suddenly here. All I can see are black uniforms; all I can hear are the sounds of jackboots. And all I can smell is anger.

And in that split second, I know it is too late.

CHAPTER THIRTY-NINE

PARIS, SUMMER 1944

Kit

A church bell rang through Paris. Soon, the single bell that was tolling one lone note was joined by another, and another, and another, until it seemed the whole of Paris was swelling with the sound of bells.

Kit grabbed his bathrobe, securing the tie around his waist, and almost threw himself into the living room.

Josephine and the dressmaker were in the kitchen. He could see through the open door that Josephine was trying to fumble with switches on the wireless that sat on the bench.

"Has it happened?" Kit stumbled, joining them, crowded around the wireless, while outside, the air was filled with the sound of bells. Now, they were no longer playing in time, but their continuous ringing was a constant, single note of hope.

"It started with Notre Dame," the dressmaker said. She turned to him, her eyes shining like that of a young girl. "Soon, it will be safe to go and find my daughter!"

Josephine's fingers flicked the dial of the wireless around, but every station was playing music. There was no news about the momentous liberation of Paris.

The door to the apartment opened, and Josephine's husband, Lucien, burst inside. Kit swung around in time with Josephine and the dressmaker, but Lucien shook his head. He held up a cautionary arm. "My contacts are telling me that this is not the liberation. Bells are ringing because the Allies are on the outskirts of Paris, but there is a way to go yet."

The air was rent with the sound of machine-gun fire, and several explosions boomed into the air. Kit rushed to the window with the others, peering up at the endless blue, which was now tainted with brown smoke.

"The Nazis are having a final go," Lucien murmured. "Reprisals. They are being merciless when it comes to the underground. I'm afraid you must stay here until we get the all-clear."

Kit nodded, and Lucien drew Josephine into his arms.

"I thought it was over," she said. Tears rolled down her cheeks, and her shoulders shook. "For one second, I thought it was finished."

Kit caught Lucien's eyes over the top of Josephine's head.

"It has been a long time," Lucien said. "And my wife has been incredibly brave."

"You all have," Kit said. He turned to leave the room with the dressmaker to give the couple some privacy. He sensed her anticipation. Soon, they would be at the fabled Ritz Hotel, reunited with her daughter. And he would leave no stone unturned to reconnect with the Allies and find Charlie.

It was a few days later that Kit was helping Josephine peel potatoes for lunch. The wireless had been chatting in the background, and then suddenly, the sounds of "La Marseillaise" rang throughout the room. Next, there was the announcement.

"Paris is liberated! Vive la France! The occupation is over!"

Kit's hand stilled. Ridiculously, he was holding his potato peeler in midair.

Josephine turned to him, two bright pink spots appearing

on her cheeks, and her face lighting up almost in disbelief. They stared at each other and hugged, jumping up and down.

Lucien thundered up the staircase, opened the door wide, burst into the room, and gathered Josephine up into his arms.

Kit hugged the dressmaker and held her close. She sobbed for her daughter. She cried for Paris.

The sounds of cheers rang through the street, and people were singing along with the national anthem on the Allied wireless stations that they had not been officially allowed to listen to for four long years.

Paris was liberated. The wireless announcer began explaining the details, how the great French army had stormed the streets. Tonight, for the first time in an age, bars would be thrown open, dance halls dusted off and swept, for a night filled with dancing and drinking and celebrating, and there would be no need for anyone to stay home.

The curfew was banished, as were the Nazis. Those who could had fled back to Germany; many had been arrested. No longer was Paris the playground of a government that would go down in history as one of the very worst; now it was back in the hands of the free French.

Lucien was dancing around the room with Josephine and leading her to the door to take her down to the bar where their loyal friends had sat out this dreadful, dreadful war.

"Come," he said. "Come, my darling, let us drink and be merry."

Kit went and leaned on the windowsill. Outside, people were dancing in the street. He was one step closer to getting home, to reuniting with his family, and his brother. The dressmaker came and stood next to him.

"Thank goodness," she said in her quiet way.

That evening, Kit walked with the dressmaker through the crowds that lined Paris's streets. He kept his gaze trained on the back of the determined mother, walking as fast as she could to get to her daughter.

Nearby, boys were tearing down the swastikas that had hung like monsters over the grand buildings of Paris, cheers rent the air, and every bar swelled with music, people dancing on the tables, others desperately clamoring to buy a drink.

They worked their way toward the crowded river Seine, the little dressmaker weaving through the crowds. The Place Vendôme, she told him, was just a few minutes' walk away. Soon they reached it and the grand façade of the Ritz Hotel stood as proud as ever and as grand. If any building could protect a young woman, then surely this was it.

An American military jeep was parked outside the swinging front doors, and Kit pushed his way forward through the crowds with the dressmaker. But right outside the Ritz Hotel, they were forced to stop, and Kit shook his head in disbelief. For there, emerging from a jeep that had parked at an angle outside the front door, was a face and a figure that left everybody in awe.

A hush had descended over the milling crowds as a figure from Paris's early literary days, the days when American writers graced the boulevards of Montparnasse, alighted from the vehicle, turned to the people, and raised his hands.

"It is my pleasure," Ernest Hemingway shouted, "to liberate the Ritz Hotel myself. This is an icon of Paris, and I intend to move in and stay here for as long as I like!"

Kit stood next to the dressmaker while the great writer pounded up the front steps and in through the glass doors. A bellhop stood aside for him, and Kit let out a wry laugh.

But then, the dressmaker gripped Kit's arm. And he saw her face turn pale.

A woman was being hauled out of the entrance of the Ritz and dragged unceremoniously by a pair of self-styled gendarmes. But they were not wearing the uniforms of the men who had driven them so graciously around France. No, they were wearing the rough clothes of the Resistance. They were holding a pair of makeshift rifles, and the expression on their faces was grim.

Kit watched helplessly. The dressmaker only paused momentarily before pushing her way toward the hotel entrance, one small woman drowned out by the jeers that were coming from the street.

"Femme tondue! Femme tondue!"

Kit recognized the famous film star Arletty. He had heard reports that she had been having an affair with a Nazi and living in great luxury throughout the war. A man stood behind her, holding her long dark hair. The people had left a space around her, and they were gathered in a circle.

Kit turned away from the grisly spectacle and followed on behind the dressmaker. Soon he was close enough to hear Arletty's barber's words. "You shall enjoy prison. And when you are brought to justice, you can think of all our loyal friends who sacrificed their lives for the likes of you. Traitor! Collaborator," he snarled.

Arletty's head was thrust back, the whites of her eyes showing and bulging, like those of a terrified wild animal.

Kit stared in horror at the clink of the man sharpening a knife.

But he had to find the dressmaker. He pushed his way into the grand lobby of the Ritz and found himself standing in the double-height, stunning marble lobby.

A group of fascinated staff were standing in one corner of the lobby, and among them, Kit spotted several maids in uniform. The dressmaker was lost somewhere in the crowd. Immediately, he started to try to push his way across to the maids. He knew exactly who he was looking for, because he remembered the girl in the photograph in the dressmaker's home.

But right in front of him, the great writer blocked his way, brandished his gun, and marched across the elegant lobby, his boots stamping on the polished floors. "Where are the Nazis?" Hemingway asked no one in particular. "Show me where they are, and I will get them all out. I am here to liberate the Ritz!"

Kit sighed heavily as Hemingway thundered up the grand stairway of the once beautiful palace and disappeared into the heights of the hotel, shouting that he would oust any remaining Nazis if it was the last thing he did.

And right then, Kit froze.

For there, in the very front of the group of staff that were hovering at the edge of the grand lobby, was a girl, her blond hair tucked up into a maid's cap. And running toward her, pushing her way through the people, was her mother. Tears streamed down the dressmaker's cheeks.

"*Louise!*" she called.

The sound of gunshots from the top floors of the hotel rang through the building. A bellhop trotted downstairs, proclaiming, "Monsieur Hemingway is determined to shoot things out, in case there are any Nazis lingering here. He has just shot the washing, the sheets hanging on the line on the roof, in case there was anyone untoward hiding behind them."

Kit pressed his forefinger into the dent between his eyes.

The dressmaker rushed toward her daughter, but the girl looked about in confusion, as if trying to find the person who was calling her name.

But then, a rabble of Resistance workers came running into the hotel.

"*Louise*!" the dressmaker shouted.

But, to Kit's horror, the rough men grabbed the dressmaker's daughter and pulled her outside. Kit pushed his way after them, aware of the dressmaker calling and crying hopelessly like a mother bird whose baby had fallen out of the nest.

Outside, everything was chaos. Kit barged his way through the throngs of jeering, shouting, fist-waving inhabitants of Paris. And then he stopped.

Kit tried to force his way through the crowd, but he could not see, and yet all around him were the taunts and jeers of the crowd. He'd lost the dressmaker. He pushed his way around, trying to find her, calling for her. But in the chaos, and after he knew not how many minutes, there was a truck, and there were three girls on it, swastikas painted on their foreheads, their heads shaved, the expressions on their faces terrified, and then four. And the crowd roared.

"No!" Kit yelled. He pushed his way through the rows of people that gawked and stared at the truck. "Get away," he yelled. "You fools," he muttered, yanking aside two burly men who were standing holding shears. "You have the wrong woman. She is no more a collaborator than you or I. You lower yourself to exactly that which we have fought against for the last five years."

The two men looked at each other, and, in that split second, Kit hauled himself up onto the flatbed of the truck. He kneeled by the terrified dressmaker's daughter, his eyes searching her face. Below the red swastika that had been branded on her face, one tear rolled down her cheek.

Kit took her hands, even as he sensed the two burly men trying and failing to leap up onto the back of the truck behind him.

"Louise!" The dressmaker battled her way through the crowd and climbed up onto the back of the truck and came to a standstill. The girl searched the dressmaker's face.

And then there was a dreadful silence as the dressmaker and the young woman stared at each other for what seemed like minutes.

"Who are you?" the dressmaker whispered. "Where is my daughter?" Her voice was so soft, and yet dread settled in Kit's stomach and spread.

The maid looked directly at the dressmaker. "My name is Sasha."

CHAPTER FORTY

PARIS, PRESENT DAY

Nicole

Andrew has come to Paris to join me. We sit opposite Arielle in her office in a semicircle. Me, Andrew, Pandora, her husband, and Aunt Mariah. Mia Louise sits on Pandora's lap and sends great toothless smiles to Arielle.

I curve my hand over the soft rise of my belly. "Arielle, you seem adamant that the photograph is of our granny Louise. My question is, why are you so certain?"

Arielle is standing behind her desk. She leans on the chair but does not sit down, and the expression on her face is hard to read. "I am certain, because the woman in the photograph is Louise Bassett, but she also is not."

Aunt Mariah mumbles something, and Andrew's hand comes to rest in mine.

"There has already been enough damage done," Mariah says. "Please, tell us the truth."

Arielle sighs. "I am sorry for what you have been through, but I didn't know myself until recently what the true story was behind the image, and it shocked me." Her brow is drawn and her expression clouds. "The photograph is of a woman who, after the war, went by the name of Louise Bassett, but it was not her real name."

There is a silence, and Pandora holds Mia close.

"Please go on," I say. I am feeling faint, as if everything I knew was as fragile and ephemeral as a bank of clouds. If Granny was not Louise Bassett, then who was she? She never changed her name to Harrington after she married my grandfather, Kit, which was highly unusual in those days. But I remember him telling me that her name was very special to her.

But now am I to believe that the name she went by was never hers at all?

Arielle clears her throat gently. "I know the girl in the photograph from 1944 is also the woman who called herself Louise Bassett, because I cross-checked the old photograph you brought against the few photographs that were online of your grandmother. It seems she was quite well known in her local area in Sussex for her garden. There were several photographs of her over the years in the local gardening magazines. I have had the photographs analyzed and we are confident that your grandmother was also the woman standing outside the Ritz Hotel in 1944."

I swallow and wait. This makes no sense. I think there must be some mistake. I glance toward Mariah. Now I am the one questioning Arielle's veracity, but Mariah is focused on the archivist, her eyes narrowed, her fingers toying with her necklace.

"However, the reason I was so confused the first time I saw the photograph is because the woman in it is also my aunt," Arielle says.

You could hear a butterfly pass by in this office. It is as if there is a collective holding of breath.

"My aunt's name was Sasha Frölich. She was my mother Mathilda's older sister, and grew up in Heidelberg in Germany, but my mother's older sister, Sasha, disappeared after the war."

"What?" I say. "So, you are telling me Granny was German?"

Arielle nods sadly. "My mother always told me that Sasha was staying at the Ritz during the Nazi occupation of Paris, and that her cousin, a French woman named Louise Bassett, who was the daughter of my uncle Joachim, was working here as a maid at the same time. My mother, Carol, and Louise Bassett's father, Joachim, were brother and sister."

"Her cousin? Granny impersonated her French cousin until she died?" I know I am gaping and barking out questions, but I feel as if the very foundations of my world are falling apart.

Andrew squeezes my hand. "Are you okay?" he asks.

Silently, I nod. "Go on, please," I say to Arielle. The only way I can get through this is to let Arielle speak on, but I am beginning to completely understand why Mariah bristled so much in our last meeting here.

Arielle sends me an entreating look. "My mother, Mathilda, was unable to trace either her French cousin Louise or her older sister, Sasha, in the maelstrom and the chaos of displaced people in Germany after the war."

"Oh dear," Mariah says. "How tragic. The situation surrounding missing people after the war was chaotic."

"It was terrible," Arielle confirms. "My aunt Sasha and her cousin Louise both simply disappeared, and, in the end, my mother gave up her heartbreaking search. But I began searching again after my mother died, because I saw how the unexplained loss of her sister and cousin depressed my mother. That is why I work at the Ritz."

I glance across at Mariah. But she is fixated on Arielle.

Arielle lowers her gaze. "My mother, Mathilda, died several years ago, and my grandmother, Mathilda's mother, Carol, passed away not long after the war." Arielle shook her head. "My grandmother Carol was in an even worse state than Mathilda. Carol had lost her brother, Joachim, Louise's father; her beloved husband; and her oldest daughter, Sasha, to the Nazis. When you came with your questions, it stirred up terrible memories. I instantly knew who the girl in the photograph was. But I needed to verify things. I couldn't just make assumptions on a whim. I am deeply involved in this too. I was trying to be professional. To put the archivist in me first before I said anything to you."

"I'm sorry," I whisper.

Arielle continues, as if each word gives her pain. "The photographs of my aunt Sasha that we have at home in Heidelberg look exactly the same as this girl whose image you brought me to investigate." Arielle reaches into her desk drawer and pulls out an old envelope. She hands it to me.

I slide the envelope open and pull out several old photographs.

Granny...Sasha...as a young woman, standing near the river in the old city I recognize as Heidelberg, the castle on the hill rising spectacularly behind her, and she is smiling and confident. Her blond hair pinned back. That Marilyn Monroe smile. The photographs continue, Granny standing under a pair of medieval gates, sitting on a seat at the university, with several students around her and in the background.

I hand the photographs around, and we all look at them in silence.

"Sasha wanted to fly airplanes, according to my mother, Mathilda," Arielle says, her voice filled with sadness. "Mother always said that Sasha was the adventurer in the family."

"My father, Kit, was a pilot during the war." Mariah lifts her head and gazes at Arielle over her reading glasses.

I smile. Again, this is something Grandad never talked about when I was small and he was alive. I like to think of him as a pilot. I know he was American, but I don't know much more.

"But why the secrets? I still don't understand why my mother never told us the truth. Never told anyone the truth."

"That is easy to answer," Arielle says. "It would have been unthinkable to be a German in an Allied country after the war."

My shoulders drop and I sigh heavily. Of course. "But how did she end up in Paris in 1944?" I still don't know how Granny ended up outside the Ritz.

"She had been working for a very high-ranking Nazi officer and came to Paris with him from Germany."

This time, the silence is as thick as butter.

"The military governor of France during the occupation, no less. Sasha would hardly have been well regarded in an Allied country in the years after the war."

"Von Stülpnagel?" I gasp. I feel heartbroken. Heartbroken for the fact that Granny could never tell us who she was, that she was German. But also the unthinkable preys on my mind. Was she a Nazi? Was she correctly accused?

Arielle smiles at me sadly. "Don't worry; Sasha was on the right side. Her boss was involved in the Valkyrie plot to assassinate Hitler, and she came out to Paris as his aide just before the assassination attempt."

We are all staring at Arielle in disbelief, and as the story unfolds, I feel like the layers of Granny's silence are being brutally exposed. I feel that we are betraying her secrets, but if she was a hero, bravely involved in an attempt to remove Hitler, why did she end up accused of collaboration?

I only wish she was here to tell her tale in her own words. But she did not want to. I sigh and let Arielle continue.

"Sasha would have been too scared to reveal her identity in Britain straight after the war, so it seems she took on the name of our French cousin, Louise Bassett. Louise had grown up in France, was working as a maid in the Ritz where Sasha and her boss were staying, and hers was the safer identity."

I sigh heavily. "And so, she never changed it? She never changed her name back to Sasha again."

"No. She must have felt she carried things on too long. That it was impossible to go back," Arielle continues. "Perhaps she felt that you would be ashamed of her for not telling you who she really was for so many years."

"I never would have been ashamed." I wipe a stray tear from my cheek.

Andrew squeezes my hand.

"But what happened to Louise?" Pandora asks.

My heart sinks. I hate to hear the answer to this question.

"Louise Bassett, who was half French and the daughter of my great-uncle Joachim, and who worked stoically as a maid in the Ritz Hotel, was captured by the Gestapo just days before the liberation of Paris."

I catch Pandora's eye. My cousin. Sasha lost her cousin. I don't want to lose mine again. Pandora sends me a heartfelt look across the table.

"The Gestapo mistakenly assumed Louise was her cousin Sasha and involved in the assassination plot against Hitler."

"Oh, dear goodness. And she was French and innocent too," I murmur.

"Of course," Arielle says. "What's more, from what my mother said, Sasha and Louise were very close. Louise even came to Germany, risking her life to try and find her cousin when she thought Sasha had been arrested and deported from France with her accused boss in the Valkyrie plot. It was when she returned to Paris after discovering that Sasha was actually alive that she was captured by the Gestapo."

"In 1944?" I ask.

Arielle nods. "After this, Sasha, it seems, was still in France working at the Ritz until the liberation of Paris and the accusations against the horizontal collaborators when Sasha was mistaken for Louise and hauled up on the back of the truck and humiliated, her head shaved."

We all take this in.

"We managed to reach out to a descendant of one of the other staff members in the hotel, who told us that Sasha was rescued from her plight on the back of the truck by a handsome British air force lieutenant called Kit Harrington, who whisked Sasha off to Britain where they married not long after the war."

"Unbelievable," Andrew whispers.

"Very romantic," Pandora adds.

"And did she have a happy life? Your Louise? Our aunt Sasha?" Arielle asks.

I nod, and tears prick my eyes, for the woman who could never admit who she really was in a world that was divided in such an uncompromising way. "Yes, I believe she was happy. She and my grandfather Kit were two of the happiest people I ever knew. She loved her life, and now I see why. She appreciated every day." I wipe a stray tear from my eye. "But why would Sasha have never gone back to Heidelberg and to her family, your mother, Mathilda; and Mathilda's mother, Carol?"

Arielle smiles sadly. "The years after the war were so hard for anyone who was German. Germans were still being rounded up and were hated. As time went on, I imagine she felt guilt too. Guilt at the fact that she lived, and her cousin Louise died in her place. Those on both sides of the war in that generation had to live with such guilt that some of them could hardly face themselves in the mirror. They would turn to anything—*anything*—to get away from the truth of who they were, and of what they'd had to do in those years. But it was particularly bad for anyone German or in Germany."

We are all quiet.

"Well then," Arielle says. "Here we all are, drawn back to the Ritz Hotel. You know, I have decided it's time that Louise Bassett is no longer invisible and is no longer only remembered as a name in a book in this hotel. And I'm about to tell you why."

"My word," Mariah breathes.

Arielle smiles at her. "I think we need to have a little tribute to her in the hotel. To the real Louise, and to Sasha, who made the most of the life that Louise could never live. Would you like to know more?"

We all nod.

"You see, we have discovered while researching your photograph that Great-Uncle Joachim's wife, Violette, Louise's mother, was the daughter of one of the bravest leaders in the Resistance in northern France. We do know that Violette, the dressmaker, lived in Saint-Germain-en-Laye and helped your grandfather Kit to safety when his aircraft was shot down by anti-aircraft gunners in northern France. So you see, this is a real family story."

Family. When I came to France at the beginning of the summer, I thought I had no real family left. I thought my unborn baby's chances of knowing extended family were zero. And now look.

"The dressmaker worked with a famous Resistance worker called the butcher, who was released from Fresnes Prison after the war. My understanding is they married...So you see, you did have family in France, Nicole."

"Yes," I say, smiling. "You, and..." I sweep my hands around the room.

"But your lost family would have been almost impossible to trace without the connection to the Ritz."

I think back to my exhausting visit to the town hall and shake my head. Now, I feel at home in this grand old hotel, possibly like Louise did. And I am thankful that this place kept Granny, Sasha, safe after she was being hunted by the Gestapo.

Tragedy surrounds poor Louise, though. I am only glad that Arielle is going to put up a tribute to her in the hotel.

I stand up, and my aunt Mariah approaches me.

"Nicole, I wonder, would you like to work with me to find out more about the dressmaker's daughter? About the lost story of Louise Bassett?" Mariah asks.

"I would love that," I say, meaning it. I'm glad that my connections and interest in the past will not have to fade when I go home.

My aunt nods, and we smile at each other.

This was a time of history that seems incredible to us now, and yet that is only a whisper of a generation away, and I realize one thing is true. We cannot change what has happened, and we cannot fight it, but the best thing we can do is to understand, and to honor the members of our family who fought so hard for our freedom.

It was not because Claudine, whom I later knew was Louise, was my only companion that we grew close. No, she went to every length to ensure both my mental and physical well-being were taken care of. Louise, realizing that I loved to read, procured for me an excellent selection of books from the much-desecrated library of the Ritz Hotel.

Among these books, there was a copy of Grimm's Fairy Tales, *which you, Nicole, have preciously in your hands today.*

It was I who inscribed the message in the front pages. It was a bit of a joke on my part, because the book was not mine to give away, but I decided that the Nazis had stolen enough from France, so I would give one of their German books away!

Forgive me—such things had to keep us amused in these dark days.

However, the Ritz was like a home to Louise and it was a sanctuary to me, so we felt extremely safe there.

I perhaps took our safety for granted in the end and Louise was murdered, tragically, by the Gestapo. At first, I thought that they had caught up with her for protecting me, but it turns out she was mistaken for Sasha—her cousin, as you now know.

If you were to ask me whether I fell in love with Louise, my answer would be yes.

We talked, oh, we talked of all things, and I think we both became protective of each other, and naturally felt very close from that initial attraction the very first time we met to an opening up of minds, and gradually hearts, that beat the same tune under a very cold and lonely gray sky that was over Europe at that time.

You know what happened to Louise, but I did not know until after the liberation, when Louise's cousin Sasha and your father and grandfather, Kit, came bursting into my attic room to rescue me.

A few days earlier, Louise had stopped coming to bring me meals. A nondescript maid had started coming in her place and she had no desire to talk to me. She seemed terrified, poor girl, and this only highlighted to me how brave Louise was.

When Kit and Sasha came into my room, my first reaction was complete relief and joy at the sight of my brother. Sasha, you see, had connected our stories after Kit dramatically rescued her from being accused as a collaborator paraded around Paris with a swastika painted to her forehead.

After that, the three of us returned to London, where Kit and I resumed our duties in the air force, carrying out missions over Germany. Sasha accompanied us, devastated by the loss of Louise and unable to return to Germany as she was a fugitive from the Nazi regime, wanted for her part in the conspiracy to murder Hitler.

It was Louise's brave mother, Violette, who organized false passports and identity documents for Sasha to get to the United Kingdom.

Violette insisted that Sasha take on her dead daughter's identity, her cousin's identity, because Frank had issued Louise's fake identity papers in Sasha's name. They looked the same.

You see, Violette came across as a very practical woman to me, and I think she felt that her darling daughter would be happy that her name was living on and her cousin was able to find the freedom that Louise died for. Forgive me; I am finding tears forming in my eyes at the memory of Louise.

Sasha, Kit, and I set up home with our father in St. John's Wood.

Sasha made a great impression on all of us, but especially on Kit. She was grieving for the loss of Louise, as was I, and Kit was falling in love with Sasha, a German girl whose spark and bravery astounded him.

Kit and Sasha married in April 1945.

I returned to America at the end of the war, and never forgot Louise.

When I finally had the money put together to open my own bookstore here in Dallas, Texas, I called it Charlie and Louise, because I want to keep her memory close, because my bookstore is a place for conversations about all the good things in life, and these are the things that remind me of Louise.

These are the things that keep me going when the memory of her starts feeling distant or when things seem too tough.

All I have to do is close my eyes, choose a book, and remember her, and everything is all right.

With my love,

Charlie Harrington

A LETTER FROM ELLA CAREY

Dear reader,

I want to say a huge thank-you for choosing to read *The Paris Maid*. If you did enjoy it, and want to keep up-to-date with all my latest releases, just sign up at the following link. Your email address will never be shared and you can unsubscribe at any time.

www.ellacarey.com

As many of my long-term readers will know, I am endlessly fascinated by Paris. Having the chance to set a book in the famous Ritz Hotel was a dream come true for me, especially during the devastating years of the Second World War. Nicole's story came to me a bit later in the process, as I found myself wondering what I would do if I learned that a beloved family member had been accused of something unspeakable. And then what would other family members think? Kit's story was very personal to me, as my father flew in the British air force dropping parachutists over France for the French resistance.

I hope you loved *The Paris Maid,* and if you did, I would be very grateful if you could write a review. I'd love to hear what you think, and it makes such a difference in helping new readers to discover one of my books for the first time.

I love hearing from my readers—you can get in touch on my Facebook page, through Twitter, Goodreads, or my website.

Thanks,

Ella *x*

facebook.com/ellacareyauthor

@Ella_Carey

AUTHOR'S NOTE

Arletty was a French actress who was born to a working-class family near Paris under the name of Leonie Bathiat. After her father's death, she left home and became a fashion model. At the age of twenty-one she became an actress in music halls, then went on to star in plays and cabarets. She then became a film actress starring in such roles as Blanche in the French version of *A Streetcar Named Desire*. In 1945, Arletty was imprisoned for her wartime affair with Hans Jürgen Soehring. She was paraded through the streets of Paris with her head shaved and her skull painted with a swastika.

Blanche Auzello was a New Yorker who hid her Jewish identity throughout the German occupation. Blanche was the wife of the managing director of the Ritz, Claude Auzello. She was arrested for her anti-German wartime activities in the hotel after celebrating D-Day with her good friend and fellow Resistance member Lily Kharmayeff at Maxim's. Blanche was transported to Fresnes Prison, and never saw her friend Lily again. Blanche was thrown into solitary confinement and resisted all attempts to extract information from her about Lily. Eventually, she was released by the Gestapo after screaming at them that she was Jewish in order to distract them from their questions about her friend. The Gestapo eventually decided Blanche was crazy and let her go. Barefoot, she made her way to the Ritz and back to her husband, Claude.

• • •

Frank Meier was the head bartender at the Ritz in Paris and worked against the Nazis during the occupation. His bar was later named Bar Hemingway. Frank Meier was Austrian-born and also part Jewish. He was famous not only for creating the classic Bee's Knees cocktail, but he also helped the French Resistance, helped Jewish residents obtain fake documents, saving them from the Vichy government's deportations to concentration camps, and passed coded notes for von Stülpnagel as he planned the failed assassination of Adolf Hitler. It is said that the idea for the failed assassination attempt may have been hatched in Frank Meier's bar.

Pearl Witherington was one of the most famous World War II resistance fighters. She was known as "Pauline," and commanded a band of thirty-five hundred French Resistance fighters. She was a special agent for the British Special Operations executive.

Henry C. Woodrum's story of evasion from the Nazis in occupied France with the help of the Underground inspired Kit's journey to Paris, along with stories my father told me of his years as an RAF pilot dropping parachutists over France for the Resistance during the Second World War.

ACKNOWLEDGMENTS

Huge thanks to my brilliant editor Maisie Lawrence at Bookouture, to Kirsiah Depp, and to everyone at Grand Central Publishing for publishing this beautiful edition of the book. It is always such a joy working with you, and I value your editorial guidance enormously. Thank you to everyone else at Bookouture who has worked on this book, copyeditor Jade Craddock, proofreader Anne O'Brien, and my thanks to Sarah Hardy for her guidance with publicity. Thank you to Debbie Clement for your beautiful cover design. Thanks to everyone in the marketing team, and to Mandy Kullar for coordinating everything.

Thanks to the wonderful Hannah Todd and Giles Milburn at the Madeline Milburn literary agency for managing my career and for your incredibly appreciated ongoing support.

Huge hugs and thanks to my family and friends, to the wonderful bloggers and reviewers for reading advance copies of the book, and to my readers all over the world. This is for you.

YOUR BOOK CLUB RESOURCE

READING GROUP GUIDE

DISCUSSION QUESTIONS

1. Did this book affect the way you see Paris? Do you think you will feel differently going there from now on if you travel to France, knowing the history of what the people went through during the Second World War? Did the book inspire any travel plans to Paris for you?

2. How much did you know about the Nazi occupation of Paris before you picked up the book? Did you know about the Ritz Hotel during the occupation?

3. Did you agree with Sasha's decisions? Why or why not? What do you think was her biggest struggle?

4. How did you feel about Mariah's attitude toward her mother? Could you understand and see how two members of the family (Nicole and Mariah) could have such completely different feelings about their mother and grandmother? Is this believable?

5. Did the events in the book spook you? Or get under your skin? What did you find most reprehensible about the way humans treated others during that time in the book?

6. How did the setting impact the characters' lives? To what extent were these characters a product of their generation, and how was this shown in the book?

7. Do you think that Kit and Sasha would have made a good couple? Did this feel right that they came together after the story finished?

8. How did you feel about Arletty? Did her behaviour invoke a strong reaction in you either way? What was that reaction? Did you know about the way women who were accused of being Nazi collaborators were treated after the Allied landings in France?

9. Whose story did you find more emotional? Louise's, Sasha's, or Kit's and the Dressmaker's? To which character did you most relate or empathize? And why?

10. How did this book compare to other books written by Ella Carey with which you might be familiar?

QUESTION AND ANSWERS WITH ELLA CAREY

What is the inspiration for this book?

The inspiration for this book is the true story of the top-ranking Nazis who lived in the Hotel Ritz in Paris during the Second World War. I have walked past this beautiful hotel many times and feel it has a fairytale quality, and its wartime history felt like an extraordinary setting for a novel.

Is there a particular theme you are exploring in this book?

Apart from looking at war, and the effects of the Nazi occupation on women in France, the book also explores the theme of family, and what happens when one member of the family is blamed—either wrongly or rightly for something. The novel looks at the nuances behind this.

What period of history particularly interests you? Why?

The 1930s and 1940s interest me particularly, perhaps because of the incredibly powerful history and the potential for romance, and because my parents were in their twenties in this era but did not really talk about it.

What resources did you use to research this book?

I use books from the library and bookstores! I like to read sources from the period as much as I can, such as letters. I read diaries and journals, as well as drawing on my many visits to Paris, which helped me to conjure up the feel of the setting.

As for the internet, I do use that as well for visual details—photos of clothing that people wore, and for fact checking if something comes up along the way as I write.

What is more important to you, historical authenticity or accuracy?

My instinctive response to that, and something I would adhere to after reflection, is that historical authenticity is more important than accuracy. While you need to be careful with accuracy, while accuracy is important and publishing houses have copyeditors to ensure that things are correct throughout the book, I think authenticity is something deeper than accuracy—it's about being true to the time about which you are writing. If, in general terms, the story, characters, and setting are not authentic, or true, then I think nothing works, the story won't resonate or ring true. In short, readers need to believe that the story seems real, as if it all could have happened—as if it did happen. I think that is at the essence of storytelling no matter what.

Are you a plotter or a pantser? How long does it generally take you to write a book?

I'm a plotter who turns into a pantser once I start writing—and it only gets worse with each draft. I do start with a synopsis so that I know I have a story, and then things change as I write. I have had several novels published in the last eight years and it generally takes me a few months to write each book from start to submission, but then they go into the revision process, which takes another four or so months, then there is a lapse of several months before the book is released, while the book is produced and covers designed.

Which authors have influenced you?

Late-nineteenth-century women authors—the classics—especially the Brontës, for dramatic, tragic love stories (they are the best kind!). *Wuthering Heights* and *Jane Eyre* are probably my two favorite novels. *Anna Karenina* is wonderful. I love E.M. Forster and Edith Wharton, along with Evelyn Waugh. I admire Hemingway's style of writing, his spare prose and his use of dialogue. In terms of contemporary writing, I am reading Michael Cunningham's *Day* at the moment, which I am loving for his beautiful prose. I'm always open to discovering new authors—I love to read.

What advice would you give to an aspiring author?

Don't give up, do educate yourself on the craft of writing to the highest level which you can achieve, and do not send your work out until you are sure it is the best it can be—you'll know when it is ready when you can't possibly give it any more of yourself. And surround yourself with people who are supportive of your writing, as much as you can—that is important.

A CITY THAT WON'T SURRENDER

I've always loved the fact that writing and reading have the ability to transport me to another time and another place, but writing and researching my most recent novel, *The Paris Maid,* has transformed the way I feel about Paris for good.

I am now incredibly moved in ways that I have not properly understood or felt before when I look at photographs of Paris. Writing and researching this book has brought my respect and compassion for the people who lived in the city between 1940 and 1944 to a new level. I have a far greater depth of understanding of what Paris suffered, and an appreciation for the beauty, grace and courage that epitomizes the city, that was never allowed to die.

I am certain that next time I go to Paris, and sit outside at one of the sidewalk cafés, I will not just be thinking about food, and art, and people watching. No. I will be imagining what it was like for my characters to walk the streets of the city with not only incredible courage, under the watchful eyes of the Nazis, but with constant fear laced in their hearts.

However, it was setting my novel in the iconic Ritz hotel in Paris's luxurious Place Vendôme that has really deepened my understanding of the complexities that were brewing in Paris toward the end of the Second World War.

The Ritz was officially a neutral hotel because it was owned by Swiss proprietors. The hotel was not supposed to be on one side or the other. However, this did not deter the Nazis from taking full advantage of one of the most beautiful and opulent buildings in occupied France.

From the Imperial suite, decorated with silk canopies and exquisite furnishings, Göring orchestrated the blitz, along with some of the most reprehensible acts that occurred during the Second World War. Coco Chanel lived in the other side of the hotel with her German lover, the Nazi Hans Günther von Dincklage. However, one of the most fascinating characters I found while carrying out my research was the film star Arletty, who throughout her lengthy career as an actress, had moved from dance halls, to theaters, to pictures, culminating in her playing some of the silver screen's most iconic roles. Arletty also tucked herself away in the Ritz for the duration of the war, forming a liaison with Luftwaffe officer Hans-Jürgen Soehring. Ultimately, it was Arletty who fascinated me, and so she became a character in my book.

When the Nazis moved into the Ritz, the French guests were moved from the grander Place Vendôme side of the hotel to the less exuberant rooms that looked over the Rue Cambon. Top-ranking Nazis moved into the suites overlooking the place Vendôme, and filled the restaurants and bars with what was often regarded as indiscreet chatter, overheard by many of the Ritz's loyal staff. The hotel was like a cauldron on the boil. In a situation that was officially neutral, everybody had to choose a side. Many people were double crossers, and it is said that the Place Vendôme was filled with spies. What a fantastic setting for a novel!

In the bar on the rue Cambon side of the hotel, legendary barman Frank Meier oversaw a string of resistance activities. The manager of the hotel, Claude Auzello, orchestrated the widespread underground network amongst the staff in the hotel. His wife, Blanche, was an important figure in the French resistance, only to be captured by the Nazis in the summer of 1944. I think Blanche was wonderful. She had to go into my novel as well.

However, ultimately, I wanted to explore what it might have been like not to be one of the grand and illustrious guests in the hotel. I wanted to write from the perspective of someone decidedly un-grand in a grand setting. Someone who, if I had not written about them, might slip behind the scenes, who scuttled around unseen, unheard, unnoticed. Louise Bassett, therefore, is a maid working in the Ritz hotel. She has an excellent memory for numbers and attracts the attention of Frank Meier, who asks her to join the underground network that is operating amongst the staff.

Frank is initially interested in the fact that Louise can remember strings of numbers, words, and statistics without any effort at all. She can recall which Nazis stayed in which rooms on which dates, and who visited them. The underground network in the Ritz hotel operated by sending coded messages to the Allies in neutral territories informing them which Nazis were staying in the hotel and when. I have to admit that my ability to remember long strings of numbers—phone numbers of my childhood friends (still!), car license plate numbers that just stay in my mind when I see them—inspired Louise.

I always wonder if I would have made a good spy! Once, when I was doing a spy tour, I was asked to carry out a fake spy act, and I managed to pull it off while no one in the tour group noticed. Perhaps I missed my calling!

For Louise, the opportunity to do something truly brave while using her extraordinary memory is an offer that is too tempting to turn down. What's more, she wants to be recognized for more than her abilities with numbers and letters. Here is her chance to truly be part of something human and real.

While Louise may only be a simple maid, she has eyes and ears everywhere. She is the perfect person to be a spy because she knows how to scuttle around the hotel without drawing any attention to herself. Who is more invisible than a maid? While Arletty has become famous by drawing attention to herself, Louise has done the opposite.

At times, the Nazis were known by vegetable code names. Louise thinks it is hilarious that Göring is referred to as a potato! In her daily rounds, she cleans his magnificent Imperial suite, running her fingers through his bowls filled with sapphires and rubies and emeralds, and dusting around his saucers filled with illicit amphetamines.

Arletty comes to trust Louise, and this becomes problematic. Louise is drawn into Arletty's complicated relationship. But when a Jewish friend of the once-famous actress is murdered at the hands of the Nazis, Arletty is forced to make a choice that ultimately is going to determine her own fate. For the lives of the women in the Ritz, life was never going to be the same again once the Allies arrived. Seeing all of this drama through the eyes of a maid was fascinating, but then, my maid Louise was faced with an impossible dilemma of her own. Her life took an unexpected turn, and suddenly, she was thrust into the spotlight of her own story, even though she had tried to hide away in the hotel from her past.

But it was outside the Ritz that the true tragedy of the war was playing out in the homes of Paris. Starving, freezing through long winters, and not able to afford to buy clothes or shoes for their families, the citizens of Paris must have felt terror in their everyday lives that seems to be all but wiped clean from the Paris we know now. It's certainly not something I ever thought about when I first visited Paris as a teenager, or even on subsequent visits, not having looked so emotionally at what happened there during World War II.

And I think this is the power of fiction. It is an emotional art form that is unique because it is about being able to inhabit a person from the past and understand their hearts and minds, and the decisions they had to make.

In *The Paris Maid*, my story threads outside the city as well into the northern countryside of France, where an Allied air force pilot must abandon his plane. He parachutes straight into St. Germain-en-Laye and is thrust into the countryside of France, forced to rely on the kindness of the underground network in order, simply, to survive.

This part of the novel, for me, is inspired by a personal story. My father was an Allied air force pilot during the Second World War. He dropped parachutists over France to aid in the French resistance, and reading accounts of what they saw, experienced, and felt was also an incredibly moving experience for me.

Recently, I have had the chance to read his diaries—he kept extensive diaries during the war, all handwritten beautifully, but...pages are cut out. I think this was my mother, because any reference to my parents' love affair has been redacted. That's another story, which I explore in my subsequent novel, *An Italian Secret*.

It is also the sense of place that I find so overwhelming and powerful in writing fiction. Imagine hearing the sound of a prop engine on an aircraft groaning and grinding like a sinking ship as it is about to go down, the way the whole plane would have shuddered, and the shaky view of the patchwork fields of France spreading out below as you opened your silver parachute and headed straight into Nazi ground.

Paris, for me, is now enhanced. More beautiful, more fascinating, nuanced, moving, and, most of all, poignant. For I truly think that it is only through novels that we can really feel the past. This is one of the true inspirations for me, and one of the most powerful reasons why I write.